Published by Camilla Monk AKA "Yaypub"

Cover design by Camilla Monk

ISBN: 978-1-64316-079-5

CAMILLA MONK

TABLE OF CONTENTS

This book is dedicated to all the losers, dropouts, and "troubled teens" out there. You are, indeed special snowflakes. And there's nothing wrong with that.

I

Officially, this is not my story. It's not my face you saw on CNN and Rai News after it was all over. I didn't lose my mother at a young age; as far as I know, she's still alive, probably doing fine. My paternal grandfather wasn't a world-class historian, and I didn't enroll in Harvard at seventeen to follow in his footsteps—I was never really good with books and studying. Just didn't have the brains for that.

But I was there. I went to Rome to visit my dad at the time—booked a round trip ticket and six nights in a budget guesthouse with my tips from Tuna Town. I know, I know . . . Keep your jokes; I've heard them all. We had the cheapest tuna rolls on Broadway, though, and fresh most of the time. Anyway, I hadn't seen my dad since I was seven, so it might sound like the adventure of a lifetime. It could even have been my story: this girl who decides to burn her meager savings on a trip to Italy to find the mysterious genitor she hasn't heard from in thirteen years. There's a tearful reunion, they sort out their issues, and she moves to Rome at the end—to start a new life and all.

I'll get to that part, but let's start with the afternoon right after I landed. I was sitting on a bench in a tiny park square tucked by the Piazza di San Marco—little more than a patch of grass under a few parasol pines. With my ripped jeans, my old Eastpak, and a can of beer tucked between my knees while I munched on a two-euro slice of margherita, I probably looked like your average gutter punk to the untrained eye. The October sun was warm in my hair—a messy bun dyed a washed-out turquoise. I liked that color, even if my blonde roots looked a little greenish.

Washing down the pizza with a slow sip, I watched over the rim of my can as buses came and went from a station on the square. Tons of buses, white and red, vomiting families of tourists coming to visit Roman ruins and that castle thing overlooking the piazza. It kinda looked like a Greek temple, with columns everywhere, white marble, and a statue of a guy on a horse in front of it. Old stuff, very nice. I took a couple of pics, mostly to pass the time because I couldn't muster the courage to hop on a bus and go knock on my dad's door.

I had his address saved in Google Maps; well, I hoped it was his, anyway. I'd found it not long after discovering his Facebook profile a few weeks ago, but he hadn't replied to my friend invite. Maybe social media wasn't his thing. He must be in his mid-fifties after all, which, to my twenty-year-old self sounded like some sort of pre-mummification stage. I set my beer down on the bench and took out my phone to check my Facebook feed for the hundredth time. I chewed on my nails. No new notification.

A few taps and a tiny profile pic of a fifty-something guy with graying blond hair appeared. Big grin, a tan, and sunglasses—taken during a vacation, I gathered.

Gabriele Lombardi.

Lombardi . . . the last name I had never worn. The name of a quiet Italian dude who'd sometimes visit our Brooklyn flat on Sundays and take me to Coney Island for the afternoon. We never did any rides, just strolled up and down the Boardwalk and shared a hot dog. He didn't know what to say to a six-year-old, so he'd be like, "Guarda, dei gabbiani!" *Look, seagulls!* Meanwhile, I'd eat my half of our hot dog in dignified silence because I already knew what a seagull was. I would have wanted to hear about his job instead, or if he'd left Rome because of all the slavery there, like in *Gladiator*. And maybe, if I'd been brave enough, I'd have told him about the secret weighing in my chest and keeping me up at night, but I was too shy—too awkward for any of that.

I had no idea, back then, that Italy was even farther than Florida, and that this occasional Sunday dad of mine didn't have legit visitation rights because he'd never filed for paternity in the first place. I didn't know there'd be one too many fights with my mom over alimony, one too many threats of suing his lazy ass, one last Sunday, one last hot dog, and that I'd never see him again after that afternoon, when the seagulls paused in their flight above our heads for a short eternity.

Whatever. Tough shit, I guess. I chugged another gulp of beer and listened to the city's noise, the cars, and the laugh of strangers, getting reacquainted with what little Italian I'd learned from my dad as a kid, like a song I wouldn't remember well, but whose melody lingered. The notes threaded with Roman voices to fill the gaping holes in my vocabulary, and I could tell that those two women worked in a hospital, or that the guys sitting in the grass were checking their phone to see how to get to Quartaccio—wherever that was. Not bad for a high school dropout with a record 0.6 GPA. I gave a snort when I noticed an ad on the side of a bus with the words *test di admissione*. College, the final frontier . . .

I manspread wider on the bench with a bitter sigh and craned my neck to look up at the azure sky. Maybe I should message him again, and say "Hey, I'm here in Rome"? But what if he thought I was a stalker and he freaked out? What if he didn't want to be found? Okay, that one was far-fetched; he was on Facebook, after all. And yet goose bumps bloomed under my hoodie in a familiar mix of shame and dread. It was kind of too late for that, but I was starting to realize I'd fucked up—again. I'd pictured myself starring in my very own Lifetime movie and blown $700 on a stupid impulse. Now I couldn't even find the balls to call him and simply ask, "Do you remember me? Do you want to see me?"

"Okay," I announced, to no one in particular—scared a couple of pigeons though.

I slammed my beer on the bench. Night wouldn't fall for another couple of hours, at least. Museum tickets and tourist stuff were expensive, but I could always take a stroll around the piazza to clear my thoughts—the forum with the old Roman ruins was right behind that palace with the horseman. No need to pay for a ticket to check it from the street and snatch a few pics. I grabbed my backpack and beer. I frowned down at the almost-full black can. Honestly, that shit tasted worse than a Natty Daddy you drink alone for breakfast, and I didn't want to be the girl who drowns her sorrow in grandma's rubbing alcohol.

But I didn't like to waste either. I decided to leave it up for whoever wanted to grab it—a bit of street solidarity never hurt. I'd barely shrugged on my backpack before this old guy with dirty track pants and gaping sneakers popped up behind me. Bumdar alert: dude hadn't even bothered removing the cardboard sign around his neck—a few lines in Italian hastily scribbled with a Sharpie. I made no attempt to decipher it; his toothless grin spoke for itself. I flourished my hand toward the can with a wink.

He took the can and toasted me with it, chewing out a few

words in a raspy singing voice. It took me a couple of seconds to make sense of the jumbled syllables—he wanted to know what a nice girl like me was doing in Rome.

My lips parted to reply. No sound came out. A loud and familiar beat in my chest muted my voice. His. Everyone else's.

Oh God. Oh no . . .

It always started like this: a pulse inside me, like a warning before the tide surged, roared . . . and froze everything. The bum had raised my beer to his lips; golden drops remained still in the air above his open mouth. The tourists stood paralyzed mid-stride. The children's grins were empty masks; their legs were coiled, ready for a jump that wasn't coming, like birds about to fly away. The cars and the buses had stopped. Over the suffocating silence, all I could hear was the blood drumming in my ears, my neck. I staggered back, buried my face in my hands. I didn't want it anymore—this hideous disease I could tell no one about.

It'd been weeks, perhaps even months since the last time, and like always, I'd almost allowed myself to believe it'd never happen again. How the fuck do you sit down in front of a shrink—or worse, your social worker—and tell them that you're doing great, except when time stops, and everyone and everything is frozen but you? *Don't worry, though, it's been like this since I was a kid; I'm used to it. I mean, sure, I freak out a teensy bit when I wake up at night, and I see a drop of water hanging midair from my kitchen faucet, but it's not as bad as it sounds. Nothing the right kind of meds and a straitjacket can't fix, right, Doc?*

It wouldn't last. It never did. I massaged my skull and kept my eyes screwed shut, repeating the words in my head like a mantra: *It's almost over. It never lasts. Never.* Just long enough to make me freak out in the middle of Central Park among frozen joggers and their dogs. Wax statues everywhere whose clothes wouldn't wrinkle when I tried to touch them, water that wouldn't wet my hands, and the silence, the *silence* drilling into my eardrums. I breathed through my nose. In. Out. Slowly, ticking endless seconds in my head until the hallucination passed.

Reality rushed back to me in a deep exhale. A car honked somewhere across the piazza, and the bum chugged down the rest of my can with a reassuring gurgle. A fat kid bumped into me; I was so out of it that I was the one who kept apologizing over and over as I stumbled away from the bench and toward the sidewalk. I needed to get away from the noise, the people. Right now. Scratch tourism; my new plan was to run straight to the guesthouse, check into my room, and stay curled in the dark until tomorrow.

Fighting the urge to climb on the first bus I saw, I resolved to ask for directions instead. Because my day hadn't been shitty enough yet, might as well stack some cringeworthy social interaction in a language I hadn't spoken in over a decade on top of it. I waved awkward fingers at a sweaty driver who sat slouched behind his wheel. "*Quale . . . Autobus . . . Appia Alba?*" Which . . . bus . . . Appia Alba?

My stuttering efforts were rewarded with a compassionate wince before he motioned at another station across the park with a doughy arm. "*Può prendere l'ottantasette.*" I remained stuck in place, my jaw hanging limply as I slowly processed his instructions. "*Ottantasette*," he repeated, before thankfully adding, "Eighty-seven."

I gave an eager nod. "*Grazie mille, signore.*" Thank you very much, sir.

Well, things were looking up. If the bus didn't freeze on its way to my guesthouse, I might even consider the trip a small victory. I strode toward the station at a brisk pace, passing the bum I'd given my beer to earlier. Dude had collapsed on the bench, using his cardboard sign to shield his leathery face from the sun while he napped. I thought of that old Phil Collins song: 'Just Another Day in Paradise," but I wasn't really sad for him because I knew there were good and bad days on the streets, and to him, a sunny afternoon and free beer probably made for a good one.

Lost in my own thoughts, I didn't pay attention to the elegant silhouette catching up with me until a soft voice said, "*Em?* Is that you?"

II

Two words: *Oh* and *Shit*.

I took a step away from the doppelganger of Audrey Hepburn smiling at me in her neat trench and navy cigarette pants. Lily tilted her head, and it made her sleek, jet-black ponytail bounce prettily. I gulped a breath that stayed stuck in my throat. What were the fucking chances? I mean, flying 6,000 miles away from New York all the way to Europe, I'd been ready to deal with a lot of weird shit, starting with bidets and tourist scams. What I hadn't counted on was running into my stepsis. To be honest, I thought I'd never see Lily again, or maybe someday she'd walk past me down Broadway, and she wouldn't recognize me—or she'd pretend not to.

"Em?" She tried again. "Is that really you?"

My mouth opened, ready to reply, "No," and maybe babble something in broken Italian, but Lily would probably see through my bullshit, and it'd make things even worse. I took an instinctive step back. "Wow. You're, like . . . in Rome too?" I tried to sound cool, but I couldn't filter the dismay from my voice, and she picked up on it.

Her lips quivered into a nervous smile. "This is just crazy . . . I actually live here. I'm doing a gap year before my MA."

Of course, she was. See, back when I was a teen and my self-centered, Slipknot-fueled angst more or less peaked, I developed this theory that if God existed, He'd sent Lily just for me, a stepsister to slowly torture me by being everything I wasn't and could never be. A wholesome girl with top grades, amazing friends, an amazing dad, a heart of gold, you name it. But I had it all wrong. God, or whoever, had not sent Lily for me. He'd sent her for my mom. God had looked upon that loser Gabriele, his rust-bitten Honda Civic and Sunday hot dogs in the guise of child support. God had taken good note of the bizarre and apathetic kid my mom was stuck with—and don't get me started on her cramped one-bedroom right above a laundromat.

And so, in his great benevolence, God had sent her a reasonably hot, mild-mannered, widowed art-gallery owner named Richard and his sweet little girl—Lily. To replace us both. *Thanks, God.*

"Em." Lily was still standing there, expecting some sort of reaction from me, I gathered. Her pale hand reached as if to catch me before I flew away. I stiffened. She dropped it back at her side just as soon. "I'm just really happy that you're okay. We even thought—"

I cut her off with a tight chuckle. "Well, I'm not dead."

She shook her head just a little too emphatically. "No! I mean, of course not. We were just worried . . . because we didn't have any news."

For two years and four months. From the second I turned eighteen, and I was able to erase myself from the background of their family portrait for good. "I lost my phone," I said lamely.

She winced. "I guess it happens. So, are you here on vacation . . . or maybe to see your dad?" she added hesitantly.

"Yeah. Just left him," I replied, looking straight into her big, brown eyes.

In the space of an unsteady heartbeat, I nearly regretted my lie, wondering if Lily of all people would buy it. She'd witnessed enough fights between Mom and me that'd end up with Mom grabbing her Blackberry from her purse and tossing it on the couch with all her strength—she missed and shattered the screen, once—yelling, "Well if we're not good enough, call your father! Come on, Em; *call him!*" Of course, I didn't have his number, and I don't even think she had it either, after years without hearing from him. So yeah, I'd never really opened up to Lily about all that, but she basically knew.

I braced myself for a doubtful frown on her part, but her face lit up. "That's great. I'm so glad you two reconnected."

I gave a lopsided smile in response. "I'm glad, too, I guess." My eyes darted around, seeking a way out—an excuse—anything to cut this train wreck short. "Okay, um, I don't want to hold you or anything. You must be really busy with work and stuff."

A couple of awkward seconds ticked by, during which I waited for Lily to wave me goodbye and run off to call my mom and let her know that oh-my-God I wasn't actually dead or turning tricks in Mexico. But she didn't move. Instead, she replied, "Yes, work's been a little crazy lately. I'm interning for an archeological foundation. I'm helping them on a research project, and they offered me a grant to translate an incredible piece they're excavating"—she quivered with excitement as she added—"on the Palatine!"

I gave a robotic nod. Far as I knew, the Palatine was this big hill full of ruins, and you could get a combined ticket to visit the whole thing along with the coliseum for twelve euro, which was a fair deal compared to the Sistine Chapel and the Vatican—sixteen euros? Get out! But I figured that Lily didn't care about that. I pursed my lips in appreciation—of what, I wasn't sure. "Sounds really cool. It's great that you still study . . . history."

I hoped we were done with small talk and she'd just leave now because I had officially run out of things to tell her. All I knew was that she'd enrolled in Harvard five years ago. I still remembered the day my mom had called to give me the great news. Normally, she'd only call when she received my report cards from Saint-Henry—a unique boarding institution empowering differently abled learners since 1904! Their words, not mine. Mom had said, "Lily has been accepted into Harvard"; then she'd asked, "And what are *you* going to do?" I knew my card was full of Fs and shit like, "I have never seen this student in my classroom," or "Emma's disruptive behavior is preventing her from exploring her potential to the fullest," so I kept quiet. My mom had sighed and hung up, like always.

I didn't realize I'd zoned out until Lily tilted her head again like a pigeon. "Em?"

My gaze snapped up. "That's me. Well, um, I guess I'll be on my way."

Her shoulders hitched; she flashed me a pleading look. "Are you doing anything else today?"

My poker face wavered, and I forced a smile on my lips as I kept lying my ass off. "I was going to visit . . ." *stuff.* "The coliseum."

"Oh my God, are you serious? Actually, I was on my way there. Our digging site is behind the Coliseum, near San Bonaventura." She grinned. "Come with me, I'll give you a tour no ticket can buy."

I had no idea what she was talking about, but one fact stood out from this slow-motion crash: I had lied my way straight into a concrete wall. I scanned the Piazza, the buses and a couple police cars blaring their sirens to pass them faster. Still no providential cop-out in sight and my brain cells were running on empty. I shrugged helplessly.

"Okay, follow me, then!"

Congratulations, Em. You played yourself.

Well, fuck me. All the turns I'd taken in life had officially taken me back to square one. Except in Rome, and in a mirror reality where Lily and I were on speaking terms, strolling down the *Via dei Fori Imperiali,* along old brick buildings and ruins. I wasn't even sure we'd exchanged a single word the last time I'd seen her. I'd been seventeen our last Christmas together—Lily coming back from Harvard to celebrate with the family, me from Saint-Henry because . . . they closed during Christmas break, and there was just no way around it. I made a point to spend as much time outside as possible, only to crash on the couch in Richard's home office around 4 am, long after everyone had gone to bed. So, this was probably the longest conversation I'd had with her since . . . ever, maybe.

I took some pics of the ruins and columns you see on all the postcards while Lily basically gave me a course on Ancient Rome, the imperial forums—sorry, *fori*—how politicians and merchants gathered there to do their business, the baths, the basilicas . . . Honestly, it was a little too much info at once what with all the names and dates, but I didn't interrupt her. I liked the distance it put between us that she was ranting about stuff I didn't really care about.

We'd just passed the massive stack of arches of a basilica, and Lily was telling me about emperor Constantine and how he kicked the ass of another emperor named Maxentius to take the throne, and after that guy drowned in the Tiber, Constantine grabbed his basilica too because these people obviously had no chill. She stopped in her explanations all of a sudden, and I knew my luck had just run out.

"What about you? I've been talking for ten minutes straight, and I realize I didn't ask about, I don't know, your life."

I retreated behind yet another shrug. "Well . . . I just work, and I guess that's about it."

"Where?"

"At a restaurant on Broadway."

The flash of compassion was easy to read on her dollface, but even with her fricking Harvard degree, she couldn't see when it was time to drop the bone. "You're a cook?"

"I work the dining room." I figured it sounded classier than just telling her I was a waitress.

"Oh. That's great." There was a lot loaded in that single *oh* that I prayed we wouldn't unpack.

"Money's okay," I quickly added. "I got my own place too." A shoebox efficiency in the Bronx, but I was pretty proud of it nonetheless.

Lily's mouth rounded in admiration, but I couldn't tell if it was sincere. She said, "That's amazing!" and reached for my hand, but I snatched it away discreetly. Undeterred, she went on, her voice a notch quieter. "I'm happy for you, you know. I know it's not always been easy . . . I'll be home for Christmas; maybe we could organize something with Mom—"

"I've already got plans," I snapped, a sudden pressure welling in my chest. I hated the way she said it, *'Mom.' Her* mom. Not mine.

Lily took a sharp breath and fished for her phone in her black Dior tote. "Okay . . . I'll give you my number anyway."

I pulled out my own phone and gave it to her. She noticed the Minions case; it made her smile. Her fingers skimmed across the glass screen, creating a new contact. Lily. When she was done, she handed it back to me with a hopeful smile. "Text me so I have yours?"

I clutched the scratched plastic case hesitantly. On a rational level, I'd rather get full-body herpes than give her my number, but I was also painfully aware of this tiny part of me that still wanted to belong somewhere. I watched my pride fly away and flip me off and chewed the inside of my cheek as I texted her. "That's mine."

After I was done, Lily pointed to the coliseum in the distance. I wasn't sure why, but there was something vaguely threatening about its worn stones and the multitude of empty arches. A dead building, long-gutted from its inside. Creepy. It looked even more massive up-close; I felt like an ant in the shadow stretching across the square all the way to the avenue. Colossal stuff indeed. I followed Lily around a mile-long queue of tourists trampling the pavement impatiently, fanning themselves with colorful leaflets.

"It's often difficult to get in, especially at this time of the year," Lily noted. "But I can use my Katharos pass to take you for a private visit after hours. Tomorrow night, maybe?"

"Katharos?" I asked, to change the subject.

"The Katharos Archeological Foundation; that's where I'm interning. They're very active here in Rome. They finance expensive excavations, publish books about their finds, and they raise funds to protect sites from developers."

"Cool." I shot a doubtful look at the spotless red varnish of her loafers. "So, you're digging and, like, dusting stuff?"

She shook her head and laughed. There was no bite to it, but I still felt dumb. "No, no. Most of the time I help analyzing the pieces we find. I draw them, and then I do research to see how they fit in our current state of knowledge about a given period. I do translation too. I want to do a thesis on proto-Italic alphabets, and the foundation has incredible pieces to study."

"Okay."

As we kept circling around the coliseum, the crowd became scarce, save for a little cluster of old people bickering around a souvenir shop. Lily stopped in front of a single arch standing a hundred feet away from the arena as if it'd been randomly dropped there. It was the size of a building, and there wasn't a single square inch that hadn't been sculpted with guys in skirts, horses, columns, Latin text . . . you name it. I took a pic because everyone else was. Lily watched me do so with a proud grin.

"It's the Constantine Arch. He had it erected to commemorate his victory over Maxentius."

"The guy he took the basilica from?"

Lily nodded. "You see the stylistic differences between the top and bottom half?"

"Sure." *Not at all . . .*

"It's because the arch is kind of a collage. The artists reused pieces from Trajan and Hadrian's period and added their own, but the late Roman style was already veering away from the classical Hellenistic one. It was less realistic, less refined," she droned, nodding with a frown of concentration. "Constantine's Arch is a perfect surviving example of that stylistic dichotomy, and some would argue, of the decline of the empire at that time . . . Em?"

Someone, shoot me please . . . "Yeah, it's . . . very cool." *It's the same bearded guys in skirts. Everywhere.*

I drew a quiet breath of relief when she walked us away from the dreaded arch. We made our way in blessed silence toward a green hillside where pines shadowed ruins emerging from the ground. A little farther down the trail, a tall scaffolding fitted with building wrap shielded a big chunk of the site from prying eyes. I stared up at the stone profile printed on the wrap and the sober black logo over it. Katharos Foundation.

A pair of beefy guards in dark suits guarded the entrance to the site. Lily flashed them her pass and a smile they didn't return, and we were in. Honestly, the wrapping looked more exciting than the piles of dirt and the excavators it concealed. Lily motioned for me to follow her. "Come, it's this way."

I didn't want to take her hand, but when she threatened to twist her ankle for the third time on protruding rocks, I let my hand dangle near hers in a silent invitation. She laced her fingers with mine, a smile on her lips. As we got closer, I stuck to my first impression that there wasn't much to see around here, except . . . a big hole. Workers wearing blue helmets bustled around a pit some fifteen feet wide and so deep I couldn't see the bottom from where I stood.

I watched them set up pickets and yellow tape around the hole and yell stuff to each other in Italian under the attentive eyes of a black guy who looked all business in a classy gray suit and camel coat. At his side a younger dude with a navy sweater and jeans ran two hands through his curly brown hair, looking awestruck. Lily waved at him excitedly, but he didn't react. His gaze was set on the hole, eyes wide and unblinking, and I couldn't place why his fascination sent a chill of unease crawling under my skin like that.

III

"Dante!"

Alerted by Lily's squeal, the younger guy's chin jerked up. He turned to acknowledge us with a ridiculously white smile.

He kind of almost winked. She blushed. I sensed an explanation coming. "Dante and I—" she began.

"—are fucking," I completed in a matter-of-fact tone.

Lily's jaw went slack, but her shock soon became a guilty grin. "He's my boyfriend. He works for Katharos too. That's how we met . . ."

"Not judging." I shrugged, my palms up.

Why wasn't I surprised that Lily's boyfriend looked like an Armani ad, on top of digging top-secret archeological holes? She ran to him like in a movie and hugged him. It made my chest tighten a little because I couldn't remember the last time I'd hugged anyone like that—maybe as a little kid? I averted my eyes and pretended to be super interested in the excavator gathering a big pile of rubble away from the hole instead.

When he tipped his head to look at me over her shoulder, she whirled around. "Dante, this is Emma Nielsen, my stepsister. Em, meet Dante Alessandri."

He waved at me with a good-guy grin. I waved back. Again,

awkward five seconds. The black guy walked up to them to whisper something in Dante's ear, his face completely blank. If he noticed me, he gave no sign of it. I took a few cautious steps toward the hole to get a better look because I had no idea what to do with myself, but also, admittedly, because I was a little curious. It went much deeper than I expected, at least a hundred feet. Ropes hung all the way down from several reels, and a few workers equipped with climbing harnesses were busy scraping dirt from some sort of large circular stone plate half-buried in the earth among broken columns and cracked slabs of rock. With each swipe of their gloved hands, symbols appeared that looked like letters, but nothing I could decipher.

I stared, feeling a little . . . off. I was hyperaware of the noise of the engines and the voices ricocheting my way from the bottom of the hole. My ears were buzzing, and I thought maybe I'd drunk more beer than I thought.

Dante's suave Italian accent filtered through my daze. "Chronos's Table. It was part of a small shrine to Cronus—or Chronos, for the Greek. The building collapsed in the fifth century during a landslide, and the table was thought to have been destroyed." He shifted closer to me with Lily latched around his arm. "It's a completely unique piece."

I stared down the hole at the concentric lines of characters covering the stone disc. "It was a table?"

"Not made for eating, though," Dante said with a chuckle. "Rather, a ritual artifact."

"What kind of ritual?" I asked.

Lily's smile wavered. "We don't know yet. We need to translate the inscriptions."

"That's what you meant when you said Katharos had incredible pieces," I mused, eyeing Lily.

"Yes. The inscriptions on the table are a form of proto-Canaanite script like nothing we've ever seen before." When my face remained stuck in a grimace of mild confusion, she explained, "What we call proto-Canaanite is a very early alphabet that was used to transcribe Semitic languages. It's basically the ancestor to Greek and Latin, derived from hieroglyphs, but here, the characters are different, and so far, the table's alphabet seems twice as crowded as Phoenician, for example."

"More letters, more sounds?" I ventured.

"That's the idea," Dante confirmed. My lips quirked in fleeting pride as he went on. "It could be a written trace of an archaic language we've never encountered before, with a broader, more complex palette of phonemes."

"And that it just awaited us for all this time inside a Roman temple; it's insane," Lily added in an awed breath.

I gave a slow nod and silently thanked Dante when he thought it useful to provide just a teensy bit of context. "We think the table largely predates the foundation of Rome—middle of the Bronze age, probably. Ancient Romans tended to either assimilate or erase older civilizations as they expanded—like the Etruscans, for example—so it's extremely unusual that someone took the pain to preserve the table throughout the centuries and place it in a Roman shrine."

"So that it can end up in a museum," I noted dryly, watching workers position huge belts under the muddy slab of granite.

If he picked up on the sarcasm, Dante chose to ignore it. "And it's all thanks to the next professor, Professor McKeanney," he chuckled, wrapping his arm around her shoulders—God, did these two ever stop cuddling? "We would never have found the table without Lily's research."

I tilted my head at her. "Professor McKeanney? Like your grandpa?"

Her gaze grew wistful. "I'm not quite there yet; I'll need to get my PhD first. It's his discovery anyway, not mine. I just used his final notes and filled in the blanks." Her eyes met Dante's, who gave her shoulder a light squeeze. She smiled. "I owe him everything."

"As do I," Dante replied, in the kind of husky and tender voice I thought you only heard in movies.

Lily gave a happy nod. "He must have been watching over us, somehow."

Ah, the legendary grandfather—my mother's pride and joy. Back when we were kids, she never missed an opportunity to slip it into any conversation that the father of her trophy husband was a distinguished professor of archeology who'd been featured in several BBC documentaries—on TV. Just in case you didn't get that right; he had been on *TV*.

Joke aside, the old McKeanney had been Lily's childhood hero, some kind of Indiana Jones, but without the whip or the adventures. He'd written tons of books, taught at Harvard, and they'd even set a memorial plate there after he killed himself, a few months before I dropped from Saint-Henry. I didn't know the details—only what I'd overhead from Richard and my mom during our final Christmas together. Apparently, the old man had never gotten over the death of Lily's mother from Hodgkin's lymphoma when Lily was three. He'd buried himself in his work for almost two decades to fight off depression until he jumped from a window.

Sad stuff, especially since he'd struck me as a decent human being the couple of times I'd met him as a kid. The kind of guy willing to pretend he was interested in my textbooks, even when I snubbed him like a little turd. My stomach coiled unpleasantly at the realization that he had ended it here, in an apartment in Rome. I shot a sideways glance at Lily, who rested her head on Dante's shoulder while they discussed their mystic Ikea Table. It dawned on me that must be weird for her to be back here, right in her grandad's footsteps . . . after that.

She turned to smile at me while Dante droned on. Like a bucket of icy water suddenly dropping over my head, I heard my mother's voice again. *Can't you be a little less selfish? Lily lost her mother! How would it feel for you to lose me, Em?* I swallowed the bitter taste in my mouth. I knew how it felt. Like you're stripped bare and you belong nowhere.

"*Ehi! Torna qui!*" Hey, get back here!

All heads flipped where that gravelly shout came from, mine included. On the other side of the hole, some hobo with a beer in hand staggered dangerously close to the edge. Blatantly ignoring the guards and workers yelling for him to get back, he let his body tip forward, even closer to the pit, reaching through thin air with a weird cane made of gnarled wood.

Dante's eyebrows jerked a fraction, before he told me, "Sorry. They're everywhere in the center because tourists keep giving them change."

Lily watched with big sad eyes as two guards hooked their arms into the hobo's to pull him away from the hole. He dropped his beer in the grass and managed to reach for his face to readjust small round sunglasses. I scanned him, an old habit even though he posed no threat to me at the moment. Long worn coat, wrinkled and patched up. Corduroy pants, threadbare at the knees, but not really dirty. Dark T-shirt, nice steel-toes showing through his busted boots. Dude hadn't shaved in at least a couple of months, and the mess of sandy curls on his head could use a cut—or just a comb, really.

My eyes narrowed as they dragged him toward us. Mid to late twenties, probably. No red blotches on what was otherwise a fairly good mug, save for that mask of exhaustion the street eventually paints on all features. One of the guards pulled on his T-shirt so hard he nearly tore it off. Hold on—no beer belly? That toned stomach was either a great contouring job or a fine case of meth abs.

I smelled a fauxbo. Dammit, I hated those. Wannabe artists and trust-fund babies, most of the time, who played bum all night before returning to their Brooklyn loft at dawn to sleep the booze off until noon. Even so, anger zinged up my spine and directly to my head when a burly guard punched him in the stomach hard, just for show. I leaped in front of them without thinking. "Hey, hey! Easy! Dude . . . He's just a bum."

They stopped and shot an anxious glance at Dante and the black guy. Neither moved to stop me. Dante flashed me a stiff smile I gathered meant he didn't want a scene in front of Lily—whose eyes were so wide they'd roll out of her skull any moment now. The guards released their hold long enough for the hobo to brace his palms on his knees and gasp out a trickle of saliva, which he wiped with the back of his hand.

I bent toward him gingerly, picking up a whiff of booze and something sweet like candy. "You okay?"

He raised his head at me, and I nearly stumbled back in surprise. His glasses had slipped askew, and I could see that the eyes looking into mine were empty—his gray irises encased milky white pupils. Blind. I glanced down at the cane he still gripped tight in his right hand. Figured.

He grinned, revealing incisors that didn't look like he'd spent years in the gutter, even if they overlapped a little. I fought the urge to step away when he reached for my face and grazed it briefly. I shivered from the contact. He spoke, the faintest accent lingering in his raspy voice. "You smell like a tourist."

I shook off the fleeting pang of compassion I had allowed to dwell in my chest as I hauled him up. "You smell like a drunk asshole. Nice to meet you too."

A hoarse chuckle on his side. "Pizza and coconut shampoo. American girls always smell like that."

Perfect. A fauxbo *and* a C-grade pickup artist. "Seriously . . . Get the fuck out of here."

He whirled around, bowed to me on unsteady legs and lumbered out of the site with a dramatic wave of his hand. My lips twitched involuntarily. There was something about people who no longer gave a flying fuck—a spark that regular folks just didn't have.

IV

After the hobo was out of sight, the black guy took Dante aside to discuss stuff with him. There was some nodding and fleeting glances at the hole. The guy—I figured he was Dante's boss—shot a look my way before he put on sunglasses and left, escorted by a pack of bodyguards. I didn't like his whole sunglasses-in-daylight-*Godfather* vibe and how he basically ignored Lily and me. The douche was strong with this one.

Night was falling. Pink clouds stretched behind the dark frame of the coliseum like a flaming halo, and the workers were starting to set up lights around the hole, angling them at the table. Lily walked up to me. "Dante and I are heading back. Do you want to come too?" Her tone grew hesitant. "Maybe we can have dinner together?"

I flung my hand toward the site's well-guarded entrance. "Actually, I need to go to my hotel. I still haven't checked in."

"You're not staying at your dad's?"

I sidestepped the trap. "Only one bedroom."

Done typing on his phone, Dante popped up behind Lily. "Where's your hotel? Maybe we can give you a ride."

I turned the idea in my head. Not ideal, but tolerable—and free. "It's the Trionfale Guesthouse. On Via Alba."

He reached into his back pocket and pulled out his phone again to type in the address. He tapped, scrolled. Cringed. I felt my cheeks grow hot because I could read on his face what he thought of my twenty-five-bucks-a-night guesthouse. The pics hadn't looked so bad to me when I'd booked it, but now, in Dante's eyes, I saw that he and Lily and I lived in different worlds. Galaxies apart, really.

His mouth twisted, and he wrestled the grimace into a gentle smile. "You know what, Emma, why don't we arrange a room for you at the Residenza for the week?"

Lily clasped her hands, shock and delight written all over her face. I inched away from her. "Thanks, but I already paid for my room at the Trionfale. What's the Residenza anyway?"

"It's a building where Katharos houses their employees. I live there with Dante. You're gonna *love* it," Lily said.

Unlikely, because I didn't want their vanilla-flavored charity in the first place. But I *was* curious to see what the place looked like. Or maybe it was because of Lily, and the way she was looking at me, hopeful and anxious. I had an urge to jump as if I were standing on a ledge. I needed to see where it'd take me, seeing her again after all this time. Hooking my thumbs in my jeans' pockets, I made my second stupid decision that day, and heard myself reply, "I guess we can always eat something and I'll go to my guesthouse afterward."

If I hadn't been riding in the backseat of Dante's Cayenne, this would have felt like a trip back in time. We drove up a long street where literally every single building was something straight out of a period drama. Antique arch doors, wrought iron grilles barring the first-floor windows, sculpted balcony above those. We passed churches that looked so much like ancient temples that I almost expected the tourists in front of them to grow togas over their backpacks. My forehead pressed to the window, I watched this endless party of columns stacked on top of more columns. I was starting to suspect they were the generally accepted unit of measure for street cred here in Rome.

And Katharos foundation's Residenza didn't lack any. The mandatory columns framed ten-foot-tall windows, and a pair of stone monsters guarded the entrance door, poised as if they were supporting the second-floor balcony—muscular guys with goat heads and really tiny dicks. Dante slowed down and glanced at me in the mirror. "What do you think?"

My first instinct was to reply that it was cool, but I feared it wouldn't do, considering. "It looks very baroque," I told him.

He gave a wheezing sound like a laugh was stuck at the back of his throat that he wouldn't allow to come out. I never knew I was so funny . . .

In the passenger seat, Lily undid her seatbelt and turned to flash me a radiant smile. "The building dates from the eighteenth century, so it's more of a neo-classical style, but yes, some of the architect's choices were . . . baroque. Come, let's get inside!"

I followed them through a wide courtyard with lollipop shrubs sitting in giant urns. I itched to take a few pics, but I thought maybe they'd find it weird because it wasn't a museum or anything—they lived here.

"How long have you been living here?" I asked Lily as we entered a hall that looked like a movie décor . . . or Teresa Giudice's house, if that's your thing. The ceiling must have been at least fifteen feet high, and there was enough gold leaf on all those moldings to pay Greece's debt.

"Three months. Mom and Dad came over for a couple of weeks this summer to help me move in." She noticed my stony expression.

Her smile wavered, and she gave a nervous chuckle. "I think she freaked out a little when I left the safety of home for this distant and mysterious land full of Italians." She curled her fingers and wiggled them like tentacles as she recounted this.

Dante laughed. I didn't. Lily's arms fell back down at her sides. It was awkward.

She bit her lower lip. "Do you want to see my apartment? We can sit and catch up for a while before dinner." She sent an apologetic look to her boyfriend, something along the lines of, "Sorry, I need you out of the way."

As expected, Dante the sentient Ken doll, smiled and said, "Take your time; I'll go review Lucius's files in the salon." With this, he bent to brush his lips against hers, allowing his nose to linger against hers tenderly before he walked across the hall and disappeared behind a set of heavy wooden doors.

After Dante was out of sight, Lily joined her hands on her lap and squared her shoulders. She tipped her head to a double marble staircase behind her. "It's this way. I share my place with Dante."

We climbed up the stairs under the judgmental stare of a series of old portraits—sixteenth to seventeenth century, because of the big ruffs. I remembered one of my history teachers telling us about those back in tenth grade. I skipped so many classes to smoke cheap weed in the bathroom, it's a miracle I was even there for that one.

Lily led me down a long hallway with three sets of tall wooden doors. I smelled wax and detergent, and my Chucks dragged across a lavish oriental carpet. She opened the doors—no key. Did she trust the Katharos foundation so much she didn't need the most basic level of privacy?

I went in after her. When she turned on the lights, my eyebrows hit my hairline and fell back in place. Like the rest of the mansion,

Lily and Dante's "apartment" screamed old money. She went to sit on the long cream sofa standing opposite a massive four-poster bed with silky gray linen. I glanced at the marble countertops of a kitchen tucked in a corner of the room. I dropped my backpack at my feet, went to lean against the island and crossed my arms, waiting for the conversation I knew she'd never have initiated in the middle of a crowded street or in front of Dante.

Lily's smile was gone, replaced by an intense brown stare and dark circles I was only noticing now under her makeup. Her throat tightened. *Here we go*, I thought.

"Em, what *happened?*" were her first words since entering the room.

I shrugged. My tactic of choice whenever dealing with family.

Her hands wouldn't stop fidgeting on her lap. "Saint-Henry called Mom as soon as you left. She actually went to the *police*. They told her they couldn't do anything since you were eighteen already."

I fought a victorious sneer at the memory of that day. Of course, they couldn't stop me. I had been counting the days—the hours—until I could legally grab my backpack and walk free through Saint-Henry's gate. There was this young counselor, a bleached blonde who loved to compare the place to Hogwarts and say we all had powers we didn't suspect. She ran after me, said she'd call my mom so the three of us could sit down and "talk it out." Nothing had ever felt as good as my two middle fingers flipping up in response.

Lily's eyes went glassy as she recalled: "Mom was . . . She didn't understand. She's still hurt and angry about it—even now."

The tears she was trying to hold back made my own eyes ache, but I wasn't about to weep in front of Lily, of all people. "It's been over two years," I said evenly. "I'm sure she got over the loss."

Lily shook her head as if something I'd said wouldn't compute. "Where did you go? *Why* did you go?"

"I kind of just . . . traveled for a while. I settled a year ago after I got my job," I replied, purposely avoiding her second question.

Her face bunched. "Traveled *where?*"

Another shrug. I was always a black-belt at shrugging—I'd spent most of my life clamming up against people asking questions I didn't want to answer, after all.

Lily squinted up at me, and with each new wrinkle on her brow, I felt myself being picked apart, examined under a microscope. My short, bitten nails, the slight bags under my eyes, a few scars on my hands, the knuckles just a little too red, a little too rough. It was a familiar unease, spotted with a little guilt here, a little shame there, but also colorful specks of pride, in spite of it all. Not for the first time, I wondered if it showed on my face that I'd spent almost eighteen months of my life sleeping on benches and in abandoned buildings. "Where?" she insisted in a brittle voice.

I gave her my secret ninja shrug. "You wouldn't get it."

Her cheeks went ashen, and I read disgust and pity in her slightly parted lips. Maybe she thought I'd been a hooker or something. "But why didn't you call us?" she near-shouted.

I wouldn't cry about that shit, but my eyes were prickling, and I had to swallow hard to keep myself together. It was difficult to find the right words; they whirled around my head like moths around a lightbulb. I took a deep breath. "You and your dad, and my mom, you're a family."

"Yes, we're *your* family," Lily shot back indignantly.

"No," I replied. I thought it'd be harder to say it, but I felt relieved hearing that single sharp syllable burst out loud in the silence. "You guys have your own thing, and that's cool. I mean, I don't care. You lost your mom, and mine stepped in, and it's . . ." I was reaching the limits of my emotional vocabulary. A shrug was needed. My shoulders jerked once again. "It's cool. I'm cool with that. But I was never part of it. It's your story, not mine."

Lily stared at me, her breath slow and shallow. I waved a hand at the wall. No need to explain. She wasn't stupid—far from it. She might not want to talk about it, but she remembered the way my mom had latched onto her new husband's perfect kid, this "second chance" like she'd said once. In front of me. Lily remembered the suffocating anger hanging in the air after each shitty report card, which would sometimes culminate in a resounding slap on my cheek after my mom was done reading. Lily knew, like everyone else did, that it was me who kept drawing on the walls of our bedroom with her pink nail polish and tearing pages out of Richard's books—even though I always accused her with a straight face afterward.

To his credit, Richard did make halfhearted attempts to play peacemaker in the complete shitstorm that was his new marriage. He'd hug Lily's tears away, caress my mom's equally damp cheeks with whispered pleas for her to calm down, that he knew it was hard. And I watched them from behind an ajar door, seething with resentment as the three of them bonded over the hell I was putting them through.

There must have been one morning where Richard woke up, and he told my mom he couldn't go on like this, that five years of simmering war was his limit. I could still feel the silence around our dinner table, thicker than usual the night my mother had announced they were sending my ass to a therapeutic boarding school upstate— the first of three. I could still see Lily's gaze, locked on the green beans on her plate, and that second of pure, blinding hate in my chest when I figured *she* wasn't going anywhere.

The sum of all my failures wiped a tear from her eye—I wished she'd been the kind of nasty clichéd stepsis you see in Cinderella. It would have made it easier to hate her, instead of feeling like something was playing "The Winner Takes It All" in the background . . .

"If you couldn't talk to Mom, you should have called *me*, or even Dad," she argued.

"He was relieved to see me go, and you know it."

Her voice rose again, defensive. "That's not true. Dad was actually the one who always insisted you come home for Christmas, even when Mom said she was too tired to deal with you . . ." That last word came out in a sigh as Lily realized what she'd just said: that even ten days for Christmas were too much of me. No wonder I served four consecutive years of full summer school, spent sprawled at my desk in front of an empty notebook or daydreaming on a bench in the park.

My nostrils flared as Lily shook her head and murmured, "Em, I didn't mean it like that."

The wetness in my eyes was gone. I just felt angry and cold, and I kinda liked the way Lily was unraveling under my narrowed stare. I picked up my backpack. "It was good talking to you. I think I'll go now."

Lily shot up from the couch. "Em, wait!"

I walked straight to the door, ignoring her—another one of my specialties. I reached for the handle, but before I could grab it, it jerked. I leaped back in surprise just in time to avoid the door hitting my nose. I picked up a smoky, woodsy cologne and found myself standing in front of the black businessman from the archeological site. At least he'd ditched the sunglasses, but not the strict gray suit. Cold brown eyes sized me up; his smooth, perfectly symmetrical features relaxed into a smile that held no trace of any kind of warmth. He looked over my shoulder, at Lily. "Will Emma be joining us for dinner?" His voice was deep, like the hum of a bass, and with the slightest hint of an Italian accent underneath otherwise perfect British English.

I opened my mouth to decline, but Lily beat me to it and replied with a firm, "Yes, Lucius. I'm sorry; I know it's a little unexpected—"

"It's no problem at all. Emma is welcome to stay at the Residenza as long as she wants."

Like Maury would say, the fact that Lucius wouldn't even look at me as he stated this determined it was a lie.

V

That Lucius guy stared at me from across the table, leaning back in the same sort of gilded chair I sat in. He laced his fingers like an old-school villain—his lips curved. "So, Emma, how long are you staying with us?"

Approximately thirty seconds if you keep giving me your creepy fake smile, bro, was what I wanted to say. Instead, I replied, "My flight leaves on Sunday morning."

"Excellent," he said.

Lily and Dante exchanged embarrassed looks. I didn't mind the jab. At least Lucius was the straight-shooter type. I was okay with that.

As if to clear the air, the dining room's door creaked open to reveal a graying majordomo pushing a clothed cart—that one was an Alfred for sure. Or maybe Alfredo. I was used to waiting tables and handling whiny customers, but I rarely, if ever, sat in the chair, so it felt weird to see that guy do my job—much better than I ever did, by the way. He placed a plate of whitish Jell-O in front of me with smooth, controlled movements, and announced a scallop tartare with white truffle oil. I cringed and discreetly reached for the bread basket to grab a slice—you know, to go with it.

Lucius took a bite while Alfredo poured white wine into our

glasses. Sitting ramrod straight in their chairs, Lily and Dante kept stealing glances at each other, the corners of their lips quivering from the smiles they didn't dare exchange. I'd never admit it out loud to anyone, but it made me feel a little lonely that they had this whole silent world of their own, almost like a language. I looked away and hit my wine hard. The tartare sat untouched on my plate while I munched on my bread in silence. I watched the three of them over the crystal rim of my glass, wondering if the mood was always so lit at the Residenza, or if conversations and potted plants died wherever Lucius went.

It was Lily who eventually broke the silence after Alfredo had brought some fish on polenta with dots of tart red sauce all over the plate like in gourmet restaurants. "Em speaks much better Italian than I do, you know," she told Dante and Lucius before digging into her polenta.

Dante's eyebrows rose in curiosity, while his boss considered me with a sort of polite disdain.

I painted flowers with the sauce on my plate, avoiding their stare. "I understand it a little. But I don't speak it."

"I remember you sang songs to your Barbies when we were kids," Lily insisted, ramming her point home with some singing of her own. "*Primadonna, primaaadonna . . .*"

I gritted my teeth. I knew she wasn't doing it to mock me, but it kind of felt like it, and it made my skin prickle.

Dante's eyes widened with recognition. "*Ti piace Gianna Nannini?*" You like Gianna Nannini?

I gave a shrug. "Kinda."

He nodded, lips pursing in appreciation. "*È stata un mostro sacro degli anni ottanta.*" She was a huge star in the eighties.

"Ah?" I had no idea. All I remembered were the CDs playing

in my dad's car when we drove. Gianna Nannini, always, Giuni Russo, Umberto Tozzi, of course, Cocciante too . . . and so many others I had forgotten. The songs had stuck with me long after that final trip to Coney Island. I told Dante, "I just remembered the melodies; I didn't really care who sang them."

"I see," he replied, his head bobbing as if I'd said something interesting.

"Do you share your sister's interest in history, Emma?"

My chin jerked up, and the table went silent as Lucius's words cracked in the air. I could totally see him run a birthday clown biz. *Ho ho, kids, it's Pennywise the dancing clown!* My lips quirked at the thought. I stared him straight in the eye as I replied, "No. I guess I'm your average tourist."

He did that thing again, resting his elbows on the pristine tablecloth to lace his fingers. He tapped his thumbs together. "I'm certain there's more to you than this. Talent runs in the family, it seems."

"Lily and I aren't really family," I heard myself snap back. Old habits die hard.

She stiffened as if the words had burned her. Dante cast me a sideways look I just ignored.

"Not related," Lucius clarified.

"No." I took a slow breath in a bid to cool the blood buzzing in my ears.

"Strange . . ." Lucius said silkily. "I could have sworn you two were."

I snorted a laugh. Lily was this delicate porcelain doll, shorter than me. Her hair was as dark as mine was blonde—well, blue—and I knew my face looked rougher than hers, more angular too. "Thanks, I guess. That's the weirdest compliment anyone ever gave me."

The corners of Lucius's lips curled while the upper half of his face remained frozen. His eyes didn't blink for a good ten seconds.

Yeah, maybe he didn't mean it as a compliment. I sprawled back in my chair and crossed my arms like when I wanted to raise my shields against a pesky counselor back in high school. "So, you're Dante's boss? You dig up stuff too?" I asked, infusing each word with the same amount of contempt I could feel wafting to me from across the table.

"I'm executive director of the Katharos Foundation. I oversee the funding of Dante's research on Chronos's Table. My own expertise on the subject is, however, limited."

A vision of the half-buried slab of granite flashed in my mind. I saw myself standing at the edge of the pit in a mild daze, drawn to the void just like that hobo had. I frowned the thought of his blind eyes and goofy grin away. Plenty of stray dogs like him out there—couldn't afford to care about each and every one of them. "Chronos's Table?" I probed, allowing curiosity to take over my annoyance.

Lily chimed in. "Chronos is a primitive deity present in both the Greek and Roman pantheon. He's—"

"The god of time; I know that," I replied with an eye roll.

"The Foundation regards the table as a significant discovery," Lucius said pointedly.

"Because of the"—*shit, what was it already?*—"the writings on it."

Lily gave an energetic nod while Alfredo returned with dessert. Thank fuck, we were almost done. "We think its alphabet could be the key to an undiscovered archaic language. The table is thirteen feet wide with twenty lines of text arranged in concentric circles, and an additional block of text in its center. That's approximately 25,000 characters, which is . . . more than we could have ever hoped for."

"Lucius is having it transferred to the lab tonight; it'll be all ours tomorrow first thing in the morning," Dante told her, sounding like it was her early Christmas gift.

"Cool," I commented. Having displayed a sufficient amount of interest for Chronos's giant table, I dug into my chocolate cake; a weird green sauce oozed out that tasted like . . . basil and lemon. Strange, but not bad.

Lucius graced Lily with a smile that was almost human as she ate her cake. "We expect a lot from your work. Lady Montecito will visit the laboratory tomorrow."

My ears perked up as I scraped chocolate from my plate. Whoever the woman was, Lily looked impressed—nervous even. She nodded meekly. "I'll try not to disappoint."

"You won't," Lucius told her, and if we'd been in a mobster flick, I'd have taken it as a threat . . . But I figured the worst that could happen would be for him to kick Lily's ass back to Harvard if she didn't translate fast enough.

Dante smiled at her, perhaps to alleviate the effect of his boss's disastrous social skills. He nudged her shoulder playfully, like a private joke. She tilted her head and bit her lower lip. It was pretty obvious they were back into their little bubble, and I can't say it was that great being locked outside . . . with Lucius.

The latter eventually cleared his throat and rose from his chair. It worked. They let go of each other's hands under the table, and the spell was broken. "Dante, Lily, I'll see you tomorrow."

I jumped on the occasion and sprang from my chair half a second after he'd spoken. "It's getting late, so I guess I'll head back too. Thanks for the food and everything."

Lily's lips pressed together in obvious disappointment. I flashed her a lopsided smile—all I could give, really. It was nice of her to try so hard, but we were better off splitting roads. She'd call Mom to tell her I was doing fine, and everyone would have an awesome

Christmas serving tuna steaks in an elf costume—okay, mostly me. I motioned to the set of finely sculpted wooden doors leading to the lobby. "I'll go get my backpack."

"It's been moved to your suite already, Emma."

My shoulders hitched. I gawked at Lucius, wondering if I'd heard him wrong. "Uh . . ."

"Dante suggested we offer you our hospitality during your stay in Rome," was what Lucius said. But his eyes were weirdly intense, and all I heard was, *We all float down here.*

Yeah. No. "I got a room booked already—"

"I took care of that," Dante said with. A. Fucking. Wink. "They should have refunded your card already."

My throat went tight, and my cheeks felt hot from the sudden rush of blood to my head. It was almost eleven, and that flaming bag of dicks had canceled my booking behind my back. Probably because he thought a reject like me dreamed of living the good life with rich assholes like him, be it even for a week. My facial muscles felt numb, and I had no idea what kind of expression I wore right now, but if the sudden guilt brimming in Lily's eyes was any indication, I looked *pissed.*

I took a sharp breath and said, "I don't remember asking you to do that."

Unlike mine, Dante's composure didn't waver. "I wanted to give you and Lily a chance to spend more time together."

I narrowed my eyes at her. "Were you in on this?"

Her eyes wouldn't meet mine. As good as a "yes." Maybe she hadn't made the call herself, but she'd known and done nothing to stop him.

I wrestled the rage boiling in my chest into a sneer. "Okay . . . okay. I'm out of here." I turned to Lucius, who'd watched the whole drama with a poker face. "I want my backpack, please."

"Certainly, Emma." He nodded to Alfredo—dude was a ninja; I hadn't even noticed him standing near the fireplace. Talk about a public humiliation . . . After Alfredo was gone, Lucius gauged me and asked, "Would you like an umbrella too?"

My face pinched in confusion. I checked the windows just in time to see a flash of white paint on the street, almost instantly followed by the roar of thunder. Rain pattered hard on the stained-glass pattern of leaves and flowers, then *clattered. What the ever-loving . . .?* I ran a hand across my face. "This is a joke. It's not seriously hailing. It was 65 this afternoon!"

"It's not unheard-of," Dante noted.

"Maybe you can stay just for tonight?" Lily ventured, before quickly adding, "And if you want to go tomorrow, I'll understand."

I didn't want to go tomorrow; I wanted to get the hell away from them *now*. But the sound of the storm raging outside made my stomach churn. Every pellet hitting the windows brought back shitty memories of roaming up and down Madison for hours under the same weather, watching storefronts and people fighting over a cab while water seeped into my boots and soaked up my socks. It had been a while since I'd felt that familiar dread, the feeling that creeps up your spine when the sun sets, and you've got nowhere safe to sleep.

I fought back a stupid shiver. It had been almost a year, and things were different now. The bushes of Central Park and the fat pregnant bitch who'd stolen my phone at the Bethlehem Mission were far behind. It was all just a bunch of hazy scenes that'd sometimes flash behind my eyelids at night. Now I had a job. I wasn't going back on the street, not even for a night.

I nodded to myself to steel my resolve. "Okay. One night, and I'm gone."

VI

The suite they'd given me looked a lot like Dante and Lily's except there was no kitchen—although a well-stocked minibar more than made up for that. A young maid had ushered me in after I voiced my decision to stay for the night. I felt bad about the way she kept smoothing the fur throw as if she worried that the room wasn't perfect enough. I tipped her, but it was only three euros, and she gave me a dumbfounded look as if she didn't expect it.

After she closed the door behind herself at last, I breathed out. I took out my phone and earbuds, flung myself onto the king-size bed like on a trampoline. My arms stretched across the silky fur, I gazed up at the sculpted and gilded beams of the coffered ceiling. They'd painted guys in togas and half-naked women in each frame. I snatched a pic and scrolled through my playlist. If the taste police barged in and asked whether I was listening to *Despacito*, I'd toss the evidence through the window and deny. I glanced at the minibar hidden behind a small door in the cream paneling. The mini vodkas were calling my name, but I didn't want to get completely wasted at Lily's place . . .

I sat up and dropped my earbuds on the comforter. The evening's mess was still fresh in my mind—just thinking about that piece of shit Dante made me want to punch something, or preferably someone. It was like nothing had changed in six years. Lily was as sweet as ever; she still wrecked everything she touched in my life without even trying. It still drove me insane, and in the end, I'd turn nasty, she'd cry, and I'd be left sitting in a field of ruins, feeling like a turd.

I freed my hair from its clip and massaged my scalp slowly. Maybe a shower would help.

Water dripped a pale blue down my shoulders, my breasts, and pooled at my feet on the white mosaic tiling. Couple weeks from now, all the color would be gone, and I'd have to re dye my hair. I sighed in the shower's misty cocoon, pressing my head to the glass panel as the hot water hit my shoulder blades. I should have called my dad. I should do it. Now? Okay, maybe not in the middle of the night. Tomorrow.

Always tomorrow . . . I reached to my left to turn the water off. Procrastination: yet another special skill of mine. I dried my hair with a fluffy, pristine-white towel that was soon spotted a shade of baby blue. No big deal, they'd probably bleach it anyway. I slipped on a ratty T-shirt and a pair of shorts, intent on falling asleep in front of something dumb on TV. I padded to the sink and flipped on the tap to brush my teeth. For the first time ever, there was no warning—no gut feeling—just the immediate rush of adrenaline in my veins when the stream of water remained suspended above the chrome plug without hitting it.

My hand swiped at the smooth transparent ribbon, like a reflex. I already knew, even before the lack of sensation registered in my brain, that my fingers would remain dry and the water undisturbed.

Everything had stopped but me. I stumbled out of the bathroom—thank fuck the door had been open because there would have been no point in trying the handle or banging against it otherwise. Neither would make a sound or produce any kind of effect. No one would hear. No one would come.

I took a cautious step in my bedroom. On my bed, my phone displayed 11:17 pm. Outside, raindrops hung still in the night air, which wouldn't hit the windows. I drew a slow breath, curling and uncurling my fingers over and over. It wouldn't last. It was okay. It wasn't real, and when it ended, the room would be the same, rain would fall, and time would flow. Until then, there was only me, left alone with my thoughts and the soft thrum of blood pumping in my ears.

A faint clatter somewhere in the room had me dart a look at the windows, expecting the reassuring patter of raindrops against the glass. Nothing, just frozen beads, and the silence closing in on me. Another clatter, like something lightly scraping the floor. My heart rammed against my ribs in response, and I spun around to face the bathroom door.

It was still open, and light poured in, almost blinding. Not the product of the vanity light above the mirror, but the pasty glare of a spring afternoon. I tried to suck in air that wouldn't come, taking in the washed out, gum-studded floorboards, the benches, and the beach. Stripes of dull blue bleeding into each other: the sea and the sky. Beyond the door, where the bathroom had been seconds ago, the Riegelmann Boardwalk stretched along the ocean. Deserted and frozen in time.

My back was soaked with icy sweat, and every rational cell in my brain screamed for me to run away, to curl in the corner of the room, as far as possible from this . . . impossibility. But somewhere on the boardwalk, the clatter echoed again, and my legs jerked, drawn against my will to the light. I went through the door. The soles of my feet touched coarse wood that was neither warm nor cold. Seagulls floated above me in the cloudy sky, lifeless, like graceful origamis. There was no breeze. When I turned around, the bathroom door was no longer there; instead, I saw Nathan's striped canopy and hot-dog sign, with its smiling red sausage wearing a little apron and chef's hat. Behind were the colorful silhouettes of roller coasters, balloons, and flags.

The clatter guided me, sometimes coming from the left, sometimes from the right. A familiar sound I couldn't place, something I had heard all my life and never noticed before, a rhythm, beating in tune with my heart. I was walking, then running breathless up the boardwalk, past the Wonder Wheel and fast-food stalls, desperately seeking its source.

But the sound stopped abruptly, leaving me stranded, lost. I staggered around, clutching my head, digging my nails into my scalp to feel something, enough pain to anchor me back to reality and find a way out of this nightmare. And I saw them. The only two people on the boardwalk with me, sitting on a bench. Him, with his sandy ponytail hanging limply down the back of his leather jacket. Her, so young the small legs popping from her pink coat didn't touch the ground. Her half of the hot dog sat on her lap in a white paper plate.

He was staring at the sea, his gaze empty, exhausted. He wasn't yet the grinning man on his Facebook profile pic. He was a loser. The little blonde girl looked up at him, studied his frozen profile. She wasn't seeing me, but I watched her, my heart cracking and bursting and aching so bad I felt it thump in my throat, my stomach, everywhere at once. She didn't know he'd go and never return. She didn't even understand why no one else felt the world stop like that.

Her mom said it wasn't real—like Santa—and she complained to the pediatrist that she had to deal with a toddler who'd vanish faster than a ninja in the middle of a crowded department store, and whom security would find minutes later three floors up in the toy department.

I raised a trembling hand, begging the girl to turn her head and see me. She wouldn't, and the clatter thundered up my spine again, coming from behind me this time. *Tap. Tap.* A shadow, stretching along a wall before disappearing around the corner. I whirled around and went after it, followed the clatter down a deserted street, each echo booming inside my skull, my chest. *Tap. Tap.* I thought I caught a flash of something behind a truck . . . a silhouette. It was gone just as fast, and my mind reeled with panic and the desperate need to *know* if maybe, just maybe, I wasn't alone. If someone was out here too, who felt the beat of time in their bones like I did, who ran lost in the silence when it all stopped.

I ran, raced after the ghost which kept eluding me, a mirage gliding across the sleek metallic side of a minivan, licking the walls. I followed the trailing echo of the clatter until I ended up in an empty street, under the looming steel structure of the Cyclone, the roller coaster's steep hills and curls casting a tangle of shadows on the sidewalk. I went still.

A shadow stood in the middle of the road, too far for me to make out anything than the shape of some sort of long coat and maybe a . . . The honk of a truck tore through my eardrums as it dashed right in front of the ghost. The moment after, traffic resumed, and I couldn't see its silhouette anymore. Time was flowing again on Coney Island, and everything was too bright, too loud, the squawking of seagulls, the light piercing through the clouds. I tried to shield my eyes with my arms. The street was getting blurry, and it looked tilted, or maybe I wasn't standing straight—

My head hit the nightstand in my fall, and gold flashed before my eyes as I took the bedside lamp with me, its cord tangled around my arm. Over the furious pounding in my temples and the sticky fog clouding the rest of my senses, I made out my bedroom's painted ceiling. Fuck, my forehead hurt. I rasped in agony. One of my legs was still in the bed; the other lay on the floor along with the rest of my body, most of my covers, a pillow, and well, the broken lamp. I registered the sound of something light rolling on the nightstand above me. Squinted my eyes at the gleaming shape. The mini bottle of vodka fell, at last, landing squarely on my chest, like a finishing move.

It took me a while to muster the strength to move, and when I did, I sat up just in time to see my bedroom door open.

"Em, are you okay?"

Lily. Her apartment was right under mine, and, of course, she had to hear me fall from bed in a drunken stupor, freshly messed up from a nightmare that felt like getting my heart torn out of my chest during an epic shroom trip. I waved a quivering hand. "I'm good. Tossed around a little too much; that's all."

She kneeled by me, saw the vodka. I wanted to say something lame like, "It wasn't that much booze; I just had a nightmare," but it sounded pathetic even to my own ears. I let her pick up the empty flacon and place it back on the nightstand without a word.

I blinked up at her yoga pants and a blinding white smudge that was probably one of Dante's shirts. "Thanks."

"I'll help you up." She sighed and bent down again, but this time I managed to scramble to my feet without further humiliating myself.

"Don't worry, I'm fine," I mumbled, running a hand across my face. "I need . . ." *to brush my teeth. Also, cold water.*

"I was about to make myself some apple tea. Do you want some?" Lily offered as she picked up my comforter and smoothed it back atop the bed.

My eyes scanned the nightstand, looking for my phone. Almost midnight. I scratched my stomach under my tank top. "You weren't sleeping?"

Her lips pursed in a sorrowful expression. "Dante and I were going over the first scans we received of the table. It's hard to sleep when it's . . ." Her right hand twitched toward the window. ". . . awaiting us less than two miles away."

I gave a slow nod, but in truth, I didn't fully understand. I'd never been passionate about anything in my life, never really cared about anything—except weed and metal maybe, in my teens. So, I couldn't really relate to that kind of . . . well, the way Lily said it, and the way Dante had been looking at that table back at the digging site, the first word that came to me was *obsession.* They were obsessed by their huge archeological discovery, to the point that they couldn't even sleep at night. Just like their relationship, this was another bubble I could never get into. Best I could do was watch from the outside and try to figure out how it felt to love someone or something that much.

Lily watched me quietly, her arms wrapped around herself. "So, tea?"

I thought *ugh,* but I said, "Yeah."

VII

"Sugar?"

"Thanks."

I inhaled the fruity scent rising into the air as Lily poured a golden tea in my mug. She'd nudged a stack of papers and her laptop aside, to make a little room on the coffee table for a tray. Sitting across from us on some kind of designer day bed that matched their cream sofa, Dante watched the delicate movement of her hands, the hint of a smile on his lips. His eyes never really left her, even as he took his mug and slowly brought it to his lips.

It made me feel a little on edge, the way I could almost physically feel their bond even as a spectator, like particles hanging in the air, that would raise unbidden goose bumps on my forearms under the long-sleeved tee I'd slipped on before joining them.

I grabbed my own mug and gave the apple tea a cautious try to distract myself from the weird mood in the room. I'd never been a tea person, but it didn't taste as bad as I expected—sweetened water, basically.

"It sounded like you were having a bit of a party up there," Dante chided gently, glancing up at the ceiling.

Shuuuut the fuck up . . . I bit the inside of my cheek, my nostrils flaring. "I had a nightmare, and I rolled out of bed."

Lily's eyebrows drew together a fraction. "Nothing too bad?"

I shrugged and smirked at Dante. "I dreamed someone had canceled my booking."

Lily winced, but he let out a warm chuckle before taking a long sip of his tea. "I deserve that one."

Having scratched that particular itch, I allowed myself to relax a little, shifting to sit cross-legged on the couch's cushions. I eyed the stack of papers Lily had disturbed to serve the tea. On one of her books, I recognized the same kind of vaguely Greek-looking characters I'd seen on Chronos's Table back at the digging site. I narrowed my eyes at the bold line of text peeking above it. "Understanding the Principles of Ancient Magic?" I raised an amused eyebrow at Lily. "Do I need to worry? Are we gonna, like, sacrifice a chicken?"

Dante's lips quirked, but his eyes weren't smiling as they met mine. "No. I'm done summoning uncontrollable forces for tonight. I have all I need, thank you."

Lily giggled, her eyes mock-scolding him. She told me, "It was my granddad's favorite field of research. Before we were able to locate the Roman shrine, most of what we knew about Chronos's Table came from that book. He'd conducted extensive research and collected all the texts referencing it one way or another. He had this intuition the table was real, and we proved him right." She pulled the book from under the rest of the papers to show it to me. The cover featured a frayed piece of parchment whose faded text looked like the characters on the table—probably that archaic alphabet Lily had mentioned earlier.

I flipped through the pages lazily—*856! Get out* . . . Tiny, tiny text everywhere that made my head hurt just glancing at it. I noticed a black and white pic of the sculpture of a horned deity on one page.

"So, he studied, um . . . witchcraft and devil worship stuff?"

Dante chuckled, but Lily's face pinched in that kinda cute-serious expression she donned when she was about to unleash science on the unwashed masses. "He studied literally anything but the devil, as you call it." Ouch . . . I'd questioned the famous grandpa's line of work, and it was *on*.

As I summoned a memory of his hooked nose and graying temples, I saw myself again in the bedroom I shared with Lily in Richard's big condo on East 57th. I was eleven, and I lay sprawled on my bed, busy doodling a Blastoise all over my math textbook while old McKeanney sat at Lily's desk with his granddaughter, reviewing a freaking novel about the civil war—I actually wondered if her teachers even bothered to read these papers before tossing her an A+. After a while, the old man had come over to my bed and asked me, "Do you need help with your homework, Emma?"

Grandpa McKeanney had stepped in the wrong hood. Richard had asked the same thing a hundred times before, and my tactic of choice was to either mumble a contemptuous "no," or plainly ignore him until he gave up with a tight-lipped nod. I kept drawing, pointedly ignoring the old man's frown and the faint scent of eucalyptus clinging to his tweed jacket. He didn't repeat the offer. Instead, his fingers reached to graze the angry red imprint of a fresh slap on my cheek—probably for stealing stuff from my mom's dresser or talking back to a teacher at school. Ours is a generation raised by Michael Jackson. I instantly recoiled at the head of the bed like he had "pedo" written all over him. He didn't apologize; instead, he murmured, "It's a big universe, and one day you'll realize that *this*," he motioned to my cheek, "isn't much in the grand scheme of things."

At the time, I just thought he had Alzheimer's, or he was crazy, but now, thinking about it, I realized he'd been right. It was just a slap, half a second in a lifetime. Sure, I'd seen my fair share of shitty moments, but even so, the sum of all those amounted to what, a quarter of my entire life if I lived to be eighty? Always look on the bright side, and all . . .

Anyway, I was eleven; I had an attitude, and what I did was look up at McKeanney and reply, "Cruise back to your retirement home, bro."

I clearly remembered the way he'd cocked a bushy eyebrow, right before Lily's strawberry-scented eraser hit me square in the forehead. It was the last time I'd seen the old guy, and, more importantly, the only time Lily had ever been violent with me—if you can call tossing an eraser violence. She definitely wasn't cut out for the thug life.

I dropped the book on the table and offered Lily an apologetic smile. "Hey, I meant no diss."

Her features relaxed. "I know." She patted the cover. "Still, your reaction is interesting, because when you bring up *magic, spells* or that kind of thing, people immediately conjure up the late Judeo-Christian cultural cliché of women riding brooms and worshipping Belzebub."

"I guess . . ." I confirmed hesitantly, while Dante watched us from behind the screen of his MacBook with what I swore was a mocking gaze. Dude was literally sending me douche vibes from across the coffee table without even taking part in the convo.

"Well," Lily went on with a dramatic pause. "Believe it or not, people didn't wait for the Catholic church to take an interest in the occult and explore the limits of their physical reality. And that was basically Grandpa's playground: rediscovering pre-Christian occult practices, understanding their beliefs, the roots of those beliefs,"— she pointed at the symbols on the book's cover—"deconstructing their spells and the written traces they left us throughout history." Her voice faltered, suddenly tight. Her eyes met Dante's, something unspoken passing between them. More than just love or understanding. Passion for their work and each other, I figured. "Most people don't care. But it's . . . an invaluable well of knowledge that's been lost for a very long time."

I felt awkward, sitting here on that couch, listening to all this, unable to reciprocate the kind of intensity they literally oozed—okay, mostly Lily. "I think he'd be super proud of you," I said lamely.

"He would," Dante concurred, setting his laptop aside and rising to sit by Lily. He hugged her, and I realized her eyes were glistening.

And . . . now I felt shitty, and like a complete outsider too—nothing new under the sun. I squirmed away to give them some space. "I'll go to bed."

She wiped her eyes. "Oh no! I mean, you can stay if you want. Sorry, I kinda got carried away. It's just, you know . . . the pressure, I guess."

"From Katharos," I stated, my eyes narrowing a fraction as I remembered our dinner with Lucius the dancing clown. "What's in it for them, though, if no one cares about the subject? Can they do an exhibit or something like that?"

"Among other things," Dante replied, stroking Lily's wrist absently. "People may not realize the significance of this discovery, but it's possible to educate them." He flashed one of his tiny winks like we were BFFs now.

"Sure," I said with a dubious look. *Cool your jets, Dante. I still mostly hate you.* Something else clicked in my neurons as I considered the mess scattered on the coffee table. I replayed in my head that comment she'd made earlier that most of what they knew about

Chronos's Table came from Professor McKeanney's book.

"So," I said to Lily, "Katharos hired you because you were taking over your grandpa's work, looking for the table."

She ducked her chin in confirmation.

"Why didn't they just hire him directly back when he was alive?"

Dante's eyebrows jerked, and I swear he flashed me the are-you-stupid-or-what look—but he allowed Lily to answer that one. "Actually, he worked for Katharos as a consultant before he died," she replied.

"Like you," I replied flatly, struggling to keep a straight face when my lips quivered from the urge to cringe. This was more than just walking in her grandfather's steps. Lily had chosen to work for the same foundation he had and to finish his job for them. Those fifteen-page long 8th grade history essays had been one thing, but this was another level of worship.

I sent one last look at the stack of papers and Lily's precious copy of *Understanding the Principles of Ancient Magic*. Nodding to myself, I sprang up from their couch. "Okay, going to bed for real this time. Thanks for the tea, and," I padded to their door and paused, my hand on the knob. I gauged Lily's pale, tired features. "Don't forget to live for yourself at some point when you're done with that table."

VIII

I didn't see Lily and Dante at breakfast, for reasons like the fact that my hangover and I fell out of bed at noon, and we crawled together into the bathtub, curling away from the sunlight pouring through the windows like a ghoul. My eyes didn't open fully until I was done drinking a whole bottle of water and eating every last chocolate in the minibar.

Once I was human again, I shrugged on my backpack, popped in my earphones to block out the real world and hurried down the stairs, keeping my eyes down to avoid the glances of a couple of maids cleaning the hallway.

Lily had texted me to say she'd spend the day at the foundation's lab with Dante and Lucius. She wanted to know if we could see each other later. I tapped to reply and saved the empty draft. I wasn't sure what to say. My first impulse was to tell her I was too busy visiting stuff, but after all she'd told me last night, I *was* kinda curious about the next episode in her History-Channel-style adventures with Chronos's Table, or about Ken doll Dante, and just how much of a hold he had on her. Would she eat Tide Pods for him? From the looks of it, yes. With a side of bleach.

I closed the draft and shoved my phone back in my jeans pocket with a deep sigh. It pissed me off that I'd run so far and for so long, only to end up getting texts and stale Ancient Rome memes from Lily, like we were . . . Shit. We weren't bonding, were we? Striding past the goat monsters framing the Residenza's door, I gave silent thanks to Chronos for no doubt keeping everyone very busy while I tried to sort my priorities.

I rolled my shoulders, breathed in, breathed out, and took out my phone again. Google said it'd take forty-five minutes to get to my dad's address by bus. Assuming he had a job, he probably wouldn't be home until the end of the day; I could always start with a recon mission to check if his name was on the intercom. I stared down at the map on my phone, trying to imagine how he'd react if he saw me creeping around his place. Would he recognize me? Freak out? Or maybe he'd spent the past thirteen years waiting for this moment like I had, but he just never dared to make the first step . . .

I chewed on my nails, oblivious to the people walking past me. Time to move, instead of unraveling right in the middle of the street. Plus, I needed to find myself a new place for the night. I cringed at the memory of Dante's little "surprise." Just picturing his wink again gave me douchebumps, but I wouldn't let him ruin my day. I exhaled the bad vibes and strolled down the Via Tomacelli toward the Tiber, enjoying the fall sun, and idly checking clothing stores. There was a secret smile on my lips, and overall, life wasn't so bad.

As I lingered in front of a Mango, I was treated to a familiar sight: a couple of cats lounged on a pink fleece blanket on the ground while next to them a guy shook his empty McDonald's cup at tourists. My eyebrows jumped. Same mess of sandy curls, beard, and steel toes. His wooden cane rested at his side, and he wore a clean gray T-shirt under his ratty coat today. I smacked my tongue. I *knew* he wasn't a real bum—gutter punk squatting in an abandoned building somewhere, more likely.

I kept my distance and watched his little business. He was

petting one of the cats with his left hand while holding out the cup with his right. A pair of Asian girls stopped because he was talking to them in . . . whatever language they spoke, I realized. I had no idea if it was Chinese, Japanese, or something else, but he sounded pretty fluent. They held hands and listened to his bullshit for a while before reaching into their designer bags. My lips pursed in reluctant appreciation as they dropped him a ten each. Smooth pitch, I had to give him that.

After the show was over, I shoved my hands in my pockets and casually walked past him. He didn't have his glasses on today, probably to make sure everyone would steal a glance at his milky pupils and feel bad.

"Hey, hey! Pretty girl from yesterday!"

I stopped mid-stride, muffling a curse under my breath. I bet it was one of his classic ice-breakers, and I felt stupid for being the only sucker around who'd fallen for it, when I, of all people, should know better. I shook my head and resumed walking.

"On the Palatine . . . I know it was you!"

I risked a peek back. He was waving at me—or at least, in my general direction. How could he know? My bumdar yelled for me to cruise on. If I let the dude hook me, he'd bullshit me until my ears bled and I gave him something just to make it stop. Why my legs chose to turn around instead, I had no fricking clue. I planted myself in front of him, arms crossed. "Look, I'm broke, and no, I'm not gonna blow you even if you ask real nice. Now that we've gotten that out of the way, is there anything else I can do for you today?"

He raised his head at me with a lazy grin and closed his eyes as he inhaled deeply. "Hmmm . . . you smell even better now that you've showered—like chocolate."

My cheeks heated up at the realization that he had it right. I *had* taken a shower not even an hour ago and stuffed my face with Gianduiotti for breakfast. Maybe it was true that blind people developed their other senses to make up for their sight loss. I averted my eyes, even though it made no difference. "Free dating advice: ditch the cheesy pickup lines," I snapped back.

His smile stretched wider, warm and guileless—I was starting to see why those Asian girls had coughed up the cash so easily. Dude rubbed his leg through the hole in his corduroy pants, and—you may want to sit for this—here's what he served me next: "You wouldn't happen to have a Band-Aid, would you? I think I scraped my knee falling for you."

Aw, come on. I rolled my eyes, mentally picturing the makeshift trap lying at my feet. A five-inch-deep hole barely covered by two twigs and a handful of leaves. I couldn't help it, I giggled. *You win this round, cat-guy . . .*

I looked around at the shoppers hurrying past us, debating the stupidity of my next move. To hell with common sense. I was in a good mood, and, to be honest, it was just too weird to stand here and look down at him like that. It felt . . . wrong. I craned my neck to send a defeated sigh to the sky, before folding to sit cross-legged on the blanket, next to him and his cats. "Okay, Romeo, you've earned yourself a five-minute date. Sweep me off my feet."

My date's lean tabby immediately rolled closer to play with my laces while his master patted his abs. "I knew you couldn't resist. They all want a piece of this body."

I blew my bangs up and fanned myself. "God, stop . . . I can barely control myself right now." Sobering up, I asked him, "So you work that corner often?"

"Once in a while. But I prefer San Pietro. Tourists tend to give more when Jesus is watching. I'm Faust, by the way."

"Em," I replied, while at our feet his other cat, a fat black and white gutter boy, licked his balls for the world to see.

A group of Americans cruised by. Faust raised his cup and shook it, rattling the coins inside. "Spare some change for a blind veteran, sir?"

I elbowed him as a grandpa dropped a few euros in the cup. "Really? A vet?" I whispered.

He gasped in mock outrage. "Why would you doubt me?"

"Because I bet you half of the bums shaking their cup out there are veterans like you."

"It's entirely possible that they are," Faust countered.

"Okay, where were you stationed?"

"Here, in Rome, but I also went to Germany and Mauretania."

I chuckled. "Mauretania doesn't even sound like a real country. Is that your usual story, the washed-up vet?"

"I also lost my wife and son in the fire that left me blind," he noted conversationally.

I pressed my lips tight not to laugh—you never know. You hear a lot of weird shit in the street, but there's a truth hidden in each lie, like shards of glass in the asphalt. Faust didn't sound too rattled by his tragic past though.

We watched Rome breathe, run, and laugh in comfortable silence for a while, longer than the five minutes I'd first intended to spend with him, for sure. Faust would shake his cup. Sometimes it worked, sometimes it didn't. A bunch of teens tried to toss him popcorn instead of change—classic! I sprang to my feet and yelled at them to fuck off. They scattered like rats, and we gave the popcorn to pigeons.

Eventually, I checked the time on my phone, and told him, "Look, I gotta go. I actually have stuff to do this afternoon. It's been fun feeding pigeons with you."

"The feeling is mutual," Faust said, perhaps more quietly than before. As I shrugged on my backpack, I heard him ask, "Emma?"

I looked down at him, wondering one second too late if I'd ever given him my full name at any point during our time together. He was still smiling, but it was different. No longer goofy.

I fought a pang of unease. "Yeah?"

"How long are you staying at the Residenza?"

He might as well have hit me with a bag full of ice. Warnings lit up in my brain one after another, blinking a frantic red. "How the hell do you know that?" I hissed.

"My kitten told me," he joked, stroking the tabby.

"Cut that shit. Did you follow me?" It wasn't just the creep factor of it all; if I was being honest with myself, I also felt betrayed because he'd seemed like this cool, harmless guy to hang out with.

He shrugged. "Not exactly. But Rome is my city; she whispers things to me."

I had standards. I would *not* kick a blind hobo's cup, but my foot itched to send it flying all away across "his city." I ground my molars in a vain effort to control my temper. "Okay, Faust, you know what? I'm done dealing with psychos, so, you keep bullshitting tourists with your cats, and I'm out of here." I stabbed the air with a menacing forefinger—not that he cared, obviously. "If I see you stalking me again, I'm going straight to the cops."

His mouth opened to reply, but I was quicker and spun on my heels, taking quick strides away from him. I was fumbling for my earbuds when he called my name. "Emma!"

I shoved the silicone caps brain-deep. *Sorry, Em can't answer you right now because you're a creep. Please leave a message after the tone.*

"They're trying to keep an eye on you. You should get out of there."

My legs stumbled. I caught myself and staggered around, wide-eyed. My heart drummed everywhere at once in my body. The pink blanket still lay discarded on the ground, but Faust and his cats were gone, swallowed back by Rome in a matter of seconds.

IX

I kept walking, but I couldn't focus on the music in my ears or whatever was going on around me, really. The worst part was not being sure. Maybe it was the same as when I felt time stop. How could I be sure that I hadn't spent twenty minutes talking to myself in the street? The pink blanket and the cats had seemed real, but Faust, who knew my name, where I'd spent the night . . . Maybe my brain had coined him from the memory of last night's hobo. I stopped in the middle of the Ponte Cavour and leaned against the white stone railing, watching boats glide silently down the Tiber.

The murky waters and reddening trees lining the shores—this, at least, was real. I buried my face in my hands, digging the heels of my palms in my eyeballs. I didn't want to see yet another shrink and listen to them pick apart my sob story. I didn't want meds, and I didn't want the labels I could practically feel tattooed on my skin. *Absent father. Oppositional Defiant Disorder. A tendency to lie and steal . . . Hallucinates douchey hobos and frozen people . . .*

In my earbuds, Rena Lovelis's sultry voice was brutally interrupted by the chime of an incoming call. I pulled out my phone. Lily. I almost didn't pick up. I liked the idea of just staying there and simultaneously freak out and wallow in self-pity in the afternoon breeze. Lily won the battle of wills a split second before I let her go to voicemail. I tapped to take the call. "Hey—"

"It's me. I'm not interrupting anything?"

"No," I stated with a shrug she couldn't see. "Everything going smoothly with your table?"

"Yes, it's been transported to the lab, and it's just . . . incredible. Not a single crack. Everything else collapsed in the shrine, but the stone is intact, even after all this time. Dante thinks that when mud rushed inside the temple during the landslide, it created a protective layer over it before the supporting columns broke."

"Wow. That sounds . . . cool."

I picked up some rustling and whispering over the line in response. She was talking to someone. When it was done, she asked me, "Do you want to see it?"

There was a beat of silence on my side as I pondered her offer. Did I? Kinda. Maybe I was unconsciously trying to find excuses to postpone meeting my father—he still hadn't accepted my Facebook invite anyway. In any case, I heard myself reply, "Yeah, I guess."

She made a little noise, like a muffled squeal, and this time, I distinctly heard her murmur, "She said yes!"

My face bunched. "Is that Dante with you?"

"Yes, he's here with me." *Awesome.* "So, listen," she went on, "I don't think they'll let you inside the lab itself because Katharos has a very strict security protocol, but you can see it through a window, and there's also a private museum inside the Foundation's building."

"Sounds great."

"I'll text you the address."

"Got it."

It was only after I'd hung up and my phone buzzed with her text that I asked myself out loud, "What the fuck am I doing?"

Answer: what I did was follow the little blue dot on Google Maps across the Ponte Cavour, to a bus stop, and all the way to a park by the Tiber, full of centenary pines and enclosed in high brick walls. The increasing number of warning signs and the cameras atop the wall suggested the entrance to the foundation's campus couldn't be far. I eventually reached a long iron gate and a security booth inside which two guards in dark uniforms . . . didn't guard shit, because they were busy watching a soccer game on one of the TVs.

I rapped at the window. *"Scusa mi?"* Excuse me?

A roar of agony answered my inquiry. Roma was losing against Lazio.

Okay . . . I banged against the Plexiglas with my fists. "Hey! I'm talking to you!"

Their heads turned at the same time, and the oldest one wheeled himself to me. —Apparently, it was too much to ask that he get up from his chair during a game. Dark eyes gauged me under bushy gray eyebrows. "What you want, miss?" he drawled in broken English. At least it made me feel good about my grasp of Italian.

"Il mio nome è Emma Nielsen. Sono qui per vedere Lily McKeanney e Dante Alessandri," I replied, skipping the pleasantries like he had. My name is Emma Nielsen. I'm here to see Lily McKeanney and Dante Alessandri.

His lips became a thin line—probably because the game was still going strong on the TV behind him and he must have been missing some hot action. He reached for a phone on his desk and called someone to tell them that "Emma Nelson" wanted to see "Lily Bikini" and Mr. Alessandri. I tried to keep a straight face until he gave a curt nod and the gate whirred open. By the time I walked in, he had already wheeled himself back to the TV next to his buddy.

I didn't bother coming back to ask for instructions on how to find Lily's lab.

I just let my feet guide me across the park under the mottled shade of pines and cypresses. There was only one building anyway, a u-shaped renaissance palazzo—don't trust my expertise. Let's just say that it looked like Ancient Roman stuff but not the real thing, with arched windows and columns lining the façade and tiled roofs. I looked left and right, saw no one around, so I took the stone stairs leading up to a terrace overlooking the park. A set of modern glass doors stood encased in one of the arches; I made a beeline for it.

Cool air hit me the moment I entered—powerful aircon. I found myself standing in a long lobby with marble and frescoes everywhere. I looked at the vaulted ceiling some fifty feet above, where naked gods were partying around tables covered with fruits and wine. I couldn't spot a single square that hadn't been painted, sculpted, or gilded, and the whole thing was so magnificent it made me feel small.

"Miss Nielsen?"

I turned around to find a twenty-something guy in a suit standing near another security booth. "Yeah, that's me."

"Welcome to the Villa Malespina," he cooed, handing me a booklet with a pic of a marble bust on the cover and Katharos's logo atop of it. "Here you'll find all the information you need on our collections."

I considered the thick, glossy paper with an appreciative pout. "Thanks."

"Follow me, please."

"Sure."

He led me through a couple of rooms where people worked in silence at their glass desks, surrounded by that same crazy décor where antique statues watched them from every corner and the coffered ceilings contained . . . more coffers. Meanwhile, I flipped through the guide, my fingers pausing with a slight start when I noticed a pic of Lily's grandpa. It must have been taken during a party. He wore a tux and stood next to an eighty-something-year-old guy whose arm snaked around the waist of a beautiful young woman in a shimmering black cocktail dress.

The text on the opposite page was basically Katharos's history, how it'd been founded back in the late nineties by baron Giancarlo Montecito, an old and rich Italian industrial. Apparently, his wife had taken over presiding over Katharos after he died a few years later—the young gold digger in the pic, I presumed.

Lady Montecito will visit the laboratory tomorrow.

Remembering Lucius's frosty remark, I side-eyed the rows of antique statues lining the hallway around me. Okay, maybe I was being a little harsh; clearly, Lady Montecito had a genuine interest in history, and she'd dug out a lot more than just gold.

We reached a flight of stairs and an elevator whose steel door seemed at odds with the sculpted garland of leaves and flowers encasing it.

"The laboratory is this way," the guy said, before reaching inside his jacket to retrieve a transparent plastic pass, which he handed me. "Miss McKeanney told me that you would visit the private collection as well. Please keep your pass on you at all times," he warned, pointing to his own badge.

"Okay, thank you." I fumbled to fasten it to my hoodie collar as the car lowered to sublevel two within seconds.

No marble and frescoes here. The walls of the hallway still showcased the ancient stones the palazzo rested on, but a sober gray carpet covered the floor, and here, too, the doors were made of glass, through which I could glimpse a few people coming and going among cluttered desks and shelves stacked with ancient books.

A petite silhouette in a white lab coat waved at me from across the room. Lily's ponytail was as bouncy as ever as she came to open the doors with a badge of her own. The dark circles under her eyes told another story, though . . . She ushered me into the open space I'd seen through the windows.

My gaze fell on her plastic gloves. "You work in an actual science lab?"

"Yes and no, the gloves are just to avoid contamination while we're working on the table. The foundation had lab technicians run some tests on the granite, but I'm not in charge of that."

"Okay."

Lily used her badge to take us through a couple of steel doors leading to a dim circular hallway. Floor-to-ceiling windows all along showcased the closest thing I'd ever seen to an operating room—I hoped it'd be a while before I saw a real one. The table rested on a metal platform supported by thick steel cables hanging from the high ceiling. Now that it had been cleaned, the smooth granite surface reflected the glare of a surgical lamp positioned above it.

Dante was inside, bent over a section of the table, his fingers slowly tracing the characters engraved in the stone. For a second, I saw him again, back at the digging site; he wore the same expression, his gaze oddly vacant despite the lines of concentration on his brow. I averted my eyes to the wall behind him instead. His zombie act was making my skin crawl a little, for some reason.

Lily clasped her hands. "I really can't take you inside the room. But Dante and I were about to take a break, so I'll just finish reviewing my notes with him, and we can join you afterward."

"Cool," I said absently, my eyes following her as she joined him in the room.

I watched them shuttle back and forth between their laptops and the table for a while in the chilly hallway. I didn't hear the doors open, but the trail of goose bumps along my spine alerted me to Lucius's presence before my brain was even done scanning the two figures who'd just come in. There was a woman standing behind him. My brow jerked when I recognized the girl in the cocktail dress— Lady Montecito—but holy shit! The pic in my booklet must have been taken twenty years ago, so she must be in her forties, at least, but she looked barely older than Lily. Pale and smooth skin, not a wrinkle, no asperity whatsoever on her perfectly symmetrical features, and just the right amount of makeup to bring out her aquamarine eyes even in the dark. All the plastic money could buy, and then some.

I waved at Lucius. "Hey. I came to visit Lily."

He raised an eyebrow but didn't return my greeting. Montecito nudged him aside delicately and came out of the shadows. Her hand lingered on his arm a little longer than I expected, and I wondered if maybe they were together. We gauged each other, her gaze trailing over my torn jeans and messy turquoise bun, while mine scanned her black suit, high heels, and the gold-embroidered shawl thrown over her shoulder.

"Emma, I presume?" she asked with a soft Italian accent.

I tried to smile, hoping to make a better impression than I had last night at dinner. "That's me, and you're Lady Montecito, right?"

She inclined her head elegantly and returned my smile, but I felt no trace of warmth in the gesture. "Please call me Leonora. I'm delighted to meet you, Emma. I understand you'll be spending the week with us?"

I couldn't stop my grimace. "Um, no. There was a problem with my booking last night, but I'm gonna find another room."

She frowned, a subtle twitch of her eyebrows that didn't crease any wrinkles in her skin—Botox for sure. "Is that so? I was told you enjoyed our hospitality, despite a minor incident in your bedroom. Is your forehead all right, by the way?"

In other words, she knew about last night. I clenched my jaw, nostrils flaring. Had Lily told her everything? But why would she do that? Camera in my bedroom, then? The memory of Faust's warning raised a trail of goose bumps on my nape. *They're trying to keep an eye on you* . . . Okay, no. Slippery slope. I should *not* start trusting my hallucinations—even if they had accurately predicted that those Katharos people were a bunch of privacy creeps. "I'm fine now," I mumbled, eyeing Montecito warily.

Her prune lips curved, gleaming like a saber blade under the hallway lights. "And we wouldn't want it any other way."

She sounded like me when I used to look counselors in the eye and tell them I was done with recreational drugs once and for all. I responded with a smile that was just as sincere as hers. "Thanks for your concern."

"Lucius," she said, flicking her wrist at him like he was her servant.

He gave an obedient nod and used his transparent badge to unlock a door leading into the room where Lily and Dante were still operating on their table. As they were about to enter, she paused in the doorway and turned to me. "Aren't you coming, Emma?"

I blinked. "Um, I was told to stay outside."

She flashed me a flawless white grin. "And miss this opportunity? My heart would break for you. Come."

I had a hunch there was no heart to break under that shiny shawl, but she was right about one thing: why miss the opportunity? I shrugged off my backpack and dropped it against the wall. "I don't suppose pics are allowed?"

"No," Lucius replied, the single syllable cutting the air between us.

I raised my hands in surrender. "No problem."

I went in after the two of them. Lily and Dante looked up from their notes as soon as they saw us. I read surprise on both their faces, but it was quickly overshadowed by a sort of quiet deference. Montecito was definitively the boss around here. She walked to the table and caressed it slowly, trailing her fingers across the mysterious inscriptions as if they were braille. "Have you made any progress?" she asked, without looking up.

"The table has been scanned entirely," Dante recited, his shoulders straight. "We're running the results against our pattern recognition algorithm to isolate new words or sentence structures. We're starting to get leads, but the circular structure is making things . . . more difficult."

She raised her head to look at him, and she did that frown again, that made no wrinkles on her skin. "Why?"

Lily stepped in. "It's all *scripto continua*, and the language could be even more ancient than we first believed. The pattern doesn't fit our current data, and as a result, we're not entirely sure where the text starts."

I gazed down at the rows of concentric circles of signs engraved in the stone. No space anywhere, no break. Just letters spinning around without a beginning or an end. I blinked hard, but the letters wouldn't stop whirling before my eyes. Faster and faster. My heart was beating loud in my ears, and I felt lost, as if the room were expanding around me.

It was happening again. My chest heaved with the need to throw up as the silent wave washed over me. Across from me, Lady Montecito stood lifelessly, her gaze absent. Lucius might as well have been his usual stoic self, but I knew better. Lily's fingers hung frozen midair as she showed something on the laptop to Dante, who had turned into a statue.

Air rushed through my nostrils in frantic intakes. *Breathe. It won't last.* Old memories flashed in my brain. I saw a young Lily, petrified mid-stride in Central Park, still among the iridescent bubbles she'd been blowing a second before. I knew what would happen if I tried to touch her. Nothing. There'd be no warmth to her skin, no wrinkle in the folds of her lab coat. I knew all that, but couldn't stand the silence, the indescribable void in the absence of time. I took a trembling step toward her, leaning on the table. "Lily," I whispered.

"Em, no!"

Lily's horrified squeak erupted before I even realized my hand was resting flat on the stone. I stared wide-eyed at my splayed fingers and the signs engraved in granite underneath, my heart beating all over my body. Time had resumed flowing, but Lily's voice was a distant echo, and I felt so far away, so immensely alone before Chronos's Table. When I managed to look up at last, the surgical light above blinded me. Beyond the glare, I saw Lady Montecito, staring back at me, Lucius's shadow standing guard behind her. I blinked frantically, my gaze flittering from Lily's shocked face to Lady Montecito's impenetrable features.

I didn't feel his presence—I hadn't even seen him move in the first place. Yet Dante was here, behind me. My eyes snapped to his gloved fingers, wrapped loosely around my wrist.

"Please don't touch it, Emma."

I jerked my wrist free and staggered back, gasping for air like I was swimming my way out of a bad trip. "I-I'm sorry. I just . . . spaced out, I think," I said with a forced laugh that did nothing to smooth the lines of worry on Lily's brow.

I raked a hand through my hair. I wanted out of there. I needed to think—away from them. "Do you know where I could find some water?"

Dante's face lit up. "Oh, we have a kitchen; just go back to the open space, and it's the door across from the meeting room." Clearly, he wanted me a mile away from their table.

That worked for me. I gave Lily an awkward smile. "All right, I'll just go get myself a glass of water while you finish."

"Okay. Take your time. We shouldn't be too long, and meanwhile, you can also check the private collections if you want."

"Second floor, right?"

She beamed. "Yes!"

Lady Montecito tilted her head at me. I felt my insides coil in response. "It's been a pleasure meeting you, Emma. I hope to see you again very soon."

I wasn't sure the feeling was mutual, and my T-shirt still clung to the cold sweat dampening my back. I stepped back and stole one last glance at the table before I let Lucius open the lab's door for me. I tried not to look at him as I slipped out, but I could feel his eyes on me, digging holes in my back. I didn't need to turn around to know that *he* was looking at me.

X

At least the Coke was free. After I was done sipping my can in the silent kitchen reserved for Katharos employees, I hopped down from my bar stool and tossed the empty can into a bin standing across the room. *Em Nielsen scores a three-pointer from thirty feet!* A nerd with tortoiseshell glasses walked in on me moonwalking to celebrate. Awkward. I took my backpack and strutted past him with a challenging look, smirking to myself when he averted his eyes.

Despite the sugar rush, the unease crawling under my skin wouldn't subside as I dragged my feet back to the hallway. I was unraveling. Fast. Counting my nightmare back at the Residenza, this was my third hallucination in less than twenty-four hours. Also, Faust . . . okay, possibly *fourth.* I closed my eyes as if a second of darkness would somehow untangle this complete mindfuck. What if he *had* been real? What if he'd really been stalking me and he knew stuff I didn't about Katharos? I caught my reflection in the glass wall lining the hallway, and I felt sick to my stomach just seeing my taut features and the mess of blueish strands hanging limply in my eyes. *Hey Em, why don't you check your own fucking Facebook instead of desperately trying to find something wrong with Lily's life?*

I grabbed my phone from the pocket. Of course, there was no message, because this whole trip was a disaster, and the problem wasn't Lily's unresolved issues with her grandpa's death, Dante's smothering presence, or even Lucius and Montecito being pretentious douchebags. The problem was me, crashing into a picture where there was no place for my mentally unstable ass.

I reached the elevator and waved my badge in front of the screen to open the doors. My phone vibrated with an incoming text. Lily.

Joining u on 2nd floor in 15mn.

My hand reached for the ground level button anyway. Hesitated. Lily was trying hard to build a bridge from the wreckage that was our childhoods, even though she didn't have to. Didn't I owe her at least a proper goodbye before I vanished for good? I sucked in an unsteady breath and punched two. The doors closed, only to sigh open seconds later, revealing the same sort of marble extravaganza I'd seen in the lobby. The soles of my sneakers squeaked on the checkered floor of a long gallery. Light poured from the floor-to-ceiling windows I'd seen from outside, bathing sculptures and broken crockery displayed in glass cases.

Sitting on a chair at the other end of the room, a guard watched me take cautious steps among reclining nymphs and naked athletes. The room itself was actually even more impressive than the treasures it contained. I gawked up at the cupola looming above my head. Specks of rainbow-colored light rained on the walls from a giant crystal chandelier. Definitely worth a pic. I reached into my hoodie pocket for my phone, but the guard saw it and shook his head. *Aw, come on...*

I kept going, thumbs hooked in my pockets, gazing absently at Katharos's treasures. I stopped in front of a marble piece, intrigued. A naked, blindfolded guy knelt at the feet of another, whose body was half-covered by a loose toga. The naked one clutched a dagger in his hands directed at his own chest. Art wasn't really my thing, but there was something gripping about the man's straining muscles, his grimace of despair while his counterpart towered over him and just coolly watched him killing himself, it seemed. I risked a finger to trace the curls in his beard, the delicate knot of the blindfold in his short hair.

"A unique piece."

I snatched my hand away and swiveled around. Lady Montecito stood in front of me, her smile etched on skin that seemed made of the same smooth alabaster as the statues around us. I pressed a hand to my racing heart. "Sorry. I didn't mean to touch it." My eyes darted to the guard's chair. He was staring straight ahead with an obvious effort to give us some privacy.

Lady Montecito waved my apology off. "Feel free to."

"Thanks. I take it Lily and Dante are done?"

Her smile grew impish. "Not quite, but to tell you the truth, I find technical details terribly boring."

"Same here," I admitted.

She trailed the back of her fingers down the blindfolded man's cheek, the corded muscles in his neck. "Do you know who he is?"

I shook my head.

"Faustus."

My eyes widened at the familiar syllable, and I tried to force a neutral mask on my features as she added, "There's only a handful of intact pieces left in the world documenting his myth, and ours is certainly the most valuable."

I circled the marble, the pulse in my neck steadily increasing. "What kind of myth?"

"A Roman legend dating back from the first century—probably a distant ancestor to the later German myth." She tilted her head, perhaps waiting for some sign that I knew what she was talking about. When I gave none, she went on. "Faustus was a praetorian serving under Emperor Caligula, perhaps originating from a Batavi tribe, according to some sources." She gave a faint snort like that detail was funny. It wasn't. None of this was funny. I kept listening, tense as a guitar string. "Caligula was well-known for being a cruel and mercurial ruler. One day, while he was listening to a group of senators to whom he had granted an audience, he grew bored with them and ordered Faustus and the rest of the imperial bodyguards to slay those men on the spot. Faustus refused, and for this, rather than killing him, Caligula had him blinded. His wife and son were executed in the circus, and Faustus was thrown on the street to live the rest of his days like a beggar."

I watched Lady Montecito's long nails linger on the sculpted blindfold, a sickening weight settling in my stomach as I processed her words. A blind vet who'd lost his wife and child and lived liked a bum . . . It could have just been a coincidence. Or maybe Faust did know about the legend, and he'd kind of tweaked it and made it his own—he wouldn't be the first to do that on the street. But *I* had never heard this story before in my life. I couldn't possibly have made it up three hours ago. The realization hit me like a slow-motion panic attack.

Oh God. Oh shit . . .

That could only mean Faust had been . . . real. As real as his warning about Katharos. Had he been here before, inside their HQ? Was that how he'd heard of that Faustus guy? No, it went deeper than that. He'd been hanging around their digging site, and he *knew* I was staying at the Residenza. He had something to do with Katharos. Disgruntled former employee maybe? That'd explain a lot . . .

I gritted my teeth, praying Lady Montecito wouldn't notice how stiff I was. "So, the guy in the toga, he's Caligula? Why is Faustus killing himself?"

Her shoulder shook with silent laughter. "Oh no, you don't understand." She placed a hand on the second man's powerful arm. "This is not Caligula. Allow me to finish. After his ordeal, Faustus went mad and wandered the streets of Rome until he found shelter in a temple dedicated to Cronus, the God of time." Her voice took on a pleading tone as she mimicked the rest of the story. "There, Faustus implored the deity to grant him revenge on the emperor, but he was a broken shell of a man. He had nothing left to sacrifice in exchange for the fulfillment of his wish."

I gazed at Faustus's grimacing, desperate profile, and I understood. "He gave his own life," I completed, feeling my skin grow cold and clammy. I remembered Dante's words, minutes before Faust and I had met for the first time. *Chronos's Table. It was part of a small shrine to Cronus.*

"He gave his humanity," Lady Montecito corrected, her lips curling dangerously. "Cronus appeared to Faustus and offered him a deal: eternal slavery in his service, in exchange for Caligula's death. One can only assume that Faustus accepted since Caligula was assassinated only a few years into his reign."

Okay. Breathe, Em. Don't freak out. Montecito's tale could mean two things.

Option one: the hobo I'd fed pigeons with this afternoon was a psychotic Katharos reject painting himself in the role of an immortal slave serving the god of time—which made him even crazier than I was.

Option two: Yeah . . . no. I wasn't going there. Not if I wanted to retain what little sanity I had left. Faust was a *regular* human being, with cats, and a host of issues I couldn't solve for him. It was sad that he was blind, and he was on the street, but it wasn't emperor Caligula who'd put him there. Two thousand years ago.

Montecito watched me decompose with a soft laugh. "You seem troubled, Emma. It's only a legend."

I mustered a stiff smile. "I know. I guess it's just a bit dark."

She crossed her arms and tilted her head at me like I was a book she was trying to read. "It's human nature at its finest. Wouldn't we all do the same, after all? Would you, Emma?"

"Would I . . . what?"

"Sacrifice your soul for something you truly desire."

I didn't like the way she said it, the edge under the silk in her voice. And what I hated the most was that she'd hit the nail on the head. I thought of my parents, of what it would have been like to love and be loved in return like the other kids. Lady Montecito had it wrong, though; I wasn't a bitter-ender like Faustus. I was a proud loser. "No," I eventually replied, forcing myself to look into her pale blue eyes. "I don't like to work too hard for stuff I want. I prefer to just do without."

Her perfect features froze, until the corner of her mouth lifted into a smirk. "How very Epicurean." Before I could ask what she meant by that, she looked over my shoulder and raised a delicate eyebrow. "I believe Lily is waiting for you."

She was right; across the room, Lily was waving at me, with Dante taped to her hip like a conjoined twin, as usual.

"I'll see you at dinner, Emma. There's a lot more I'd love to discuss with you," Lady Montecito cooed, turning on her heels to leave.

Discuss with me? "Hang on, I'm not … I told you I'm not staying."

She didn't look back, but there was steely certainty in her next words. "I'm certain you'll reconsider."

My first impulse was to snap back "hell no!" but my gaze fell on Lily as Montecito glided past her and I was reconsidering already. I needed to speak to Lily alone, grill her about Katharos, and try to find out why Faust had gone through the trouble of stalking me to warn me about them. If there was any truth to what he'd said about Katharos spying on me, then it meant Lily wasn't entirely safe working for those creeps either . . .

XI

"I'm so pumped you're staying after all!"

I gave Lily a thumbs-up from the backseat while Dante parked his Cayenne in front of the Residenza. Back to square one. "By the way," I asked her, as we unbuckled, "can we talk a bit more before dinner? In my room?"

She gave an eager nod. "Sure."

Dante grinned at us. "They refilled your minibar; you two call me if you need help finding your way back to our apartment afterward."

Lily giggled and shook her head at him. I managed a cringing smile at Dante's subtle jab.

After we'd made our way into the Residenza under the disapproving gaze of the goat guys guarding the entrance, Lily pressed one last kiss to Dante's cheek, her fingers lingering in his. I watched her let go at last with a secret sigh of relief.

The tension in my shoulders only eased once we were in my room and I dropped my backpack on an armchair. I pulled out my phone from my hoodie pocket for a quick Facebook check. Nothing. There was a familiar pressure in my chest—the clinical sign that I felt like shit. I tucked my phone back and ignored it. Maybe he'd eventually reply, and if he didn't . . . whatever. I'd made it without him for the past thirteen years. Tons of real orphans out there who had it worse than me.

I went straight to the minibar as Lily sat on the couch. I took out a bottle of water. "Want some?"

She shook her head, I opened it and gulped some before plopping myself in a blue brocade armchair across from her. Lily's hands were folded on her lap. She wore a guileless smile, but she wouldn't speak first. So, I did.

"I didn't decide to stay because I'm comfy at the Residenza," I told her. When she tilted her head expectantly, I added, "I stayed because . . ." *I'm getting red flags about Katharos from a hobo who should write pilots for HBO.* Okay, no. Bad idea to tell her about Faust. "Because you looked kinda on edge last night. I know you've got a lot on your plate, but just wanted to make sure you're more or less okay before I go and resume ignoring you, Mom, and Richard for the next decade." There. Compassionate tone and vague excuse—perfect.

Lily's lips quirked. She looked at me like she thought I was a kitten pretending to roar. "Em, I'm okay, I promise, and I hope we can meet for drinks from time to time while you'll be ignoring me."

"I'll think about it," I said regally. Before she could enjoy that small victory though, I veered back on track. "I just think Katharos is putting a lot of pressure on your shoulders, and maybe it's too much on top of having to fill your grandpa's shoes every day."

Lily didn't reply. She leaned back in the cushions, crossed her arms, and her eyes avoided mine. It might not sound like a big deal, but it felt supremely weird for me to see her play my role. I wondered if my teachers and counselors had felt as useless and confused as I did right now when I would wall myself in the same silence. I snapped my fingers at her. "Hey, earth to McKeanney," I said it with a playful grin, so she wouldn't feel awkward and clam up even tighter—totally a counselor thing too.

She sighed and wrenched her hands. "It's been a little harder than I thought," she managed. "At first, I just loved having this connection to him—working with his notes, living here." I let her go on, my gaze set on her pale fingers. "But I think . . . being here, it started to bring up memories. I was so young when my mom died. I didn't remember her, and Dad didn't want to talk about her. But Grandpa would tell me about her all the time, and he was . . ." Her voice cracked. "He was my bond to her, in so many ways, and he meant so much to me. And I wanted to do this; I still want to be here and finish this for him." She looked up, and her eyes were glassy. "But it's just been hard."

I swallowed, thinking of my father, of the abysmal void that mere stranger had left in me. The same void Lily's grandpa had left when choosing to leave her. "I get it," I said tightly. "But I don't think living and breathing Katharos is helping you. You know, you could try renting a place elsewhere in Rome. I mean . . ." I waved at the gilded ceiling. "None of this is worth it if you don't feel right."

I honestly thought she'd burst into tears, but she straightened and shook her head instead, brushing a finger over her eyelids to dry them. "No. I'm right where I need to be." Her gaze hardened as it swiped around at my bedroom's paneled walls. "I needed to start over where it ended."

My chest constricted. "What do you mean?"

She clasped white-knuckled fingers on her lap. "He had an apartment at the Residenza. He always stayed there whenever he was in Rome." Her lips pressed bitterly. "One of the perks of working for Katharos."

I digested the news with a shudder. "Was it—"

"No," Lily reassured me, reading the question as it formed on my lips. "He didn't die in your bedroom."

"Please tell me it wasn't yours either," I breathed. This whole situation was fucked up. And it seemed to get worse with every detail I learned. I stared down at the bottle of water still resting in my hands. My Facebook invite drama and ugly duckling complex suddenly seemed almost trivial compared to the amount of grief Lily had been through, and I couldn't shake a pang of shame that I'd been too selfish to truly care until today.

She tipped her head to the ceiling. "It's on the third floor."

"You've been inside?"

"Yes. I thought . . . it might help me understand."

"Did it?" I probed, already knowing the answer.

But again, she surprised me. "Yes. It helped me see the path I needed to follow."

I took a slow sip of water to soothe the unpleasant dryness in my mouth. "Find the table and complete his work."

"It's the same for you," she replied, lightening up all of a sudden. I waited for the rest with a cautious frown. Her voice was softer as she added, "You're not wandering aimlessly."

Wandering. The first image her word conjured up was a vision of myself, a year ago, sitting on a sidewalk and watching Apple ads play on a flat screen in the windows of a Best Buy. I'd seen the same iPhone ad over and over until I was braindead. I forced a chuckle and rolled my eyes. "Of course, I'm not . . . wandering."

She shook her head, grinning. "I didn't mean it literally. It's more like a metaphor. Do you know the story of the three fates?" I shook my head, casting her a doubtful look. "It's a myth the Greeks and Romans shared, a metaphor for destiny. The fates are three women who respectively spin, measure, and eventually cut the thread symbolizing each person's life—mortal or immortal. They knew the beginning and the end of one's life and . . ." She waved her hands as if she were trying to turn the concept around in them. "Dante would explain it so much better than me, but the idea is that this thread—this path—shows you that no matter what happens, there's a fate written for you; you're going somewhere, and you'll influence other lives on your way. Things can happen a thousand different ways, you can make a thousand different choices, but eventually, they'll always lead you where your path is taking you."

I ran a tongue over my lips and gulped some more water, absorbing this information under her bright, expectant gaze. She didn't see what it could mean for someone like me. To her, it was probably a poetic way to say that even she'd lost her grandpa, and it couldn't have been avoided. It was also in her cards to meet Dante and experience this huge love, like in Disney movies and *Fifty Shades of Grey*. The real deal that made your knees weak and melted every brain cell of an otherwise healthy college student.

To me, it was like looking down at a frayed thread knowing it'd never get better than this; that no matter what choices I'd have made, my mother wouldn't have wanted me, and my father wouldn't have stayed. If that path Lily was rambling about existed, mine led to Tuna Town at best, or out on the street. I ground my molars together. *Fuck that.* She could believe whatever she wanted. I chose to believe that it was bullshit and that I didn't walk around with a thread tied around my ankle.

"Sorry," I said tartly. "I'm not into that kind of spiritual stuff."

Her lips parted to reply, only to be interrupted by a soft rap across the room. Dante's voice came muffled through the door. "Lady Montecito has arrived."

Lily sprang up from the couch with a blissful smile. Jesus, all it took was hearing his voice, and I could already see her brain oozing fast through her ears. "Yes, we'll be there in a minute."

I followed her to the door, but once she was standing in front of it, her hand paused on the handle. She turned around, her gaze searching mine, always so clear, so open. I had this thought that she'd always get hurt badly someday if she didn't learn to shield herself better.

"Em . . ."

I raised an eyebrow to indicate she had my full attention.

"I should have said something." The words escaped her in a strangled sigh like she was confessing a triple homicide. "Every time she compared us or when she hit you, I knew it wasn't normal, but I never said anything. I was afraid she'd hate me too . . . that she'd leave Dad. I think it was the same for him too." She balled her fists. "We looked the other way. It wasn't right, and I'm so sorry—for everything."

At first, I just stood there, my mouth hanging open dumbly. It didn't last. My auxiliary system took over, and I waved her apology off with a flick of my wrist. "Fair's fair. I was a toxic little piece of shit."

"It's not true," Lily insisted. "Families stick together, and we messed up. I just wish I'd been stronger back then."

My eyes were prickling a little, and with it came a wave of shame. Because I still couldn't get rid of those old bruises inside, because Lily had not only taken the love my mother couldn't give me, but she had it in her to pity me on top of that. I mustered a superior smile and rolled my eyes. "I got over it."

She gave a shy nod. "Okay. I guess it helped, reconnecting with your father, right?"

I mumbled a vague, "Yeah." Lies; they pile up so fast.

Lily took my hands and squeezed them. I let her. "I'm just glad we can have a second chance."

Her words registered almost like a foreign language in my brain.

I turned them over, dissected them. A second chance? More like a slew of sketchy coincidences and my usual gift for finding trouble faster than it could find me. And yet . . . Lily and I were here, talking, sharing more than we ever had when we were living under the same roof. Maybe she was right, and there was a second chance squeezed at the bottom of that barrel of lemons.

XII

When I was sixteen, before Mom sent me to Saint-Henry, I got myself fired from this other school which had a wilderness program called "Young Wings." The whole idea was that we were birds who hadn't yet learned to fly and dropping our asses in the middle of the woods with military rations in our backpacks and psychotic vets to shepherd us would somehow work wonders. One of the kids tried to hang himself from a tree.

I didn't do that. *I* took off while the adults were busy cutting the rope. I made it to the road and hitched a ride to the next gas station from a fifty-something biker—a true gentledude, who not only bought me a bud light, but rescinded his offer to take me to a nearby motel when I told him I was underage, and therefore jailbait. Decent guy overall: 10/10, would hitch again.

Anyway, I got caught and ended up being lectured by the undersheriff of Hamilton County, sandwiched between my mom and Richard. Now, I'd like to stress that all of this—the undersheriff warning me that I could have been raped by that biker and gotten pregnant; my mom feigning outrage and swearing to the guy that she had *no idea* I drank alcohol; Richard staring vacantly at a pair of moose antlers on the wall—all of this went better than my second evening at the Residenza.

Sitting stiffly on a long brocade couch next to Lily and Dante,

I watched Alfredo pour two fingers of scotch over the ices cubes in my glass. I could feel Lily's mildly alarmed gaze on me as I brought the drink to my lips. Apparently, I should have asked for a glass of prosecco like everyone else in the room. She seemed to shrink under the weight of Dante's hand on her shoulder when I swallowed the first gulp with a contented hiss. Nice burn.

In the couch opposite ours, Lady Montecito watched me down my scotch and toasted me with an impenetrable smile. Lucius stood behind her, his back to a tall window showcasing the palazzo's darkened courtyard.

"Is the whiskey to your liking, Emma?" Montecito asked suavely.

I pursed my lips in approval. "Yeah. Really nice and smoky."

"Nothing better than a heavily peated malt," she concurred, dipping her red lips in the light golden prosecco in her glass. Her eyes gauged me over the crystal rim. "I'm so glad you decided to stay with us after all."

"I love it here," I replied, my face deadpan.

"And we love having you." Her voice had grown cool, an echo of my own. My unease dialed down a bit at the realization that we were playing the same game. She saw me for who I was—a bitch—and I saw her for who she was—see above.

"So, Em, what did you think of the foundation's private gallery?" Lily's unsteady voice broke through my staring match with Montecito, her eyes pleading with me to shelve the brass knuckles and be a considerate guest.

I didn't look away—it was a matter of honor—but I said, "It was beautiful, and I had a great guide too."

Montecito's mouth twitched, and she turned to Lily. "Emma was very interested in our marble of Faustus." She set down her glass on the colorful tangle of vine and flowers of an inlaid stone coffee table. "I think she was moved by the poor man's plight."

Lily gave a timid nod while Dante sipped his wine, a silent spectator to the tension sizzling between the three of us. "My grandfather told me this story," she acquiesced. "He even used it to open one of his conferences about Pagan concepts of immortality during the Empire." A genuine smile stirred her cheeks. "He said that in our modern world where we trust that money will someday buy immortality, he liked the idea that the only man Chronos gifted it to was a blind beggar."

"A lesson in humility to all of us," Montecito murmured, her gaze drifting to me. "Speaking of beggars, Emma, there's something Lucius and I have been meaning to ask you—and I hope you'll forgive our curiosity . . ."

I went rigid, save for a tremor in my wrist that made the ice cubes in my empty glass tinkle softly. Alfredo glided my way without a word to take it from me. I let him, my eyes set on Lucius. For the first time since we'd entered the salon, he was coming alive, his shoulders rolling ever so slightly under the dark, shiny fabric of his suit. The low hum of his baritone echoed in the salon. "As you already know, Emma, Chronos's Table is an invaluable archeological discovery. Security and confidentiality are therefore our utmost priorities."

I cocked my head at him, mustering a laid-back sneer when my armpits were, in fact, getting damp from a cold sweat. "And . . .?"

He leaned forward to rest his large hands on the back of the couch where Lady Montecito sat. "We had an intrusion on the Palatine two days ago." His eyes narrowed briefly. "Concomitant with your visit."

*Faust . . . w*ho probably thought his disappearing act and his cats made him some sort of discount Batman. Flash update: he sucked at covert ops, and Katharos had him in their crosshair because when you waltz around completely wasted, people fucking *notice*.

Lily shot me an anxious look while Dante's arm snaked around her waist—to comfort her or hold her in place? I wasn't sure.

Keep it cool, Em. I shrugged. "I know. It was just a bum though . . ."

Montecito's features softened in a parody of compassion. "Indeed. Lucius told me what happened. He praised your display of kindness." I raised an eyebrow at the interested party. That sounded almost as credible as, *Lucius volunteers to rescue orphaned kittens in his free time.* She went on, her voice suddenly cutting. "But some people can abuse that kindness."

Lily's lips formed my name, but Lucius cut her question with his own. "Has this man tried to contact you again, Emma?"

It was as if my heart had stopped for a suspended second while I processed his question. *They're trying to keep an eye on you.* I braced my hands on my knees to stay focused. Calm, even as my pulse roared in my eardrums. "Why are you asking me that?" I snapped.

Lucius walked around the couch. I registered the rustle of his suit, the whiff of woodsy cologne as he moved to stand a couple feet away from me. His lips stirred. I avoided his gaze and locked on his hands instead, oddly smooth, and with perfectly clean and trimmed nails, like he'd never done a single second of manual work in his life. "I believe you met him again, Emma," he said, his voice a notch softer.

Oh shit! They knew about that too. Had Lucius sent someone to tail me? Or was it Faust he'd been watching? I balled my fists, seconds ticking in the salon as I walled myself in cautious silence.

Meanwhile, Lily managed to free herself from Dante's embrace and snapped out of her stupor. "Em, who's that man he's talking about?"

I hated to see that expression of betrayal on her face, a look that seemed to say, "How could you? I gave you a chance, and you completely fucked up, like you *always* do." The fear pounding in my temples became anger at myself, but also at her for dragging me here at the Residenza in the first place and starting all this. I shot up from the couch and glared at the four of them. "Look, I'm out of here. I don't give a shit about your table." My eyes set on Lily, and I loathed the tremor in my voice as I added, "and I don't give a shit about *any* of you." I turned to Lucius and Montecito. "All I know is that you're a pack of creeps breathing down people's necks for whatever reason, and I don't want any part of that."

"Emma, I'd like you to sit down and talk to us," Lucius replied, taking a threatening step forward.

I circled away from the couches and toward the salon's doors, my arms outstretched challengingly. By then, it was my adrenaline doing all the talk. "Make me, cocksucker! Give me a good reason to press charges!"

Lily's eyes nearly popped out of their sockets, and that shifty cunt Dante clasped a hand over his mouth in an obvious attempt to conceal a smirk. Through it all, Lady Montecito remained perfectly still, her hands laced on her lap. "Dante," she eventually said. "Please take Lily upstairs."

It was Lily's time to rise when she heard this. "Lady Montecito, I'm absolutely sorry. I think Emma has had a little too much to drink, and she didn't mean—"

Montecito's voice was a smooth blade cutting through her blubbering tirade. "It's all right, Lily. No one here intends to hold Emma against her will."

I drew a furious breath through my nostrils. "You better not. I'm getting my backpack, and I'm seriously out of this freak show."

Across the room, I noticed Alfredo opening the doors for me. The wave of relief that followed came laced with guilt and shame as my eyes met Lily's, glistening with disappointment. What else was new? I saw her throat move, but she wouldn't speak. She never had in the past either. She never judged, never compared us. There was no need to. Actions spoke louder than words.

I felt too shitty to even apologize, so I just bulleted past her and ran up the stairs to go get my stuff, without another look for Montecito and Lucius either. After I'd slammed my apartment door behind me and returned to the lobby, the four of them were still here, Montecito and Lucius, as impassive as ever, Dante, feigning some sort of concern. And Lily, who wouldn't lie, wouldn't try to hide her regret.

"Won't you just talk to me?" she murmured, watching me as I tightened the straps of my backpack.

"No. I shouldn't be here," I snapped before my shoulders sagged helplessly. She'd just think I was crazy if I told her about Faust, but the knot in my stomach wouldn't ease. Something wasn't right in Katharos's heavenly bubble, and I felt shitty for running away like that. I forced myself to look her in the eye, purposely ignoring Dante standing next to her. "I just want to say . . . that you should keep your distance." I waved in Lady Montecito and Lucius's general direction, who gave no sign they had noticed—or that they minded my warning. "They're weird," I concluded lamely.

Her eyes darted to her employers. Apologetic. She shook her head at me. "Em, I don't understand, and I can't help you if you just storm off."

I did what I knew best. I shrugged and walked past them. Lily went after me in the courtyard. "Em! Where are you going to spend the night?"

My legs nearly missed a step, but I caught myself. I waved her concern off without turning back, ignoring the sudden weight in my chest. "Don't worry; I'll find myself a room somewhere."

XIII

The clerk who cashed me out in that tiny supermarket near Piazza Cardelli gave me a weird look. Her puffy eyes snapped from my shuttered expression and messy blue hair to the cheap snack cakes and Pepsi bottle sitting on the conveyor belt. Didn't help that I kept looking over my shoulder and through the shop's windows, expecting to find Lucius's conspicuous gorillas following me, hiding behind sunglasses at 10 pm and keeping a finger taped to their earpiece. I guess she must have thought I was a junkie tweaking out and going on a sugar binge to tide herself over until her next fix.

Pretty much all shops were closed, and tourists were getting scarce. I wanted to find a place to sit, unwind, and use what little data I had left to find a cheap guesthouse that would let me check in even in the middle of the night. I hurried down a narrow street, along cracked façades and ancient sculpted doorways, scanning my surroundings for a bench, or just steps. I eventually found myself standing on a wide avenue, crossed it, and kept dragging my feet in vain.

I eventually settled for the ledge of a rectangular fountain in front of a tall building whose façade was decorated with ancient Roman mosaic—naked dudes doing stuff like working the fields and . . . carrying a tiny boat with smaller naked dudes in it. Remember kids, don't do mosaic when you're high. I retrieved a mini cake and my Pepsi bottle from their plastic bag and set the bottle between my feet, before tearing the cake's wrapping with my teeth to start my picnic. Contrary to the wrapping's claims, that filling was anything but chocolate, but the cake was otherwise okay. Good value.

There were no sketchy bodyguards on my trail after all—not a soul, really, save for the occasional car speeding down the street—and at last, I allowed the tension accumulated in my muscles to dissipate. I took out my phone in between cake bites, wondering if Lily might text me in the wake of this disastrous night. There was nothing. It was better this way, but I was left with an ache, a void inside me I couldn't place and that no amount of soda and junk food would fill. I checked Facebook as if a notification from my dad would solve everything. There was none, of course, and it'd been a while since I'd felt so low, so lost. I closed the app and loaded Yaytravel.com instead, narrowing my search to the cheapest—and likely sleaziest—hotels in Rome.

A flash of black at the edge of my vision had my fingers pause on the screen. My head slowly whirred left. A black Mercedes had just stopped on the avenue, barring access to the street. I watched it from the corner of my eye, expecting it to either turn or park along the other cars in the street. The engine stopped.

I gripped my phone with clammy fingers, trying to look chill even as I darted looks left at the Mercedes. The rear doors opened and two men came out. I didn't recognize their faces from that far away. But the dark suits, the heavy and determined stride, those were all too familiar. I casually tucked my phone as they walked toward me. Braced my feet against the pavement.

Breathe . . . Now.

I lost sight of them for a millisecond as I shoved my phone in my pocket and exploded forward. Soles immediately clattered on the cobblestone in response. They were coming after me. I raced down the street, fueled by a panic that damn near gave me wings. It was really happening. Montecito and Lucius had actually sent their goons after me. All because of Faust? Because I was their only link to a crazy hobo trying to get near their table? My skull hurt; I couldn't breathe over the din of my thoughts.

The sound of heavy steps slamming the pavement grew closer. Tires screeched somewhere ahead of me. A black SUV pulled up to block the other end of the street. I ran—faster than I ever thought I could—but the searing pain in my chest and legs told me I couldn't keep this up much longer. I blinked frantic eyes at the cold façades looming over me on the right and the low wrought iron fence running to my left. A length of black tarp covered most of it, advertising the renovation of the Mausoleum of Augustus. I had no idea what it was, and I could barely make out the shape of trees and ruins beyond it. All I knew was that I was running fast toward a dead end and that the men racing after me couldn't be more than thirty feet away.

I veered left and covered the distance to the fence. If eighteen months on the street had taught me anything, it was how to efficiently climb any obstacle when security guards showed up, and it was time to rise, shine, and take off. Fast. I leaped, gripped the iron bars, and propelled myself over the flat railing. The landing was rough. I yelped when my knees hit dirt and cutting gravel, and I went rolling down a light slope leading to a courtyard. The dark silhouettes of construction vehicles surrounded me, silent beasts guarding a massive circular building I could now see more clearly through the shadows of tall cypresses.

Behind me, the fence clanked under the powerful grip of

Katharos's gorillas. I scrambled up and ran toward the mausoleum, my heart pounding in my throat. If I could hide inside, maybe they'd give up, unless they wanted to draw the neighborhood's attention with flashlights. I slipped into an ajar iron gate and dashed straight into the building's gaping mouth, a pitch-black passageway that swallowed me whole.

I could still hear the men running after me, skidding on gravel just like I had seconds ago, while I rushed into a second circular courtyard. I fumbled my way through the ruins, overwhelmed by the scent of damp stones long reclaimed by ropes of ivy and bushes of weed. My legs shook with every step, every panting gasp. The adrenaline pumping in my system was no longer enough. I stumbled, fell to my knees, and this time, I didn't get up. I crawled among the remains of a collapsed wall, and curled there, my teeth gritted so hard I thought they might shatter.

They entered the courtyard seconds after me, their steps slow and cautious on the uneven ground. Shadows crept toward me, closed in on me. I stopped breathing, willed myself invisible when they glided mere feet away from my hiding spot, and the shape of a gun barrel caught a trickle of moonlight. *Oh shit . . . shit . . . shit . . .*

"Emma." Lucius's baritone rose in the courtyard. A soft, dangerous thrum I could feel raising the hair on my forearms. "I know you're here."

A shadow detached itself from the wall, and I picked up a hint of woodsy cologne. I gripped my knees with quivering hands, listening, trying to gauge how close he was. I managed a croaky exhale when I realized he was now shuffling away from me and toward the center of the courtyard. He vanished, his inky frame merging with that of a round building—the cold heart of the mausoleum.

His voice slithered along the ancient brick walls. "We have

more in common than you think, Emma. I, too, was once an insignificant roach. I was not born a free man."

But you were born an asshole, I thought, holding onto the thin hope that he'd keep searching the tomb rather than the ruins outside. I couldn't see his men anymore, but the faint echo of feet crushing gravel behind me had me shrink to a microscopic ball against the ruins of the wall shielding me.

"But Lady Montecito picked me up from the dirt, and she gave me everything a man could dream of," Lucius went on, probably unaware that he sounded like the brainwashed follower of a cult. Also, this was getting weirdly personal, and I prayed, *prayed* he wasn't about to lose the few marbles he'd left. He came out of the tomb through a door I hadn't noticed in the dark, and suddenly, he was closer than ever. Close enough that I could make out the strangely smooth skin of his hands, sculpted by moonlight. I sucked in a panicked gasp.

Lucius's voice grew ominously louder as his moonlit profile came in sight. "Your presence here in Rome is no coincidence, Emma. You have a purpose to fulfill."

You're not wandering aimlessly. Lily's voice echoed softly in my mind, mingled with his. Had she been fed the same kind of bullshit by Lady Montecito—No . . . I remembered now, what Lily had said: *Dante would explain it so much better than me.*

Meanwhile, Lucius still believed he might coax me out Barry White style. "There's no need to hide, Emma. Come with me, and Lady Montecito will reveal the secrets of the table to you. Be one of us."

Hang on, hang on, hang on . . . The secrets of the table? My shoulders hitched, or perhaps it was my legs, jerking imperceptibly. Whatever it was, it made the earth whisper under me. Lucius went still. His head turned slowly. His fingers twitched, and I thought I saw something. I was no longer certain I could tell dream from reality through the curtain of my terror, but I thought I glimpsed a fleeting curl of smoke, swirling around his wrist as he moved.

He flicked his hand, beckoning his henchmen. Their footsteps ricocheted around the mausoleum's barren walls, growing nearer. Blood roared to my temples; they were moving to trap me.

"Step back," Lucius ordered them. "I will handle this."

The next words he spoke were a hurried whisper, mumbled in a foreign language I could make no sense of. Yet I sensed the urgency vibrating in the deep bass of his voice, raising the hair on my nape. Instinctively, I knew I was listening to a prayer. Then the words died as Lucius went quiet.

I waited, every cell of my body in a state of suspended terror. He raised his arm, and one single thought detonated in my brain: he must have a gun, too, and he was going to shoot me. But his hand was empty, his fingers curled over thin air and a thin ribbon of ink-black smoke. Maybe I was hallucinating this too, the way the smoke seemed to expand around his wrist, until it became a wide black ribbon that stretched and spun gracefully in the air, guided by his hand. *What . . . the . . . ever-loving . . .?*

It went too fast for panic to even register in my brain. The smoke ribbon hissed above my head and sliced through the remnants of a column like butter, snapping it cleanly in half. Several tons of granite hit the ground with a shockwave that ripped through me from the bottom up.

Fear returned to me like a whiplash, and at last, my legs remembered how to move. I scrambled to my feet and tore across the courtyard, away from him and his goons. Forget guns. That shit was *magic*, and nothing made sense anymore. All I knew was the all-powerful fear of death, and the instinct to run as long as my body could. But I was too slow, and my feet too heavy when the shadowy ribbon drew a wide arc above me and whistled down, fast as an arrow. All I could do was shield myself with my arms as the smoke whip hit me full-force.

I kept my eyes squeezed shut for a whole second, expecting agony that wasn't coming. When it became obvious that I was still alive, I mustered the strength to turn a fraction and peek at Lucius through trembling forearms. He stood transfixed, watching the smoke dissipate in the air around me. His brow jerked. Furrowed. A second of complete daze ticked between us until his shocked expression disintegrated into a hateful snarl, and he pounced.

I leaped and ran, feeling his feet stomp the ground behind me. His goons came from the sides to block my escape, emerging from the shadows once again. The ruins were spinning around me in tune with the wild beat ramming against my ribs. *No way out.* Lucius, his terrifying smoke ribbons, the guns . . . there was nowhere left to run, nowhere to hide as the two men lunged at me. I glimpsed their suits, tried to shield myself, to crawl away, even as their hands tightened around my arms, threatening to break the bones there.

I never knew I could scream so loud. The sound ripped out my throat, burning everything in its wake, amplified by the gigantic walls of the gutted mausoleum. "Help! Someone help me! *Aiutami! Aiutami!*" I arched against their grip and howled at the top of my lungs, kicking blindly to ward off Lucius as his men dragged me across the courtyard. My hair came loose, and through the blue curtain, I glimpsed Lucius's fingers, reaching for my neck. I coughed a whimper, unable to escape his touch, like dead branches wreathing around my throat. I think he tried to squeeze, but he snatched back his hand just as fast as if he'd been burned. A growl of surprise rose between us—his.

Lucius's eyes grew wide. He took a step back, holding up his hand that had just touched me. His skin . . . *Holy fucking shit*, his skin was . . . rotting, peeling off dried-up bones and tendons. My lungs constricted, pumping for air in vain, but I couldn't breathe through this absolute terror. "Don't get near me! Don't touch me! Don't *touch* me!"

I kept straining against his goons' bruising grip, howling in vain for help that wouldn't come. My head, my ears were buzzing painfully, so loud I couldn't hear my own screams.

It always started like this. A wave that washed over me, twisting my insides. The hands clawing at my arms became a stone embrace. Lucius was still staring at his decaying hand, gripping his bony wrist with the other one. A trickle of moonlight glistened, reflected in the white of his eyes. Time had stopped.

XIV

I stopped believing it was real around the age of seven—not long after my mom told me Gabriele had returned to Italy and she wasn't sure when he'd return. I didn't cry. I wasn't the kind of kid who cried, and my mom wasn't the kind of parent who cared anyway. I waited, and as months passed and Lily and Richard became a part of her life, I stopped believing. At some point, a kid shrink from Bellevue taught me the difference between child's play and hallucinations. Once I understood what that word meant and what happened to people who had hallucinations, I never told anyone about mine again.

But tonight, my heart was drumming out of control—everywhere at once in my body. Because it was real. I knew, deep in my bones, as sure as I'd seen Lucius's magic smoke and rotting hand, that time had truly stopped, and that it wouldn't last.

I forgot to be afraid. Long-buried reflexes came back, from a simpler time when this frozen world was no nightmare, but my playground. I let myself go limp and slip out of the gorillas' lifeless grip. I fell on my ass without disturbing a single speck of the gravel in the mausoleum's courtyard. Inert as a statue, Lucius still held his ravaged hand. His eyes were wide open, but he wasn't seeing me as I raced out of the ruins and toward the wrought iron fence. I hoisted my body atop the railing for the second time that night. The landing on the sidewalk was rough, but I barely felt the pain in my knees; I was free.

The SUV I'd seen earlier had moved. It was now parked right in front of the Mausoleum's closed gates—waiting for Lucius and his men to drag me screaming inside, I realized with a wave of nausea. Perhaps for the first time in my life, it fully dawned on me that I was gliding at the edge of my own future. They could have taken me, or maybe I'd have managed to free myself, and I'd have found refuge among the steel skeletons of construction engines. Would I have lived? Or died? It had taken a jump into the twilight zone for me to rediscover this curse of mine with the eyes of the child I'd once been.

For the first time in thirteen years, I stood wide awake outside time.

Inside the SUV, a petrified driver sat behind the wheel, his head tipped as if to check something in the street. It almost felt as if he were watching me through the tinted windshield. I caught a flash of blue in his mirrored aviators—my hair. I frowned. There was another shape moving too.

Behind me.

Blood turned to pure ice in my veins. I swiveled around, and I saw *him. Moving.* I stepped back on shaky legs. Oh God, I wasn't alone. I was no longer alone, and it scared me more than anything else ever had. He was walking in the middle of the street less than a hundred feet away. His gnarled cane hit the asphalt with every step, like a pulse, a familiar clatter. *Tap, tap.* I took in the steel toes, the worn coat. The mess of blond curls and the empty eyes. Faust waved at me, and I was seconds away from pissing myself in complete terror.

He grinned. "Emma! It's as if time stops every time we meet."

Holy . . . ever-loving . . . fuck. I wanted to scream, but the sound was trapped at the back of my throat; all that squeezed out was a breathless gasp.

His face fell. "I thought you'd find this one funny."

Oddly, it was only after he said this that the full weight of the situation hit me. It was like getting whipped by live wires; my brain shut down and my legs went into survival mode. I spun on my heels and exploded forward, past the SUV—away from him.

I registered his puzzled shout behind me, the only sound in the absolute silence. "Emma . . . are you running from me?"

Hell yeah! I pushed beyond the burn in my muscles, racing down the deserted street in the opposite direction, as fast as my legs would take me. I had no idea how much distance I covered. Buildings were flashing past me, and there was a crossing ahead. An engine roared to life somewhere behind me as the traffic lights blinked green. Time was flowing again, slipping fast through my fingers as the reflection of Katharos's SUV glided in darkened windows and gained on me. The lights switched to orange, then red. I ran, spurred by the threatening rumble of the engine, growing ever closer. But it was too late already.

The driver hit the gas and veered left. The sleek black body drifting toward me became my entire world, and I knew I just wasn't fast enough. Tires screeched as a red minivan barreled from the right and smashed the brakes to avoid the SUV. I couldn't process any of this, couldn't find a way out of this slow-motion nightmare. I raised my arms to shield myself from the impending crash. My heart skipped a beat, and I saw myself, the cars, the lights, and the buildings as if that single second had been shattered into a hundred shards flying in all directions.

The SUV's bumper grazed my knees. I felt the heat of the grille against my skin where my jeans were torn, but the impact didn't come. I wobbled backward, my entire body shaking so hard it was a miracle I could still stand on my legs. It was happening again. Behind the windshield, in the driver's gloved hands, the wheel had stopped spinning.

I risked a look at the frozen minivan. The rear door was open, allowing me a glimpse of the passenger inside. I just saw his coat—his face was partially hidden in the shadows. His fingers were wrapped around the cane, his voice soft and eerily calm as he asked, "Emma, can I offer you an Uber?"

I thought: *fuck no*—screamed it inwardly, in fact—but there was no denying that I stood inches from a three-ton SUV about to paint me along the white line. I figured it was one of those moments when the fire looks effectively safer than the frying pan. I breathed in, breathed out, and bolted to the minivan. I flung myself in the backseat next to Faust—I'd have ample time to question my life choices if I survived to see the dawn.

In the driver's seat, an old guy with a tracksuit and flat cap sat behind a flashy red racing wheel, frozen like everything else. Faust extended his hand to me. "Do you have a cell phone?"

My mouth fell open dumbly. I understood each word and the question they formed. Yet none of this made any sense.

His fingers flicked impatiently. "Emma, please?"

Short-circuited, numb, my brain commanded for my hand to reach into my jeans pocket. A distant part of myself watched me drop the phone in his hand . . . only for him to toss it through the door. I jolted back to my senses when it crashed on the asphalt. "Hey! What the—"

Faust ignored my protest and raised his cane. "Are you ready?"

Ready for *what?* I curled in the seat, hyperventilating. "N-no!

I'm not . . . I don't want—"

"Excellent," was Faust's reply, before he lowered his cane.

I felt it then, pulsing deep in my marrow, my veins, like never before, the familiar shockwave when Faust's cane hit the floor mat.

Time roared back to life.

I was instantly crushed against the backseat as the minivan dashed away from Katharos's SUV. I inhaled cigarette and car freshener—the latter dangling from the mirror—as the doors slid shut automatically. We bulleted past a blurry ribbon of buildings, the wheel spinning fast in the old dude's evidently expert hands. In the mirror, I saw the SUV make a 180 in the middle of the street to race after us.

A grunt reached us from the driver's seat. "*Cintura.*" Seatbelt.

Faust complied with an easy smile, while my own hands were shaking so bad it took me several tries to clasp it right. We took a series of sharp turns that shook my internal organs like a martini, while sad Italian rap blared from the speakers. I gripped the roof handle like a lifeline with one hand while the other clawed at the seat. A warm touch on my fingers had me snatching my hand off and tucking it safely between my knees.

Faust's hand still rested next to my thigh on the seat. He tilted his head to me, and I could have sworn he could see me, somehow. Yet his gaze was unfocused, the kindness in those silvery depths directed at a point past my shoulder. "It's going to be all right, Emma. Silvio is a five-star driver."

My eyes bulged out from my head as the Uber drifted left and right in a maze of small streets. I blinked at the lampposts flashing by, looking for the Mercedes tailing us. After I realized we'd lost them, I managed to stutter a coherent sentence. The only one that mattered to me at the moment. "Y-you did this! Holy . . . shit. You did this . . . with your cane."

I caught the old driver checking us in the mirror, but his sunglasses snapped back to the road just as fast. Faust scratched his beard, while in the speakers, the rapper wailed that God had abandoned him. "Well, it's complicated—"

"No, it's *you!*" I shrieked, panting from the mounting realization of all it could mean, the staggering consequences of this overwhelming truth.

"It is me," he confirmed with an apologetic smile.

I thought of the clatter of his cane in my dream, of that day when the seagulls had stopped. I tried to breathe, ride this wave of shock, collect my thoughts, and my second question was, "How?"

The car had slowed down and was now gliding silently down a deserted avenue. Faust's right hand rested on the cane while he reached with the left one to rub a tattoo circling his wrist that I hadn't noticed before. A flash of coppery light from the street splashed it. I clenched my jaw when I recognized a row of the same ancient characters that were engraved on the table. He sighed and leaned back in the seat, retreating behind his trademark easy smile. I sensed bullshit loading in the chamber. "Well, Silvio happened to be in the neighborhood, and he called to tell me, 'Oh, aren't those Katharos employees following our new friend Emma? Shouldn't we—'"

"You had him follow me . . . What the fuck is going on?" I near-yelled.

"To be honest, I was hoping to ask you the same, Emma." Faust's mouth twisted as if he weren't sure what to say next. "I was quite surprised to find you . . ." He cleared his throat. ". . . unaffected by my intervention."

Unaffected. Able to move when everyone and everything else

went still. I held on tight to the roof handle, my stomach lurching as if I were freefalling from the sky, seconds away from the final crash. He was the one *stopping* time, and he'd just said I was a glitch in that . . . thing. He could stop anything but me. Memories rushed back all at once, all those times I'd prayed people would move at last and time would resume flowing. Faust had been out there, somewhere, unaware of what he was doing to me. "It's never worked," I rasped. "Ever since I was a kid. I've felt time stop. I can move, but if I touch people, it does nothing. It's like they're dead. Nothing happens."

Faust stayed silent for several seconds, his expression blank for the slight 'o' of his open mouth. "All your life?"

"Yes."

His eyebrows twitched. "Every single time I—"

"Yes!" I snapped. I didn't want to think of the seagulls. Not now.

His head lolled as if he meant to nod, but his neck wouldn't cooperate. "All right. This is new." His fingers rapped fast on the hilt of his cane. "I like new things. I can work with that."

I cast him a desperate look. "So, you don't know . . . why I'm like that?" I wasn't sure what I expected—maybe some huge reveal that would suddenly right my world and help everything make sense. What I got instead was this:

"To be honest, I didn't even think such a thing was possible. I'm sorry, Emma." He offered me an apologetic smile. "I have no idea what you are."

What—not who. Funny how a tiny word can send your toes curling inside your sneakers. A powerful roar of the minivan's engine hauled me back to immediate reality. I suddenly remembered our driver and flashed a panicked look at his back while he casually ran a red light.

Faust waved my concern off. "Don't worry. You can speak

freely around Silvio." He winked at the old guy in the mirror. "*L'ho conosciuto da quando era bambino.*" I've known him since he was a child.

One of Silvio's hands let go of the wheel to respond with a thumb up. A thousand goose bumps popped all over my body in response. Dude must have been what, sixty, sixty-five at least? And Faust couldn't be a day over thirty. *Oh shi . . .* I hoped they were just trying to mess with me. He couldn't be . . . It wasn't possible.

Cronus appeared to Faustus and offered him a deal: eternal slavery in his service, in exchange for Caligula's death.

My stomach was doing funny flips, and I was probably going to throw up. Or cry. Or maybe both. I risked a peek at him, mentally comparing his sharp profile to Lady Montecito's sculpture of Faustus. No. There had to be another explanation. A beard doesn't make you an immortal hobo. *Nothing* makes you that.

I ran a hand across my face. It was harder to think now that exhaustion was washing away the rush of adrenaline in my system. A hundred puzzle pieces whirled together in my head, stirred by a mild headache: Faust wobbling around the digging site yesterday, Lady Montecito's story, Lucius's magical smoke ribbon—or whatever it was—the way his hand had rotted off, and his claim that Montecito could show me the table's secrets. Then there was Lily: did she know about any of this? Dubious: Montecito had tried to get her and Dante out of the room to question me, back at the Residenza, and Lily had seemed genuinely shocked to hear about my encounter with Faust. Dante, though . . .

The primary source of my headache fished for an old smartphone in his coat pocket as Silvio parked the SUV in a narrow-paved street. He swiped across the glass, guided by a digital voice describing every item on-screen. He opened Uber and proudly announced, "*Cinque stelle!*" Five stars, his own voice echoed by the app's metallic accent.

Hilarious.

I sunk in the backseat and buried my head in my shoulders. "What do you want from me? Why did you drag me into this?"

His head jerked up. "What do you mean, *drag you into this?*"

"Katharos knows . . ." My voice faltered when I realized I'd been about to say, *Katharos knows who you are*, but I couldn't put that surreal notion into words. Couldn't accept it. "Katharos knows about you. The only reason they went after me is they thought I had something to do with you—like I was your accomplice or something. They saw you talk to me in the street, and they freaked out." Even I knew there were a lot of shortcuts, and things left unsaid in this summary, but it was the best I could do when my mind had been continuously blowing in slow-motion for the past hour or so.

Silvio kept staring at us in the mirror while Faust's thumb rapped on the knots of woods on his cane. "Listen, Emma, I wouldn't usually be so direct on a second date, but I'd really like to take you home." His lips pursed. "For a little chat."

I instinctively reached for the door handle. Locked. I drew a shuddering breath and smacked my tongue, the sound thunderous in the car. "Sounds like a kidnapping."

Silvio shook his head. "*No. È come su Tinder.*" No. It's like on Tinder.

I dragged a hand over my face. Tinder, of course. Where you swipe right, no one looks like their pic, and you end up stuck in a car with a psycho bum who may or may not have struck a deal with an ancient deity two thousand years ago.

I turned to Faust. "How do I know I can trust you?"

A grin cracked through his beard. "You don't." As he said this, Silvio unlocked my door and let it slide open—probably to lessen the overall creep factor of this "second date."

Faust winked at me. "Maybe a little privacy will help you relax."

His cane hit the mat before I could ask what he meant by that.

XV

It could have been an ordinary night in a deserted Roman street, forever suspended in time. Faust and I treaded away from Silvio's minivan along dirty ochre facades. I gazed down at the cobblestone under my feet, studied the way the bricks weaved together. The rhythmic clatter of Faust's cane sent jolts of electricity up my spine as we passed a pair of petrified silhouettes about to straddle a bike. A couple, whose cheeks were pinched in silent laughter, empty eyes staring right through us.

"You're going to love my place," he said conversationally.

"Which bench is it?" I shot back, feeling the fight return to me.

He shook his head. "Don't worry; I only sleep rough when I'm too drunk to drag myself home. I have an actual bed. Running water, private WC in the hallway, Wi-Fi from my neighbor—all the modern comforts."

I was ready to lash out that considering all that had happened so far tonight, I couldn't care less about his no-star bachelor pad, but the smooth surface of a turquoise pool came in sight at the end of the street, and the words died on my tongue. The dramatic, temple-like backdrop and graceful statues standing on fake rocks were familiar. I just never imagined I'd ever see the waterfalls of the Trevi fountain frozen in midair.

Faust rested his weight on his cane with a smug smile. "I told you you'd like it."

"You live . . . here? Near the fountain?"

"Yes." He motioned to a vague point across the piazza di Trevi. "Back there."

A few tourists lingered on the place, sitting on the fountain's stone ledge, leaning against the gates of a church, trapped in Faust's dream. I took hesitant steps toward the aquamarine mirror and sat by the water. I grazed the surface and felt nothing. It wasn't cold, nor warm. My fingertips remained dry. Faust went to sit at my side, waiting for me to ask.

I did, my voice oddly serene even as I could barely keep together. "Are you Faustus?"

His gentle smile turned wry, almost bitter. "I wondered if you knew."

I held on to the travertine ledge with a white-knuckled grip as my world tilted on its axis for good. "You're not really . . . Please tell me you're not two thousand years old."

"I'm not." My breath of relief hitched when he added, "I'll be two thousand and five in January."

Oh God. Oh shit. I leaped to my feet; he made no move to catch me, but I held my palms to ward him off anyway. "This is . . . not right."

He gave a weary shrug. "It is what it is. Eternity is long, though, especially after the first couple hundred years."

I clasped my hands together, twisting my fingers in a desperate bid to gather my thoughts. "The table—what is it? Does it have something to do with your power? Lucius said . . . he started to say a lot of weird shit back at the mausoleum, about how Lady Montecito knows the table's secrets and she would show me if I followed him."

Faust's eyebrows shot up in an amused expression, and he

chuckled. "I'd love to see that."

I glared at him. "Well, I don't." I dragged a hand across my face and let out a sigh of mental and physical exhaustion. "Honestly . . . I have no idea what's going on. I'm still kind of wondering if I'm not actually tripping balls somewhere in a parking lot."

"You're not," Faust reassured me.

Awesome. I went to crash back by his side on the fountain ledge. "Look, this is too much to take in. I'm . . . completely lost, and I'm not sure where to start. All I know is that right now, my stepsister is working for Katharos, and she lives in the Residenza. I need to get her out of there." I shuddered at the memory of Lucius's freakish powers and rotting hand. He'd probably show up at her lab tomorrow, acting like everything was fine . . . I had to find a safe way to contact Lily and tell her everything—why would she believe it though? I sure wouldn't.

Resting his cane between his legs, Faust turned his head my way. "I'm assuming you mean Professor McKeanney's granddaughter?"

I nearly fell backward. "You know Lily and her grandpa?"

"Not personally. But Silvio and I have been doing some digging up about Katharos, and a few interesting details popped up."

"Like?"

He flicked his wrist. "Old stories . . ."

I narrowed my eyes at him. "You're not really answering any of my questions so far. You were doing the same back in the car, by the way. *What* is Chronos's Table? What does it do? What's the deal between you and Katharos?"

His chest heaved from a sigh. "I'm sorry, Emma, but there isn't much I can tell you about the table, save for what you probably already know. I'm bound by the kind of contract one does not break."

Like a contract with an old god of time. I looked around at the glass-like surface of the water, the frozen tourists. Despite the evidence, that new warped reality still wouldn't fully set in. I kept expecting to wake up on a sweat-soaked pillow any moment from now, just like I had last night.

"So, it's all true," I said tightly. "You're Chronos's slave. You gave him your life . . . for eternity. What about Katharos? What are they?"

Faust's hands moved back to rest on his cane, and he went silent for several seconds before he asked, "Do you want to hear the official pitch?"

I blew my bangs up in aggravation. "No, thanks. I read the booklet back at their HQ. It didn't say anything about Lucius being . . . Yeah, I don't know what he is, but he's not normal, I can tell you that."

"I wouldn't quite call you 'normal' either," Faust retorted.

I went tense as a violin string, overwhelmed by a rush that was at once red-hot anger at his nonchalance and ice-cold fear when I figured out what he meant. Me, here with him, outside time.

He cocked his head, the same way he had back in the car, as if he could see me. "You do realize that your case is . . . highly unusual, right?"

I clenched my fists so tight my fingers hurt. "What's *wrong* with me?"

He shook his head slowly. "I honestly have no idea, Emma. I can't say I mind your company, but, as I told you already, this is definitively new."

I couldn't take his laid-back act anymore; I inhaled deeply and detonated, jumping to my feet. "I'll tell you what's new for me! Lucius who tried to *kill me* with . . . with his smoke ribbon or whatever. That was pretty fucking new! And the way his hand literally *rotted* when he touched me. That was *new* too!"

After I said that, Faust didn't react immediately. He stared ahead for several seconds like his brain was a beer-soaked Cheeto until he eventually raised an eyebrow. "Now . . . did he?"

"*Yes!*" I gritted out. "I don't know . . . He was trying to strangle me, but his skin started to dry up and peel off." I squeezed my eyes shut and clenched my fists at the memory. I was going to need a dozen showers after that.

Without warning, Faust reached for my arm, and he felt his way down to my hand, squeezing it. He blinked, keeping my fingers captive even as I tugged to free them.

"Hey . . ." I warned.

He let go and nodded to himself. "As expected," he murmured.

"What? What did you expect?"

"Nothing. You can't rot my hand off."

"Well, *no*, and you should be glad I . . ." I trailed off when I realized what he meant. "Do you think it was *me*, not him? Lily touched me, though—"

"That just proves your stepsister isn't trying to stave off death with wonky spells."

"I'm sorry, come again?"

He grimaced and got to his feet, dusting his pants with one hand. "I'm afraid there's a lot I need to tell you about Katharos— not all good. Why don't we go discuss that in my love nest?"

Love nest. *Really?*

My jaw hung slack as he strolled past me, up the steps leading back to the piazza surrounding the fountain. When I remained stuck in place, he lowered his cane, hitting the pavement once. A soft laugh echoed somewhere across the place, covered by the relentless hum of water cascading down the fountain's stone décor. A couple embraced each other and kissed under the stern gaze of marble gods.

Faust called me. "Emma, are you coming? I need to feed my cats."

My gaze flitted back and forth between the couple making out by the fountain and Faust's fingers rapping impatiently on the hilt of his cane. What was it that Silvio had said, back in the car? *È come su Tinder . . .*

I mentally swiped right and followed Faust.

XVI

"What do you think?"

I squinted my eyes in the dark, scanning the cracked plaster façade of the house Faust had stopped in front of. "Not bad."

"It's the oldest building in the street," he noted with evident satisfaction.

It showed. The reddish paint had seen better days—and its share of tags. The first floor looked much older than the upper ones, with its worm-eaten wooden door encased in a massive stone arch. But it was kind of cool.

Faust produced a set of ancient iron keys from his inner pocket. They tinkled softly as he unlocked the front door. "Follow me."

Once we were inside, a musty hallway led to warped wooden stairs. A dusty chandelier hung from a vaulted ceiling, and a few mailboxes seemed to have haphazardly been tossed onto the wall, to see if any would stick. One of them was painted with a single, messy *F*. I treaded carefully behind Faust, cringing when the steps groaned under our weight.

"We're almost there," he said as we passed the third floor. The building might have been minutes away from crumbling to dust, but the residents' doors were freshly painted a bright azure blue, and a heady scent of eucalyptus laced the air. The landing's antique tiling had been scrubbed clean not long ago.

Once we reached the fourth and final floor, Faust waved his cane in the general direction of the wall. Tucked between two regular blue doors with name tags was a narrow plywood one. "The one in the middle's the bathroom. Don't worry, I'm the only one to use it; the other tenants have their own. I have a washing machine too if you need it. Just remember to sit on the lid during the spin cycle or else it bounces all over the place."

"Okay . . ." I noticed a bronze charm nailed to the door and shuffled closer to inspect it. "Why do you have a winged dick on the door?"

"It's a *fascinus*, for good luck. Give it a stroke before doing your laundry to prevent dye transfer."

"You're insane," I stated, but I could feel the corners of my lips curling even as I said this.

"*Superstitious*," Faust corrected while reaching up with his cane to hook it into an iron hoop dangling from the ceiling. An attic hatch creaked open and vomited a wooden ladder. Faust bowed and motioned to it. "After you."

I inspected the dusty steps. "You live up there?"

"Yes."

"Renting or squatting?" If an angry landlord was going to show up with a shotgun in the middle of the night, I preferred to know it beforehand.

Faust's brow bunched in that brand of boyish confusion he seemed to cultivate. "Neither."

"So, you don't pay rent?" I insisted, casting a wary glance at the dark mouth of the open hatch.

He shrugged. "Why would I do that?" With this, he grabbed the rungs and climbed up. I followed him and caught a flash of glassy yellow in the darkness above. An impatient meow confirmed Faust's earlier claim that he did indeed have cats to feed. I hauled myself all the way up into a darkened attic, where I could make out the shadows of a bed, shelf-covered walls and mostly . . . mess.

"Where's the light?" I asked, feeling a tail brush my legs.

"Give me a second." The hatch slammed shut, and Faust glided past me, perfectly at ease in the night where I fumbled and groped. I registered the click of a switch and light burst from a colorful Tiffany lamp hanging above an antique canopy bed. My lips quirked when I noticed the blue and red duvet where Spiderman jumped among skyscrapers.

"A Marvel fan?" I asked teasingly.

He blinked. "What do you mean?"

"Your sheets."

He shrugged. "They're blue, right? I got them from a neighbor. Her grandson didn't want them." He ran a hand over his beard with a chuckle. "He thought he was too old for them. If he only knew . . ."

My smile wavered from an ache in my chest I couldn't place. "I just thought they were cute."

He gave a happy nod. "Blue like your hair."

"You know?"

"Yes. Silvio told me."

"Ah." Good thing he couldn't see my grimace. I was no longer really afraid of Faust, but I couldn't ward off a prickle of unease at the idea that Silvio had been watching me from his gangsta Uber. Was he Faust's servitor? Some kind of stoic henchman doing his evil bidding?

The dark lord thankfully cut through my sinister musings. "In any case, make yourself at home."

I mumbled a "thanks" and set out to explore his treasure cave. Spanning over a thousand square feet, Faust's attic was crammed full of the most bizarre junk collection I had ever seen. Here, a couple of store mannequins watched over old furniture—classy stuff with chipping gold leaf. There, he kept stacks and stacks of books and yellowed magazines—I wondered if, or how, he'd read any of them—but also toys, a rusty red bicycle, and some examples of terrible taxidermy—the raccoon standing on his sideboard was especially wrong, with glass eyes bulging out of its misshapen head. Hardcore stuff.

Faust tossed his coat on a ragged velvet armchair, disturbing the pair of orange tabbies sleeping there. "Pay no attention to the mess; I'm overdue for a spring cleaning."

"When was the last one?" I asked, inspecting the many DVDs, CDs and even VHS lining his shelves.

"When I installed the kitchen, I think. I needed to make a little room for the stove."

Indeed, I spotted a fridge, a porcelain sink, and a massive pink cooking range tucked in the corner of the room. I raised an eyebrow at the rusty burners. "Either you really love retro stuff, or you bought that thing in the sixties."

Faust sighed. "As I said, overdue." He went to search a cupboard for a bag of cat food. All it took was the faint rustle of paper for a bunch of cats and kittens to come out from under a wardrobe and his leather couch. The tabbies got up from their armchair too, and within seconds, half a dozen tails twitched and twirled around Faust's legs, escorting him toward a set of dingy windows at the other end of the room. He opened them with his free hand to reveal a balcony where a plastic bowl and a litter box sat among potted plants.

I followed him. "How many cats do you have?"

"I'm not sure. They come and go. Sometimes they follow me

home, sometimes they don't."

I leaned against the iron railing and gazed at the sea of tiled roofs below while he fed his little pack. You could even see the fountain from up here, gleaming like a diamond in the dark.

Faust stepped away from the carnage, allowing the cats to huddle around the bowl. He grabbed a watering can from the floor with a happy sigh. "Now, a little water, and we're done."

I watched him bend over his plants and water them lovingly one after another. Crystalline drops ran along star-shaped leaves and hairy buds, before collecting in dirty porcelain plates underneath the pots. I squinted my eyes. "Hold on, is that . . ."

Faust held up his can with a guileless grin. "We're facing south. Good sun all day long for good weed. Now come back inside, I'll roll you a 100% organic blunt."

My gaze shuttled between the cats eating at my feet and Faust's jovial expression. "Thanks, but I didn't come here to get wasted."

He gave me a sad little boy look. "But it's nice mild sativa. It won't make you sleepy. It'll just help you unwind."

I wavered. It'd been a while since I'd smoked, and now sounded like a weirdly appropriate time to do that. "Okay . . ."

Once we were back inside, Faust went to the sideboard and moved the raccoon aside to take a rusty biscuit box. I inched closer to watch him as he retrieved smoking paper, filters and a smaller box that was evidently his stash. He opened it and took a long sniff at the greenish lump inside. "Perfect. I call it 'Faust's peanut butter kush.'"

I leaned to smell it too. "Not bad. Definitively hints of peanuts."

He dropped a generous pinch in the paper, and his fingers worked with practiced ease, tucking the filters in, and rolling two joints. He handed me one and felt near the raccoon's tail for a lighter. I watched the end of the blunt shimmer red and took a puff. I exhaled a cloud of potent and vaguely earthy smoke. I pursed my lips in appreciation. "Dank stuff."

Faust drew on his own blunt with a blissful smile. "I wouldn't settle for less. Now, wait a second. I know what we're missing." Pinching the joint between his lips, he went to open a seventies turntable sitting on a wooden stool. He felt for a box of old vinyls sitting underneath, his fingers flipping through them fast before he picked one.

"How do you know which one you chose?" I asked, watching him delicately lower the stylus to the record.

"Magic."

"And apart from magic?"

He handed me the cover with a wink. A long-haired dude with a lot of chest hair was smiling stupidly under the title. I had no idea Umberto Tozzi looked like that. I inspected the worn paper as the first languid notes of *Ti Amo* rose in Faust's attic. Someone with way too much time on their hands had pierced tiny holes in a corner of the cover, probably with a needle. Braille. I handed it back to Faust. "I am *a little* impressed."

He went to sit on his couch and drew on his blunt with a shit-eating grin. "Then my work here is done."

I leaned against his sideboard and smoked under the crazy eyes of his raccoon, feeling the tension flow away from my limbs with each puff. Good stuff, indeed. I studied him through heavy-lidded eyes, half-lulled by Tozzi's husky voice. "Just so we're clear, are you trying to set the mood to fuck me?"

Faust pointed to his chest with wide, innocent eyes. "Of course not!" He leaned back in the leather cushions, his features relaxing in an impish smile. "Not tonight anyway . . ."

"What's that supposed to mean?"

He looked way too pleased with himself as he explained, "Well, we can assume that you'll inevitably fall for me as I help you save your sister. Of course, you'll try to resist our chemistry, but we'll eventually share a desperate one-night stand, like in *Highlander*."

Yeah . . . right. I gave him a doubtful once-over. "*Highlander?* Wasn't that a song from Queen?"

Faust's mouth fell open in scandal. He leaped from the couch and went to scour his shelves, his fingers trailing along the rows of DVDs—counting them. He paused and pulled out one that he handed me. There was a guy with a sword on the cover. Eighties stuff—no mullet, but the dude's super intense crossed-eyed look was weird.

"A chef d'oeuvre," he announced, plopping himself back in the couch.

"Ah."

He gave a disapproving sigh. "I can't believe you haven't seen it."

"You haven't either," I fired back.

"There's an excellent audio commentary."

The weed was starting to hit me, I felt both lighter and sharper as I tucked the DVD back in place on the shelf he'd taken it from— really good stuff indeed. "So, what is it about?"

"The journey of a brave and handsome immortal warrior, from the sixteenth century Scottish plains to present-day New York," he recited.

"True to the source material?" I asked, fighting a chuckle.

Faust smiled and stretched his legs. "I like to think so."

I considered his answer with pot-filled neurons. "But he has a sword and you don't."

"Emma, I can stop time."

"Fair enough," I conceded, blowing a curl of smoke. "Look, do you think I forgot why we're here?"

He craned his neck, eyes closed as the peanut butter hit him too. "Behind you. Top left drawer."

I turned to open the sideboard's drawer as instructed. Inside, an iPad sat on top of a massive collection of ancient postcards. "Do you want your iPad or are you gonna tell me about your trip to . . ." I inspected a yellowed black-and-white postcard of the pyramids. "Egypt?"

He patted the empty half of the couch. "Bring the iPad. I'll show you."

XVII

I settled on the couch next to Faust while his fingers fluttered across the iPad's screen. Like his phone, it had that feature describing every icon and reading every text he touched in a fast, robotic voice. Amazing stuff. He opened a folder with dozens of scans of old papers, black and white pics, newspaper cuts. "As I told you, Silvio has been busy for the past couple of weeks," he noted.

I tapped the ashes off my blunt in a blue glass ashtray sitting on a stack of shoeboxes near the couch. "Meaning Katharos is after you, and *you're* after them."

"It seems that Lady Montecito is very eager to make my acquaintance," he admitted. "But I'm shy, and she's not really my type."

I nodded slowly. "It made you laugh when I told you that Lucius said she'd show me the table's secrets. She doesn't know them all, right?" I watched Faust's lips press together. "But you do. And you're not allowed to tell because of your contract." I concluded. Faust remained silent, but the ghost of a smile curved his lips. Bingo. Montecito hunted him to extract intel about the table from him, and *he* had taken an interest in Katharos two weeks ago, of his own admission—probably when he'd realized excavators were at work.

Faust tucked his blunt back between his lips and mumbled, "Let me show you something fun." His forefinger glided on the iPad's screen, going through a list of thumbnails. The computerized voice dutifully recited the place and date each pic had been taken, guiding him. When the voice droned, "Adulis, Eritrea, 1910," he tapped to open a cracked picture of a group of several men and a woman posing in a desert near some ruins. Those columns behind them looked like the front of a temple, maybe. It was your typical colonization era shit, with white guys in uniforms sitting on folding travel chairs, and half-naked black dudes standing on each side of the group—one holding an umbrella above the woman because it seemed racism wasn't yet a thing in 1910, but slavery still was.

"Zoom on her," Faust instructed.

I pinch-zoomed as instructed and damn near dropped my blunt. I stubbed it in the ashtray with a trembling hand—no need to get any higher. I was in space already, gazing at Lady Montecito's eerily pale and smooth features, and her clear eyes staring back at me. "*Okay* . . ." I swallowed, clasped a hand over my mouth. "Okay. What am I looking at?"

"The wife of Giuseppe De Ludovicci, governor of Eritrea from 1908 to 1914. Lady Emilia De Ludovicci." He chuckled. "She was only nineteen at the time, but she already showed a keen interest in archeology."

I struggled to do the math, caught in the silent horror of this simple portrait. "She's 126 years old!"

Shrouded in a cloud of pale smoke, Faust rolled tired eyes to the ceiling. "Still a little one."

Right. We were probably all little ones to a guy who'd been around since the time of togas and skirts. But to me . . . somehow that pic hit me even harder than the notion that Faust was 2,000 years old , because I didn't really have anything to anchor that belief into reality, save for an ancient marble and a gut feeling. But this was something I could see and understand. 107 years ago, Lady Montecito had sat on a chair in the Eritrean desert, and someone had taken her pic. My gaze drifted to the muscular ebony arm of the man holding her umbrella to shield her from the sun. His impassive face. Staring coldly straight into the camera lens.

I was not born a free man.

"That's Lucius." I gasped. "He was there too . . ."

"A faithful servant," Faust confirmed. "Or rather a slave, who entered her service during her first husband's tenure in Eritrea. The two of them went off the grid after her husband's death in 1915." He closed the picture and resumed his browsing through the thumbnails until the iPad's voice-over announced, "Cairo, 1949." Faust handed me the tablet, which now displayed an old share certificate written in English, for a company named . . . *Katharos Limited.* "They resurfaced in Egypt after the war with Israel, running an antique business in Cairo. I'm sure the name will ring a bell."

"This is insane . . ." I shook my head slowly, opened the gallery view and swiped through the rest of Silvio's findings: Spanish newspaper articles dating back from 1955 and relating to the accidental death of a prominent art collector, survived by his now rich young widow—Emilia Fonseca. A certificate of death for that same Emilia, dated from 1974. London, 1978: A portrait of a short-haired Montecito—then Silvia Federicci, the owner of an antique store specializing in ancient Greek and Roman pieces.

"She eventually returned to Rome in the mid-nineties," Faust explained, reaching in the general direction of the ashtray while looking straight ahead, past me.

"To marry Baron Montecito," I completed, taking the ashtray to gingerly guide his wrist, so he could stub his joint. He gave me that silly blissful smile of his. I felt my ears grow a little hot; there was a sense of intimacy I couldn't place about helping him like that.

Right after I was done placing the ashtray back on the stack of shoeboxes where it belonged, he raised his palms. "There you have it: a long life, well-lived—albeit at the expense of others."

I chewed on one of my nails, wide-eyed, thinking of Lucius's dried-up hand again—part of a body that should have been long-dead. What was it that Lily had called her grandpa's field of study? *Pre-Christian occult practices.* Slowly, all the pieces snapped together in my brain. Thank God for the weed; it probably helped me keep my cool as I murmured, "She's a witch . . . she's a . . . real witch."

Faust winced. "I don't like that term; a lot of mistakes were made in its name. Let's say she's a woman who let her interest in occult practices carry her much further than most."

"No shit, Sherlock! She's fucking immortal!" I squeaked, startling a tiny black kitten who jumped from the chair he'd been sitting on and went to hide behind Faust's feet under the couch.

"She's not," Faust assured me. "Judging from what you told me about Lucius, the two of them are merely borrowing a little time, but these spells come at a heavy price." He got up from the couch and went to rummage on the shelves covering every square inch of the attic wall. "Where did I put it?" I heard him mumble before he grabbed an antique coffee can with a satisfied huff. "I could be wrong, but I'm willing to bet she used this," he announced, plopping himself back on the couch next to me.

I tensed as he opened the rusty lid. Nothing ghastly popped out, though. All the can contained was a roll of really old, frayed linen. Faust took it out and unraveled it, revealing an endless strip of characters, painted on the narrow band of fabric. The same proto alphabet that covered the table and was inking all around Faust's right wrist. "You can touch it; it's harmless," he said.

I poked it once, snatching my finger back just as soon. "What is it?"

"An embalming spell. Preserves one's external appearance while the rest rots as it should."

I recoiled. "Why did you make me touch that?"

"Don't worry, I told you it's harmless. There's a whole ritual to perform for it to work, and this one's been used already, anyway. I don't think it could work again."

My stomach heaved. "*Used?*"

He unrolled more of the linen and coiled some around his arm. "You wrap it all around yourself during the ritual, like for a conventional embalmment."

I eyed the brownish stains spotting the fabric. God, I was going to be sick. "Put it back in the can. It's gross. Why do you keep that anyway?"

"It's a souvenir," he said, coiling the bandage back in the coffee can before he went to place it exactly where he'd found it on the shelves—unbelievable. He knew every corner of that attic like the back of his hand. How long had he lived here to get to that point? He returned to sit next to me. "The owner was an interesting man who lived to see twenty-two popes. He didn't understand, however, that there's no point in wishing for immortality." He sighed. "Time can't be stolen, only given."

By Chronos, I mentally completed. I gazed at Faust's features, those of a man only a few years older than me, yet who carried the weight of an eternity in his eyes. "What happened to that guy?"

"He tripped on a halberd. Pierced his heart."

I cast him a dubious look. "I'm not sure I wanna ask . . ."

Faust gave a sorrowful sigh, petting the black kitten who'd come out of its hiding spot under the couch to settle on his lap. "I was holding the halberd."

A shudder cascaded down my spine, and I inched away from him. "You killed him."

"In my defense, he had it coming for a long time," Faust whined.

All his joke achieved was to make my jaw tick from aggravation at his antics. "That's what you're planning to do to Montecito and Lucius? Get rid of them before they figure out how to use the table?"

He gave a guilty wince. "The idea crossed my mind, but there're a few things I'd like to understand first. I've dealt with her kind before, but she's not exactly the usual fare."

I shifted to sit cross-legged on the busted leather cushions, allowing curiosity to override my concerns over Faust's general lack of regard for human life—or laws. "Her kind?"

He nodded, scratching the kitten curled on his lap to a steady purr. "The power you call 'Magic'—it's not a good word for it, but let's go with that for the sake of clarity. In any case, there's not much of it left in this world, and what you call 'witches' or 'sorcerers,' I would call scavengers. They scrape the earth for what little remains of that power, in artifacts, in ancient spells transmitted from one generation to the next," he explained.

"Archeology with a twist," I summarized. "And your power; it's the same kind of *magic*?"

"In short, yes. Lady Montecito isn't the first one to bang at the walls of reality to get a glimpse of what lies on the other side—and she certainly won't be the last—but she seems unusually skilled at it. You said you saw a ribbon of smoke when Lucius tried to capture you?"

"Basically . . ."

"Would you say it was a weapon? Did it touch you, or anything else around you?"

How the hell could he know? "Actually, yeah. It sliced through a column like butter, and after that, he tried to throw it at me, but I think he missed. It did nothing . . ."

Faust's lips went thin as I recounted this. "*Telum Tenebrarum,*" he said in Latin, with an accent I could never copy even if I spent the rest of my life studying it. Faust was a native speaker of a dead language, I realized. It was just a detail, a grain of sand amidst the flow of weird I was continually struggling to process. But, somehow it impressed me almost as much as his ability to stop time. I ran his sentence against my meager Italian vocabulary. Got nothing. "What does it mean?"

"Spear of Shadows," he said slowly. Wrinkles appeared on his brow, that vanished just as fast as he chuckled away whatever dark thought he'd been entertaining. "But I'm just trying to scare myself. It's been a very long time since a practitioner went that far, and while I think highly of Lady Montecito, I don't think she's that talented. Could be a much simpler spell, or even a whip sword you mistook for something else in the dark."

"*My* eyes work fine . . ." I replied tartly. "But you said someone had done it before, that smoke spear thing."

Faust nodded. "Yes. The man I told you about, in fact. But he wasn't able to complete the spell, in fact."

My eyes narrowed. "Because of the halberd?"

He gave a sheepish shrug. "Among other things. The entire city of London was in flames, and it was overall . . . a very complicated night."

My mouth fell open in dumb shock. "The entire city? When was that?"

"1666."

Of course. The fire. In 1666 . . . I massaged the bridge of my nose slowly. I thought I'd more or less gotten over it, but the age difference was still proving to be a major issue during this second date of ours.

Noticing my prolonged silence, Faust tilted his head, his brow wrinkling in concern. "Emma, are you all right?"

"Yeah, yeah. I'm just . . ." My throat was too tight. I gave up, and I waved at him, the attic, all of this, knowing all too well he couldn't even see my hand. I sighed. "Nevermind. Look, now that I've figured that Montecito and Lucius basically eat children for breakfast, what do I tell Lily? She's never gonna believe any of this, but I need to find a way to get her away from Katharos."

"She studies the table, right?" Faust asked.

I nodded. "With her douche boyfriend."

"Dante Alessandri," Faust confirmed. "Katharos hired him eight months ago. PhD in Theoretical and Applied Linguistics from Sapienza, summa cum laude."

I raised an admirative eyebrow. "And here I thought all you did was drink and con tourists."

He winked. "You forget my passion for gardening."

My lips quirked, but I couldn't bring myself to laugh with that weight in my chest. "He's the one who helped Lily get her internship, and she's . . ." I sighed, thinking of their fusional bubble thing. "Let's just say I'm the last person she'll listen to. Dante is her whole world right now, and of course, he's team Katharos. If I try to tell him they're dangerous, he's just gonna laugh in my face."

"She's in love and living her grandfather's dream," Faust said softly, reading my thoughts. Before I could ask him what he knew about old McKeanney, he added, "We wouldn't want her to land as hard as he did."

My scalp prickled. "You know about that too?"

"That he jumped from the Residenza's third floor? Yes." His

tone cooled down a notch. "A tragedy, especially when he was so close to locating the table."

"I've been told it was suicide," I murmured. A nameless fear swelled in my ribcage, laced with tar-black anger.

"The police found no evidence to the contrary," Faust noted.

"But you?" I urged. "What do *you* think?"

He drew a slow breath, his jaw working as he carefully chose his next words. "I think that a man who spends fifty years studying a subject is bound to understand it sooner or later, and I wonder how well Professor McKeanney understood this."

"You think he figured it wasn't just all legends—the spells, the magic . . . and you."

An enigmatic smile pierced through's Faust's beard. "He wrote an insightful paper about me. It's a pity we never met."

I let that sink in for a couple of seconds, mentally replaying Lily's fond recount of her grandpa's work about Faust. The old McKeanney I remembered had been just like her—one of the good guys, with a moral compass the size of a stadium, and maybe too soft for his own good. If he'd found out about Montecito, his first impulse must have been to pull out. But as I'd learned tonight, one didn't leave the Residenza so easily. "Faust. I *have* to get Lily out of there."

His smile widened, and for an instant, I thought it looked feral, determined—two adjectives I wouldn't have associated with Faust's easygoing personality so far. "Seems you and I are stuck together until we both have what we want, Emma."

I considered him warily, my gaze lingering on the tattoo around his wrist. "Except I've got no way of knowing what you truly want because you'll be waving your *contract* in my face every time I try to bring up the table."

He ducked his head, his shoulders shaking with quiet laughter.

The kitten on his lap stirred and stared up at him with big emerald eyes. "And I have no idea why I can't still you, or what you did to that poor Lucius for him to come apart like that. Don't you think that makes us even?"

I had things to reply to that and still more questions than I'd ever had in my life, but I was also numb, drained—and okay, maybe a little sleepy because of Faust's magic peanut butter. "I can work with that," I agreed, quoting him.

He flashed me what I now mentally dubbed his happy-hobo-grin. "See? We're making excellent progress already. Now, why don't we try to get a little rest? We have a lot to investigate when dawn comes."

"I'll take the couch," I announced, eyeing the busted cushions with a pout. "Do you have . . . like, a T-shirt or something? Clean," I thought it useful to add.

He got to his feet and padded to a wardrobe whose dark wood had seen more than a few decades—or centuries—of use. "Of course. The bed is yours, by the way. It would be ungentlemanly of me to have you sleep on the couch. I'll share it with Confucius."

I blinked and looked in the direction of said couch. The cats were gone, presumably to do cat stuff in the night, but the black kitten he'd petted earlier remained, half-buried in the cushions.

"He never goes out with the others," Faust noted while rummaging in his wardrobe. He eventually produced a white tee and grinned. "My favorite."

I rubbed my eyes and tried to focus them on the embroidered design, a few lines in Italian under a drawing of Jesus on the cross. "*Prima . . .*"

"*Prima ero cieco, e ora ci vedo,*" Faust recited. I was blind, but now I see. "John 9:25. Love it. Reminds me of that time Vespasian spat in my face."

I took the garment gingerly. "Your friends are weird. I'm not really into Bible stuff, though."

Faust shrugged. "It's a great comedy. Probably the best ever written."

I rolled my eyes while shimmying out of my jeans. "Sure . . . Now, gimme that and turn around," I ordered, reaching for the T-shirt in his hands.

His face fell. "Do I really have to? It would make no difference."

"Do it."

He complied with an exaggerated sigh while I shrugged on his T-shirt and placed my clothes in his armchair. "I'm still imagining you, you know."

"Come on . . . creeping on a girl a hundred times younger than you. Shame on you, old man."

He turned around, his palms raised in surrender. "What can I say? I like to pick them young."

I shook my head with a muffled laugh and let myself fall on his bed in a concert of squeaky springs.

"Comfortable?" he asked.

Well . . . his bed didn't smell clean, but I detected no suspicious stench or icky crusty stains either. Good enough for me at the moment. I jerked my hips to test the bounce of the moaning, rolling, living thing under me. "This is worse than my fifty-bucks folding mattress back in New York, but also weirdly cool," I admitted.

"I knew you'd like it." I registered a click, and the lights went off. Faust's voice drifted across the attic, deep and soft. "Dream on, Emma."

I managed a weak smile in the dark. *Aerosmith*, uh? "You too, blind man," I replied.

XVIII

"*Ti fidi di lei?*" You trust her?

"*Non penso che stia mentendo, ma penso che c'è qualcosa che non mi sta dicendo.*" I don't think she's lying, but I think there's something she's not telling me.

"*Era ieri alla Villa Malespina. Dovresti chiederlo a lei.*" She was at the Villa Malespina yesterday. You should ask her.

"*Sai che non posso farlo . . .*" You know I can't do that . . .

A sigh. Faust's voice. The other one sounded like that Silvio guy. They filtered through the fog in my brain. I lay in bed, tucked under Faust's Spiderman duvet. The heavenly scent of coffee wafted to my nostrils, but I couldn't move my head—a warm weight pinned it to the pillow. I yawned and got a mouthful of fur as a tail slapped my face.

A chair scraped the floor. "Oh, she's awake. How are you today, Emma?"

Like an extra in The Rocky Horror Picture Show.

"Take the cat off," I mumbled, while whoever sat on my cheek wiggled, settled back, and kneaded my shoulder with sharp claws. I reached with a sleep-numbed hand to shove the intruder away and glimpsed a fat black and white ass running off to jump on Faust's cluttered sideboard. "Yeah . . . that's right . . . fuck off."

Faust walked to the bed as I stretched with my usual morning Chewbacca groan. "There's coffee, Rice Krispies, and beer for lunch if you're hungry."

"Lunch?" I croaked.

"It's almost noon," he noted, but I sensed no reproach in his voice.

"Okay . . . thanks." I scratched my thigh under Faust's T-shirt, jumped out of bed, and padded across cool floorboards to a small laminate table.

Silvio sat on a stool, contemplating two half-empty coffee bowls, the glossy black screen of Faust's iPad, and a couple Playmobils someone seemed to have forgotten there. I registered rustling behind me and turned around to see Faust rummaging in his fridge door for a bottle of milk. He opened it, took a cautious sniff, and nodded to himself. I cringed. He returned to the table with the milk and a box of cereal.

I assumed that third empty bowl was for me, so I dragged it to me and poured the Rice Krispies, watching them rain with bleary eyes. Faust must have recognized the sound—a grin peeked through his beard. "I like to eat mine with a serving of Faxe."

"What's that?" I asked between two mouthfuls. Thank God, the milk was still good.

"A rather strong Danish Lager sold in one-liter cans. Tastes like wet cardboard, but you'll get a memorable hangover for 2.50 euros. You can't beat that."

Silvio's silver mustache twitched from a gravelly chuckle. "Faxkrispies . . ."

Faust's head bobbed eagerly. "Exactly."

I kept a deadpan face as I ate, even though it was actually a little funny. They were kinda cute together. Faust with today's thoroughly wrinkled red Salvation Army T-shirt, Silvio with his sunglasses, black Adidas tracksuit and golden Stan Smiths. Like an old couple. Of losers. Plotting stuff while I slept.

I sipped the last of my milk with narrowed eyes. "So, what's the plan? How do we get Lily away from Katharos? Do we kidnap her or something?" I was only half-joking. I'd gladly snatch her in Silvio's minivan and drop her at the airport at this point.

"I'm glad you asked," Faust announced, clasping his hands.

"Hang on. Are we *seriously* doing it?"

"No." Silvio shot me a leery look from behind his sunglasses.

Faust shook his head. "She's fine for now. She's with Dante at the Villa Malespina, working on translating the table, I assume."

"*How* do you know that?"

Silvio held out the tablet for me to see and tapped to open some kind of multi-screen video feed. I watched, wide-eyed, as Lily climbed in Dante's SUV on one screen and out in another. A third screen had her walking through the villa's gates and waving at the security guards. My mouth worked in stunned silence until I managed to squeak, "Are you guys CIA or what?"

Faust's eyebrows shot up, before he clarified, "Oh no, no. It's just . . . a network of friends willing to help in exchange for a little something in return."

When my face remained pinched in incomprehension, he took on a grave expression and said, "It's bums with phones, Emma. The second and third most common commodities in any big city."

"What's the first?" I heard myself asking, as I tried to process that Faust and his mysterious—and somewhat edgy—Uber driver oversaw a network of spy bums to do their dirty work.

"Pigeons."

Okay, he was still as crazy as last night, but at least there was a method to his madness. I went to rinse my bowl at the sink, holding it under the tap as it spluttered icy water. "What's next, then? Montecito and Lucius are probably looking for the two of us all over Rome right now." And if they managed to find me, Faust and his time-freezing trick were my only chance to survive my vacation in Rome. Now that I was able to assess my situation in broad daylight and with pot-free neurons, it was becoming clear that I stood so deep in shit I was going to need waders. I returned to plop myself in my chair, and told Faust, "I hope you keep a halberd in here."

He laughed. "That's not what I had in mind. I'd like to understand what I'm up against before we move on to the stabbing part."

Silvio acquiesced with a grunt and lowered his glasses, sending me a pointed look. "We want to understand everything," he said, the words coated in a gravelly Italian accent.

Faust's eyes widened briefly as if he didn't expect his sidekick to step in. "Well—"

Silvio cut him off to ask me, "You were at Katharos's headquarters yesterday afternoon?"

"Yeah," I replied in the same cutting tone he was using with me.

"You saw the table?"

"Silvio," Faust warned softly. He didn't like any of this, I could tell by the wrinkles deepening between his eyebrows.

Silvio rose from his chair and grabbed his empty coffee cup. As he turned to go rinse at the sink like I had, he paused to drop a hand on Faust's shoulder. He gave it a squeeze, and for the second time this morning, I heard him grumble, "*Dovresti chiederlo a lei.*" You should ask her.

Ask me what, exactly? Did he mean when Faust had stilled time while I was in the lab with the others? Had he done that to get inside Katharos's HQ? Come to think of it, the time had stopped too, not long before I'd first met him on the digging site . . .

I watched Faust pat Silvio's tanned hand gently. "Don't worry my friend."

That didn't seem to particularly reassure the old man, who shot me a disapproving glance over his shoulder as he went to sit on Faust's couch. He searched the stacks of shoeboxes surrounding it and retrieved a bunch of papers that looked like administrative stuff. "Call me if things go bad," he said ominously before he started leafing the documents. Apparently, he was done with us for now.

Faust sighed, scratching one of his tabbies when it jumped on his lap. My gaze flitted between him and Silvio's hunched frame; I felt kinda guilty that I'd been the cause of a bromestic fight. I couldn't blame Silvio. From where he stood, I had just barreled into his friend's life—just like Faust had barreled into mine, actually. Silvio probably thought I was bad news, and if I was being honest with myself, I had very little to plead my case with . . .

Faust's voice cut through my musings. "Emma?"

"Yeah?"

"There's something I want to check, not far from here. Will you come with me?"

Across the attic, Silvio raised his nose from the paper he'd been reading, watching my reactions. "Sure . . ." I replied hesitantly. "As long as no one tries to kill us there."

Faust pressed a hand over his heart. "It's perfectly safe."

I cringed. You'd think he'd have learned to lie better than this after two millennia.

Faust's shower must have been built at the same time as his

building. The pipes rattled ominously against the tiling, but the hot water raining on my shoulders helped me focus. I scrubbed with his cake of olive oil soap and dried myself with a Superman towel. Apparently, Faust's old neighbor kept giving her grandson gifts he didn't want. A bottle of Lightning McQueen shampoo stood in the corner of the shower tray. As I combed my hair with my fingers, I shot a suspicious glance at the small portable washer Faust claimed could bounce all over the place. I drew a wide berth around the thing, lest it jump at my throat.

I knew it was dumb, but when I closed the door, I stroked the winged dick pinned to it. I was going to need all the luck in the world to pry Lily out of Katharos's claws, and I had a sinking feeling that Faust had other priorities anyway.

The ceiling hatch opened, and I quickly snatched my hand back. The wooden stairs unfolded, revealing Faust's cane and legs, quickly followed by the rest of him. "Are you ready?"

"Yeah. Nice shampoo, by the way," I teased.

"You should see my Babar mugs."

I chuckled and peeked up the hatch. "Is Silvio coming after all?"

"No, he needs to do some paperwork for November's property tax." He shook his head. "The rules keep changing . . . Let me tell you, Emma, you don't want to spend an eternity doing your taxes."

I gave a once-over to his threadbare pants and free Salvation Army tee. "You . . . um . . . you pay property taxes? For your attic?"

"For the building."

"What do you mean, for the building?"

He blinked. "It's the law. If you have a property, you have to pay taxes." He flicked his wrist. "It's all very complicated. I mostly let Silvio collect the rents and do the math."

I raised a quivering forefinger to the ceiling. "You own *all this*?"

He acquiesced. "My father built it when he retired from the legion, with his discharge bonus. I lost it after some minor legal trouble, but I won it back from a silk merchant in a die game . . . I think it was in 204."

He said it so easily, like it was nothing. But Lady Montecito's tragic story came back to me as he spoke, about the emperor who had blinded Faust, executed his family, and condemned him to live as a beggar. He'd mentioned a fire instead . . . which one was true? Did he remember them after all this time? I studied his peaceful expression as he counted off his fingers and went through his memories. "Then there was the sack, then we had the riots in 1242, a fire in 1757, the two wars . . . I kept patching it up, rebuilding . . . now all that's left from the original insula is the cellar."

"But why live in the attic if you're . . . rich?"

Faust shrugged. "There's not that much money left once taxes have been paid. Enough to pay for repairs, and I do have a little money on the side too. But I like it up there." His face lit up. "And I love it out there, on the streets."

The words felt like a sudden slap, smarting my cheeks, and making my blood boil. Maybe if I had been someone else, someone better, I would have seen just how awesome it was that Faust had managed to cling onto his roots for two millennia with so much tenacity, that he just happily lived on the fringe. But I was just me, and I could find nothing but resentment in my heart for a fauxbo who thought it was fun to sleep on the street because he had an entire building to go home to anyway. I zipped up my hoodie and hurried past him to the stairs. "Whatever," I mumbled. "Let's go. The sooner we can sort out that shit with Katharos, the sooner I can get Lily out of there and go home."

Faust trotted behind me down creaky steps. "Emma?"

"What?"

"Did I say something to offend you?"

He sounded like Lily, his voice laced with the same kindness, the same pity. I ground my molars together, crushing my anger between them. "No," I replied. "I don't care enough about you for that."

XIX

"So where are we going?"

"To a bookstore," Faust announced as we passed the Trevi fountain to lose ourselves in a maze of narrow streets lined with ancient houses. Ivy slowly ate away at a thousand shades of ochre everywhere I looked, dangling from balconies, winding around stone archways. Faust seemed to have no problem finding his way, as if his cane knew each long-polished stone of the pavement.

"How is this going to help us?"

"I need to check a little something to jog my memory," he replied, the occasional clatter of his cane rhythming this strange trip back in time. I wondered how it must have felt for him, to roam this changing city throughout the centuries with nothing but his sense of touch and hearing to learn its secrets. Were the streets still in the same place even though all that remained of the Rome he was born in were either ruins or new buildings standing where the old ones once had—just like his house?

"Emma."

My head snapped up.

"There's something we need to talk about." Faust's voice held its usual calm and gentle quality, but he wasn't smiling. He looked serious for once. I shivered. There it was, the discussion Silvio had meant to have with me. "Yesterday was a strange day," he noted like he'd have commented on the weather.

I kept walking, waiting for him to go on.

"Things didn't go quite as I planned."

He could have meant my leaving the Residenza, Lucius's insane powers, or even the car chase . . . but all I could think about were those few seconds back at the lab. The pressure in my chest, the white noise in my head when my fingers had grazed the table. "Stop playing with me," I snapped. "If you've got something to say, spit it out."

"You know I can't tell you about the table," he began. Aggravation zinged in my veins, but before I could ignite, he added, "What I can tell you is that my power has never failed me once in two-thousand and five years." His legs came to a stop. "Except yesterday."

The mind-blowing, blood-curdling moment of realization didn't come this time, because a remote part of my conscience had been expecting this—dreading it, in fact. I stood there while the afternoon sun trickled down in my hair from old roof tiles, my throat too tight to speak. Faust's power had stalled on him, the same way Lucius's ribbon of smoke had dissipated when he'd tried to cut me with it, or just like the embalming spell that kept him young had let him down when . . .

"I touched it," I murmured, wrapping my arms around myself as if it could shield me from the memory of that brief contact with Chronos's Table. That feeling of being so utterly alone in the face of something too big for me to ever comprehend. "I was with them in the lab when time stopped. I freaked out, and I . . . it was an accident, I just leaned on the table."

"And the flow resumed," Faust concluded.

"Yes," I gasped. Freaking Christ, something was *wrong* with me.

He inhaled sharply and released the air in a slow exhale, like that first breath you take after a flaming shot of Tequila. "Well . . . this should be fun. Remind me why you came to Rome again?"

"I didn't tell you."

His thumb rapped on his cane. "Does that mean you keep secrets of your own?"

"I just came here to see my father, okay!" I near-shouted. "Nothing else. I didn't want to see Lily—we just ran into each other—and I certainly didn't come here looking for you either. I had never heard of you until yesterday. I just . . ." My voice died in a whistling breath as I contemplated the chaos my life had devolved into in just a few days. "I just wanted to see him," I rasped.

"Did you?" Faust asked, his voice softer.

"No. It's complicated . . . Look, I don't want to talk about it."

His eyes were kind, but I sensed a speck of distrust lingering in those milky pupils. "As you wish." He seemed to consider his next words, before he said, "I have a friend, someone very knowledgeable. When I'm done checking the Libro, I'll take you to her. She might be able to shed some light on your predicament."

"The Libro?" I asked as we resumed our walk.

His sunny composure returned—if I didn't know any better, I'd have thought that easy smile was just how his lips were shaped. "Do you remember when I told you that Lady Montecito has been taking pages from someone else's book?"

"Kinda."

"I meant literally so. And I'm interested in finding out exactly which ones."

"Okay . . . and how—"

"Here," was Faust's answer to the question I didn't have the time to ask.

He paused in front of a tiny storefront on the first floor of a house whose wooden beams showed through a cracked plaster façade. Dozens of books were, indeed, displayed in the window, but I noticed there was no sign to be found above it. My mouth pursed as I examined the English-speaking offerings of this nameless shop. *Positive Magic: Occult Self-Help; 100 Spells a Wiccan Needs to Keep her Home Clean; Belzebub's Christmas Table; Empower Yourself at Work with Black Magic* . . . "Self-help for witches?"

Faust grinned. "It's what sells these days. But he keeps the real deal in the cellar—not the sort of thing his average customer is looking for."

Before I could ask who *he* was, Faust went ahead and entered the shop with a resounding, *"Bien le bonjour, Louison!"*

I followed him into a cramped space that was crammed with books from floor to ceiling, squeezed on dusty shelves, piling up in waist-high stacks on each side of the threadbare red velvet curtain leading to the back. Faust's greeting sparked some furious rustling behind said curtain before a wrinkled hand parted it. A shriveled grandpa popped out, wearing a dirty apron over a striped blue shirt and a sparse dusting of white hair on his skull. Approximate age: 150 years old.

He slammed his fist on the counter and roared, *"Fous le camp toi!"* The words rasped his throat. It sounded like French, but I wasn't sure. His name sounded French, though. When Faust kept grinning and felt for a stack of books with his cane, the old dude yelled, *"Sciò! Fuori dal mio negozio!"* Shoo! Out of my shop!

I side-eyed Faust. "Are you sure about this?"

He all but ignored me, taking another step toward the counter. "How have you been, Louison?" I gathered this time he had switched to English for my sake.

The reply flew fast and hard, with an unmistakable French

accent, indeed. "You're no longer allowed here!" Louison took a ragged breath before unleashing his full wrath on our asses. "Last time you come here, you bring a cat and the cat he piss on my carpet! Now you come back, you bring a punk!" He pointed a dramatic finger at me, his cheeks mottled red with rage. "What is the punk going to piss on?"

My own temper lit up like fireworks. "Hey, mind your own prostate, dude!"

Faust raised his cane in front of me to stop the exchange from escalating to a punch-off with a hundred-year-old guy. "*Allons, allons* . . . I came here with an offering of peace, Louison."

The grandpa watched, tight-lipped, as Faust fished in his coat pocket for a pair of tiny colorful objects. I recognized the Playmobils I'd noticed on his dining table earlier. He held them out in his palm for Louison to see, who fumbled for a pair of spectacles sitting among the papers scattered on the counter. He fitted them on the end of his potato-shaped nose and hobbled closer to inspect the toys. He took one—a little construction worker with yellow hair and a rake in his blue hand—and squinted at it, his lips pinched.

"I believe they're prototypes from the 1974 Nuremberg toy fair," Faust cooed. "Virtually unique."

Louison held the playmobil between trembling fingers, turned it around to check its feet, its red-striped jacket. "And the other?"

Faust gave him a little Indian with a plastic feather standing on his head. Air whistled in the old man's throat. "How much you want for them?"

Faust shook his head. "Not a cent."

Louison's eyes became pale slits behind his glasses. "*What* you want?"

A smile stretched Faust's beard, that might have been a teensy bit evil, or maybe it was just the light. "I'd like to take a look at your copy of the *Libro Creaturae.*"

Louison looked down at the playmobils in his hand, greed and hesitation playing across his features. "I can pay."

"But what I want is to see the book," Faust countered suavely, extending his hand to take the precious toys back.

The grandpa's fingers curled them around like claws, and he drew his hand close to his heart. He pointed his chin at me. "She waits outside, not in my shop."

I bit my tongue, seething as Faust replied, "Emma is very curious about the Libro too, and . . ." he tilted his head at Louison. "She's more than able."

Able to do what? A vague discomfort settled in my stomach, a presentiment I wouldn't like the rest of my afternoon. Louison peered up at me suspiciously from behind his spectacles, his mouth so tight it looked like his chin was about to fold over his upper lip. "You two wait here."

As soon as he disappeared behind the curtain, I jumped at Faust. "What is this about? What am I supposed to do? I'm warning you, I'm not doing weird shit," I hissed, keeping my voice barely audible.

Faust bent to whisper in my ear, the brush of his beard against my ear sending an unexpected shiver down my back. "Relax, Emma. We're just going to read a book." His fingers reached to tuck a turquoise strand behind my ear. I let him, only to nudge him away when I realized his hand was lingering and my cheeks were growing hot.

"I don't like this." I warned him, just as the red curtain rustled open to reveal Louison. Wearing a full bike suit. With a motorcycle helmet. And holding a fricking medieval sword.

A thick silence fell in the bookstore as I stared at him, my face slowly melting into a mixture of dismay and disbelief.

"Is there a problem?" Faust asked.

"He's dressed like . . . like he's trying to buy a flat screen on Black Friday. He's carrying an actual sword!" I squeaked. "What kind of book are we talking about?"

Faust patted my shoulder. "A real page-turner. Don't worry; Louison is overdoing it a bit."

The old man lifted the visor of his helmet and glared at us. "Still want to read?"

Faust's "of course" outsped my "no." Louison gave a firm nod and turned around to disappear behind the curtain. Faust's hand traveled down to rest on the small of my back, applying the slightest pressure there. "Shall we?"

I gulped, gazing at the dim and messy corridor stretching beyond the frayed red velvet. Only one way to know what was in that Libro thing: I soldiered onward, followed closely by Faust. We slipped between boxes of dusty books and magazines, guided by the clanking of Louison's sword in a scabbard secured around his waist by a black karate belt. The corridor led to ancient stone steps spiraling down to a vaulted cellar. Here, the books looked different than in the shop: thick leather-bound tomes, worn by decades— possibly centuries—of use, and all locked inside grilled cabinets. I couldn't decipher the gold letters of their titles. It was mostly Greek or maybe Hebrew stuff. On a few bindings, I recognized the same ancient script Faust's tattoo was made of.

Louison went to take a set of iron keys hanging from a small hook on the stone wall. There was a door in the corner of the cellar, whose dark wood bore the scars of time in its veins, a landscape of holes, scratches, and dents. The longer I looked at it, the more my guts coiled like a plate of spaghetti. Louison lumbered to the door in his cumbersome suit and turned the key in the lock. The hinges creaked open, oh so slowly.

Faust's thumb rapped on his cane. "Here we go," he whispered. "It's been a little while since the last time I've been in there."

I stiffened. "How long, exactly?"

His mouth twisted in hesitation. "A couple centuries."

Oh God . . . I hated to be reminded that he'd been around longer than any of the books in there.

Louison flicked a switch to light up a bulb hanging from the ceiling. The sudden glare revealed bare walls, a single table on which sat an ancient chained iron chest, and, oddly, a pair of black latex gloves. What the hell was he keeping in that box? Louison slipped on the gloves and singled out a smaller key to open the lock and release the chains. When his hands moved to raise the lid and shook a little, I braced myself, ready to make a break for the door if *anything* sprang out of that chest.

Faust's hand reached for mine, giving a light squeeze. "I'm sure you'll actually find it interesting."

Not a chance. But I'd be lying if I said I didn't stare my eyeballs out when a shiny surface came in sight, like melted silver. I blinked at the liquid filling the chest. I looked up at Faust. "I thought there was a book? It's just some kind of melted metal in there . . ."

"It's mercury—among other things," he replied, while Louison plunged his gloved hands into the glimmering fluid and retrieved a thick grimoire with chipped, yellowed pages.

I watched silvery droplets run along its cracked leather cover without clinging to it. My jaw hit the floor. "You gotta be shitting me . . ."

Faust grinned. "I told you it'd be fun."

Louison dropped the Libro Creaturae on the table and stepped back. "I'll wait outside. I'm locking you in until you're done."

Hang on a second. My gaze flitted between him and the book.

"Why do you need to do that?"

Faust cleared his throat. "There are a few things I need to explain to you before we start. It is fairly easy to open the Libro." He winced. "Perhaps too much so. Due to the nature of its content, however, closing it is a different matter. There've been a few . . . accidents in the past."

I felt myself blanch. Had the room been so cold a second before? Or was it my own blood turning to ice like that? "*Accidents?*"

There was no reassurance to be found in Faust's embarrassed smile—and even less in his answer. "People get lost so easily in a good book."

"You will find no spells in there," Louison warned. "Only nightmares." With this, he slammed the door, and the only sound left in the room was the rattle of the key in the lock. Lovely.

Faust felt for the table to rest his cane against it and grappled at the grimoire, before casually shoving it aside. "Let's get rid of the props first."

I took a tentative step closer. "What do you mean? I thought it was the Libro . . ."

"Oh no, that's just to give idiots a run for their money." He turned his unfocused gaze at me. "You see, Louison actually guards only a small portion of the Libro. Back in the days, it used to fill a pool so big you could have swam in it. But most of it has been stolen or just spilled and lost to the earth over time."

I darted a confused look at the silvery liquid in the chest. "You lost me at the swimming part."

Faust motioned to the liquid inside the chest, voicing my concerns out loud. "*This* is the Libro."

I peeked again, just in case I'd missed something. Nope. It was still silvery jizz, all right. The tension in my limbs eased a fraction as confusion took over anxiety. "So, it's not an actual book?"

"What is a book?" Faust countered.

I frowned. "That thing you just called a prop."

"No. That's just sheets of parchment bound together."

Okay, maybe I was starting to see where he was going with this. "A book is . . . the knowledge it contains?" A Fausty smile rewarded my efforts—yeah, I had an adjective for that impish and blissful grin now. "Okay, so what's inside? What does it contain?"

"Memories of those who sought its knowledge."

I turned his answer around in my head, trying to make sense of it. Did that mean that those people had used the Libro to look up a piece of knowledge from the memories of someone else who'd searched for the same thing? And in doing so, they'd become part of the Libro's memories too? Jesus, those were the times I wished I'd learned to solve a Rubik's Cube as a kid, instead of peeling off and rearranging the stickers on Lily's. I mentally rummaged through the staggering pile of intel I'd absorbed over the past couple of days. "That guy you talked about last night, the one who tried to use the Spear of Shadows, did he use the Libro for that?"

"Oh, yes, he did." There was a flicker of admiration in Faust's eyes as he said, "It takes a special kind of mind to not only enter the Libro but also understand its nature." His lips thinned. "And his was quite unique. Let us hope Lady Montecito is but a pale imitation of her predecessor."

My brow slowly rose as I caught on at last. "You want to know if she used his memories." I eyed the small pool of mercury in mild—okay, *huge*—disbelief. "The Libro could tell you that?"

Faust shrugged one shoulder. "Only if it wants to. So, without further ado . . ." He camped himself firmly in front of the chest, rubbing his hands. "Here's what we're going to do. I'll take us in, and as long as we're reading, you must *not* touch me or the Libro." His tone hardened a notch as he added, "Do you understand, Emma?"

Not at all. What did he mean by "going in?" Going *where?* When Faust's eyebrow drew together slightly, expecting an answer, I blurted, "Okay . . . I-I don't touch you, and I don't touch that stuff."

"Exactly."

Was it too late to get off that ride? I had to contract the muscles in my legs to stop them from shaking when he reached into the chest to graze the surface of the mercury. Wasn't that shit supposed to be toxic, by the way? "Faust," I gasped. "What happens if I touch you?"

His hand paused. He was no longer smiling, and that scared me more than everything else. "I believe it would have the same effect we've already observed."

"You mean the Libro would . . . stop working?"

"Yes."

Just like the table. If I touched Faust while he read the Libro Creaturae, whatever mysterious force Louison feared so badly inside that chest would shrivel and die . . . I glanced down at my clammy palms as if the lines there might hold the answer, reveal the nature of the hidden disease inside me, the poison messing with Faust's power. I drew a shivering breath, cramming that particular fear back into the deepest recesses of my brain. Now wasn't the best time to freak out about the possibility that I'd somehow caught magical Ebola.

Mercury lapped at the iron walls with soft sloshing sounds as Faust plunged his fingers into the liquid. I was so focused on the silvery ripples that I didn't immediately notice something was happening to Faust's tattoo. Around his wrist, the characters started to glow a dim red and sizzled like skin was burning. I took slow breaths, and I balled my fists to keep it together when the mercury stirred, clinging to Faust's hand as if to swallow it. Faust's lips moved, wording a silent request, and he murmured, "The Libro will guide us. It knows what we want better than we do."

I didn't hear the light being switched off over the pounding of my heart, yet in the span of a heartbeat, we were plunged into absolute darkness.

Faust had disappeared in the pitch black. My hands reached for him blindly, but I remembered his warning and snatched them back. "Faust, where are you?"

"Right here." Hardly helpful when panic squeezed my throat, and I was seconds away from a stroke, but I could pick up the faint tang of pot and outdoors clinging to his old coat, and his voice sounded close, tinged with its usual warmth.

I wrestled my frantic panting under control long enough to form words. "What's going on? Where are we?"

"Inside the Libro. You could say we're reading it as much as it is reading us."

"What the . . ." Light flickered at the edge of my vision, and my head snapped to its source, a bright orb growing in the dark, blazing fast toward us. Within seconds, it was close enough to halo Faust's silhouette with a faint coppery hue. I took an instinctive step back. "Shit. Faust," I warned him. "There's something—"

"I know. Be ready, Emma."

I was given no time to ask, "for what?" The glow became a blinding tide engulfing us, and I tumbled into the light with Faust. No—into the fire. I didn't feel the landing, but I now sat on my ass on a rough, hard surface. Golden sequins danced before my eyes at first, which progressively became flames engulfing an immense room, slithering up wooden beams, spreading to tapestries hanging from the walls. My brain felt the heat, told me my body was burning. Panic exploded under my ribs in response. I scrambled to my feet with a scream.

"Calm down, Emma." Faust's powerful voice gonged through my trance, anchoring me. The flames licking at my clothes were a cold dream; the smoke rising to the vaulted ceiling carried no scent, no heat.

"We're but guests in the Libro's memories," Faust said, more softly. "He can't see you, and I can't either."

He? I blinked dazed eyes at the burning hell we were trapped in, and I saw them. Two dark shapes faced each other in the blaze. *They can't see us. They can't see us.* I chanted the words in my head over and over, breathing my fear out, and I watched, taking it all in at once. One of the two men stood at the center of several rings of symbols painted on the room's dark marble floor—as if he'd tried to reproduce the dizzying pattern of Chronos's Table. Greasy curls fell over his ruffled shirt and dark vest. He yelled something I couldn't understand at a motionless cloaked figure—a string of jumbled syllables that were either French, Latin, or both.

Like the beat of a pendulum, I felt my heart swing once, twice, and stop. The other man's face remained invisible, concealed under the hood of his long, ragged cloak. A ghost in a beggar's attire, whose hands rested on the hilt of a gnarled wood cane as he listened to his counterpart's roaring tirade. The long-haired man eventually shook his head, an expression of despair on his youthful features.

Faust's double spoke, and it was the same soft, weary hum I knew. The same voice, 350 years apart. I couldn't understand him either, but the words rolling off his tongue sounded like a warning.

My lungs struggled for oxygen that probably didn't exist inside the Libro. "It's you, back when . . ."

"It happened a very long time ago," Faust murmured, his voice mingling with his double's in a dissonant choir.

Before us, the long-haired man extended trembling arms. Anger twisted his mouth as he recited words in a different language now, like nothing I'd ever heard. Bits of the conversation I'd had with Dante flashed in my mind. *More letters. More sounds. An archaic language we've never encountered before.* A long-forgotten rhythm I'd never heard, yet whose beat my heart synced to, like an old habit—the language of Chronos's Table, of Faust's tattoo.

The man's voice rose to the burning ceiling, loud and compelling, and around him, the characters painted on the floor started to glow red and sizzle just like Faust's tattoo had when he had taken us into the Libro. My calves tensed with the urge to run the hell away, but I stood still. I watched in a trance as the letters burned to ashes that stirred and whirled around their master, forming a black trail. *The Spear of Shadows,* a voice deep inside me whispered. *He's calling the Spear. Calling Him, begging Him. Do you feel His presence?*

I did. I felt . . . something else taking shape in the room, a stifling presence. Faust's doppelganger reacted; he lifted his cane and hit the marble once, even as the flames threatened to spread to his cloak. A familiar shockwave washed over me, stilling everything— the fire and the nascent shadows enveloping the long-haired man. The cloaked Faust drifted around him, unhurried, the clatter of his cane the only sound in the silence. He walked through the frozen blaze unscathed and felt for one of the crossed halberds hanging on a wall. He seized it, and with the same calm determination, returned to position himself right behind the long-haired man.

The cane hit the marble again, a split second before his left hand thrusted the halberd. My entire body shook in response. The man gasped, staring down in incomprehension at the bloody blade jutting out from his chest. When he collapsed, the shadows became ashes again, a cloud that swirled to the ceiling and dissipated in the fire.

Faust couldn't see me, but he guessed—felt my horror creep under his own skin, maybe. He lowered his head, regret weighing on his features. "He tried to summon a force he did not understand. I couldn't let him do that."

My fingers trembled closer to his, aching to take his hand, to find even the slightest measure of comfort in the hell of the Libro's memories. "Please," I gritted out. "I want out."

Faust's right hand moved to raise his cane. Around his wrists, his tattoo was still smoldering slowly, shimmering crimson. "It's almost over, Emma," he said. "I need you to be strong a little longer. I just want to know who else . . ." His voice faded into the same silent mumble he'd opened the Libro with. This time I didn't need to hear the words to know. I felt the mysterious language hum in the air around me. It resonated with every cell of my body as the light swallowed us away again.

My eyes fluttered open to absolute peace. Gone were the flames, the rage, and the shadows. I sucked in a tentative breath and looked at Faust. "Where did you take us?"

"Don't you recognize this place?" he asked.

A stream of bleak light filtered through the curtains of a silent apartment, while a light breeze blowing through an open window made the gauzy fabric billow gently. Stacks of books and papers covered a leather-top desk, but also the brocade chairs and sofa in the room. My gaze trailed along cream paneled walls, all the way up to a painted ceiling where naked gods embraced nymphs. My pulse picked up again. "It's the Residenza," I said.

"As expected," Faust replied, his lips thinning in his beard. "What do you see?"

"It's an office," I whispered—even though no one else but him would hear. I crept away from him to explore the quiet room. Most of the books looked like the kind of old grimoires Louison kept under lock in his cellar. "There are magic books, tons of them, kind of scattered like someone was working with them, and—" I checked the desk. "There's also a laptop." Meaning this new memory the Libro had taken us into had to be recent . . . I tiptoed closer to check the screen—an ancient drawing of Chronos's Table. Next to it sat a digital picture frame. My eyes grew wide. On the glass screen, a young Lily smiled in Richard's arms. "Faust, I think we're in Professor McKeanney's old apartment!"

His brow creased. "Are you sure?"

"Yes," I confirmed, my heart beating in my throat. "Why did the Libro take us here?"

Faust shook his head as if something didn't compute. "I'm not certain . . ."

My gaze swept around the room again frantically, looking for something—what, I had no idea, until I spotted a black shape leaning against a stack of moving boxes in the corner of the room. Lily's black Dior tote, and on the boxes, *"Granpa/Residenza"* sharpied in neat, curly cursive. "I think . . . I think it was after he died," I heard myself say out loud, as I stood shaking from head to toes in this dream I could make no sense of.

As Faust's lips parted to reply, a whimper silenced him, escaping from a set of closed doors across the room. My pulse revved to a panicked beat. *Lily.* Another whimper, then a loud, frightened sob. I raced to the doors. "Lily!"

Faust's bellow jolted me to a stop. "Emma! This isn't real."

Or was it? Lily wouldn't stop crying; her desperate wails seemed to tear through me from all directions, as if she were everywhere in the room at once, directly inside my head. I staggered back, screaming hysterically, "Make it stop! Make it stop!"

"Hold on tight, Emma; I'm taking us out," Faust shouted.

His tattoo caught fire around his wrist. I squeezed my eyes shut, waited. Nothing happened. My eyelids fluttered open, and I saw Faust's features, taut with shock as a ray of silvery light filtered from under the doors. Mercury. The Libro's essence, spilling into the room, spreading like a stain across the carpet. My breathing became a series of short, erratic pants, and my voice sounded unbelievably shrill even to my own ears. "Faust! There's something wrong! I see the Libro; it's coming from under the doors!"

Faust's cane hit the floor hard enough to make it shake. A familiar shockwave washed over me as he attempted to still time inside the book. To no avail.

Oh shit.

Gone was the carefree hobo I had met the day before. Faust's eyes were steely slits, and his knuckles were white around the grip of his cane as the liquid kept stretching hungrily to surround us, and still, somewhere in the depths of this nightmare, Lily cried—howled.

"Emma, don't touch the Libro!" he roared. "Step back and take my hand!"

He reached for me then, his fingers clawing at thin air. I extended my hand to catch his, but I felt . . . a hot breeze on my sweat-soaked skin, a whisper from above. And I looked. I shouldn't have. The ceiling was no more. In its stead were shadows, swirling, hissing in a thick, tar-black mass. They stretched the walls, bloomed on the walls like dark flowers, and my body was paralyzed. I wanted out, but even my lungs wouldn't cooperate.

I was drowning in the dark immensity of the Libro.

Somewhere very close and very far, Faust shouted and strained to take my hand as the room moved and came apart around us. "Emma!" Pain registered in my arm as he clasped it tightly. My last conscious thought as darkness became light was that I could breathe again.

XXI

"Louison, I am terribly sorry for this."

"You're never setting foot again in my shop!"

Louison's breathless outrage and Faust's apologies were a painful buzz in my skull as I tried to recover. I was still on my knees, and Faust's hand lingered on my nape, holding my hair while I spit the last of my breakfast on the dusty floorboards of Louison's cellar. I stared down at the yellowish splatter of half-digested Rice Krispies.

The Libro had tried to drown us. No, I reminded myself, it wasn't the Libro. It was the shadows. They'd been here, in the apartment where Lily's grandpa had chosen to end his life, and somehow, this mere "memory" had turned out to be horrifyingly real. Lily's desperate sobs were drilled into my head as if I were still hearing them. My head spun, and the edges of my vision blurred as I remembered those minutes of absolute terror, the black mass swarming on the ceiling, the walls . . . I managed to rise on shaky legs and leaned on the table where the Libro had been open moments before.

Louison had sealed it back inside its iron prison already, along with the decoy grimoire. Faust moved closer to rub circles on my back. "Are you all right?"

"No." I shrugged off his touch. "Lily . . . Where is she?"

Behind me, I heard Louison mumble, "Always eager to jump, never ready for the landing."

Meanwhile, Faust had taken out his phone. Voice-over's metallic voice commented each tap and swipe as he browsed to "Barbowatch"—Silvio's video feed app, I gathered. The voice droned through a list of updates on Lily's position in Italian. 15:27—Villa Malespina; 16:19—Parcheggio, Cayenne AD989DP; 16:27 Ponte Sisto, Cayenne AD989DP.

"She's all right. She's driving back to the Residenza with her boyfriend," Faust said.

"Okay . . ." I rasped. "We have to tell her—"

"Out, out, out! Now!" Louison returned to the room with a bucket and a mop, which he waved at us menacingly.

"Thank you for your help, Louison," Faust said tiredly, steering me back to the musty stairs leading back to the shop. Once we were on the street, he told me, "I don't like this. We'd better head back to my place as soon as possible."

Anger sizzled up my spine, chasing the last remnants of nausea in my stomach. "No. And I don't want beer, I don't want weed: I want to know what's going on!"

His chest heaved. "Emma . . ."

I backed away from him. "Don't even *try* to bullshit me! Lily was in there! And you actually dragged our asses into the Libro because you already knew. You said Montecito wasn't powerful enough to use the Spear of Shadows, but the Libro took us *straight* to the Residenza!" My voice broke as the full weight of this madness set on my shoulders. "They did something to Lily's grandpa, and now, she's in there and . . ." I couldn't bring myself to say it. What if Montecito tried to get rid of her too? A small, bitter part of myself thought of my mom. She'd be heartbroken if something happened to her only child.

"Let's not jump to conclusions," Faust reasoned. But there was an edge to his voice, and I could tell he was shaken too. "There's definitively a piece we're missing in this puzzle."

Maybe there was. And the longer I kept looking for that missing piece, the deeper I dove into Faust's upside-down world, the faster I'd lose my mind. I couldn't do this: magic, immortal people, liquid books that sucked you into nightmarish memories and tried to swallow you whole afterward. This wasn't my life, my playing field. Those weren't weapons I could beat Katharos with. My spine straightened. "Okay, you know what? We're done here; I'm going to the cops."

He shook his head. "Emma, you're being ridiculous; this is way out of their depth. They probably won't even file your complaint."

"Lucius chasing me down, trying to snatch me serial-killer-style, you think they won't listen to that?" I shot back. "Maybe someone other than you and Silvio heard me scream, and . . ." I rolled up one of my sleeves. "I got bruises to show. Even if they don't believe me, they're gonna have to ask Lucius about that, and it'll keep him busy for at least a couple days. Meanwhile, I'll call my mom, and I'll make her freak out, so she jumps on the first plane for Rome. Once she's here, Dante can say whatever he wants, Lily won't listen. She basically does everything Mom tells her to," I concluded with a nod to myself.

Faust listened to my one-sided brainstorming, his lips pursed in what I realized was mock admiration. "I suppose it could work; I can't imagine Katharos would dare to resist your mother."

I gritted my teeth, trying desperately to hold onto the single thread of sanity I had left. But I was cornered, terrified, and drained by our plunge into the Libro. I had only one defense mechanism left—always the same, really. I inhaled deeply and detonated. "*Fuck you*, Faust! You're the one who dragged me into that shit in the first place. You fucked my life up from the very start, and now I'm supposed to trust you? How about no? So yeah, I'm going to the cops, and when they ask me if I got any witnesses, I'll take them to your place! How does that sound?"

A little group of tourists walked past us during my screaming tirade. They kept at a safe distance, but I could feel their eyes on me, some amused, others frightened—a typical reaction to witnessing a bum fight in the street. I didn't care what they thought of me. I was too far gone, my body shaking from the bitch storm I'd just unleashed on Faust.

I waited for him to get mad, too, to give me a good reason to keep fighting and exhaust myself yelling, but he just blinked and released a heavy sigh he'd been holding while I tore him a new one. "Emma . . . you know I won't let you do that. It could get Silvio in trouble, and it's the last thing I want."

It wasn't the blaze I needed right now, but that spark would do. "You *won't let me*?" I spat. "Really? Well, freeze me!" I challenged him, arms outstretched. "Come on. Freeze me if you don't want me to go to the cops."

When Faust just kept giving me that sorrowful look that seemed to say, "Can we be done with this?", I spun on my heels and marched away from him, my head held high. I tried to stay angry with each step, but I could feel the intoxicating adrenaline rush sizzling away in my veins already, leaving nothing but shame and this vague sense of being trapped, forced to go down the road I'd barreled onto—because apologizing was out of the question.

I'd barely covered fifty feet when a familiar shockwave washed over me. I stopped mid-stride and peeked over my shoulder, practically blowing steam through my nostrils. Faust hadn't moved. Higher up the street, the bunch of tourists we'd passed had stopped mid-stride. Two teens stood huddled in front of Louison's window, permanently grinning at a phone affixed to a selfie-stick.

Faust walked toward me, armed with his cane and an apologetic smile. "I can't freeze you, but I can freeze everything else."

I chewed on my lower lip angrily. "For how long? You can't keep time still forever." At least I hoped he couldn't. But he was immortal, so technically . . . *Oh God.*

His shoulders rolled in the faintest shrug. "Long enough for you to truly hate me, I suppose."

"I already hate you," I snapped back.

A twitch of his lips. "No, you don't. You're frightened, lost, and you don't know what to make of me, but I'm growing on you." I shivered, because there was a tiny measure of truth to his assessment, and it made me feel exposed, vulnerable that he didn't even need eyes to see that. When I remained quiet, he held out a hand. "Come, Emma. I want to take you somewhere. Somewhere safe," he added, as if in afterthought.

I gazed at him, at the kind features of this man I couldn't lie to because he'd probably heard it all over 2,000 years, and I said, "I'm sorry. I don't trust you."

His eyebrows shot up. Maybe it was still possible to surprise him after all. "Emma, are we really going to have a battle of wills?"

I had no rage left to spend, only a sense of being numb—lost, as he'd aptly diagnosed. I turned around and kept walking, ignoring the clatter of his cane trailing after me, and the undercurrent of annoyance in his voice as he called loudly, "Suit yourself. I have all the time in the world!"

Well, I was twenty, and I had time too.

The rhythmic tapping on the cobblestone pavement followed

me down Via della Madonna dei Monti, then Via Urbana, past stone façades and silent bistro terraces where gracious waiters waltzed still, a tray full of drinks balanced in their hand. I kept treading obstinately along the much larger Via Cavour and its luxury hotels, housed in a string of nearly-identical nineteenth century stone buildings. My hands shoved in my pockets, I walked in the middle of the street, along the tram tracks, slaloming between buses and cars, frozen passersby and sleeping bums.

Faust followed me all the way to the big square stretching in front of Roma Termini Station. I took a right, strolling along Via Giolitti in the shade of the station's massive concrete frame, and at last, he surrendered. "McDonald's?" his voice offered tiredly, a dozen feet behind me.

I glanced right and paused in mild surprise. There was, indeed, a McDonald's tucked between two souvenir shops in a craggy building that faced Termini's monumental glass entrance. Man, he really knew every single square-inch of Rome, and the craziest part was that he couldn't rely on sounds or smells as long as we were outside time. He was able to tell his way with nothing but his sense of orientation and counting his steps. Unreal.

I turned around warily. "You're paying?"

He gave a beaten sigh. "What a man wouldn't do for the love of a venal woman . . ."

My knees gathered to my chest, I watched a coin fly and land in Faust's empty coffee cup, tossed by a backpacker.

"Either you tell everything you know, or I'll manage on my own with the cops. I'm done running in the dark," I stated, taking a sip of my Sprite. The first words I'd spoken since we'd sat against one of Roma Termini Station's mile-high stone walls. There was something soothing about the incessant roll of the crowd coming and going in waves, the ads everywhere, the voices droning from speakers that the trains would be late. It kind of reminded me of Grand Central.

Faust emptied the cup in his palm and felt for its contents—almost five euros so far, not bad. "There are things I'm not allowed to tell you."

I pondered that. Same old tune. "Then let's take the table out of the equation for now. What's the Spear of Shadows? I mean, apart from being . . . shadows."

Faust's head bobbed as if he were having an internal debate with himself and he'd just come to a decision. "Do you remember when I told you that the power Montecito and Lucius use isn't magic?"

"Yeah."

"Magic is just a word we put on forces we don't understand." His lips quirked. "Your abilities are magic to me."

My abilities . . . I gulped softly upon hearing Faust use that word. What kid never dreamed of having mutant powers or a magic wand? But these only sound great as long as they remain sealed within the safe realm of fantasy. I studied my knuckles that I'd bruised trying to escape Lucius in Augustus's Mausoleum. That I might have anything in common with people like Lucius or Faust . . . I couldn't accept it. There must be another explanation. Plus, it wasn't like I was capable of doing anything specific anyway. The way I saw it, the problem was with *their* powers, not with me. That's what you get for buying your wand at Dollar Tree.

"Let's set aside my case for now," I snorted. "Tell me about the powers you understand instead."

"The Spear is a weapon," *No shit* . . . My ears perked up though, when he added, "which used to belong to a very powerful entity who lived long before the age of men."

I frowned. "Like, during the dinosaurs?"

"After that." Faust chuckled. "What I'm trying to tell you is that humans who seek to control the Spear's power misunderstand its nature. The Spear represents what little is left of this deity's power, the remains of the soul of a titan."

My eyebrows raised slowly. "A . . . titan? You mean an actual god? Like Chronos?"

"Perses the Destroyer," Faust breathed as if he were afraid to merely say that name. "Technically Chronos's nephew, but it's difficult to plaster human notions of a family on such primordial beings."

I was having a little trouble breathing straight, but overall, I was taking this better than I'd thought. Immortal, witches . . . titans. Okay. I mean, sure. I eventually found my voice again. "So that guy we saw in the Libro, he didn't know he was basically summoning part of a titan?"

"He did," Faust replied, his thumb playing on the smooth knots of woods of his cane. "But he made the same mistake you just made."

I gave him an uncertain look, barely aware of the toddler who'd just dropped a spit-covered M&M in our cup as she waddled by with her mom. Around us, life pulsed and flew as usual, which only served to make this entire conversation eerier. "What did I get wrong?"

"No one summons a titan," Faust replied, his tone hardening. "You *beg*, lay all you have, all you are at their feet in exchange for the fulfillment of a meaningless human wish, and once in a billion times, that god vaster than you can ever comprehend choses to use you.

You summon nothing. You control *nothing*."

As I listened to him, the station's clamor and swarming crowd seemed to fade away, replaced by the burning room where the mysterious long-haired man had once attempted to use the Spear of Shadows. Faust's gloomy warning echoed in my mind . . . *before he'd chosen to kill that man rather than let him sell his soul to Perses the Destroyer.* My eyes fluttered back to reality. I saw Faust's tattoo, like a chain around his right wrist. "Is that what happened to you? You begged, and now you're Chronos's servant, but you can never know why he chose you, and you can never break out?"

Two thousand years of servitude weighed on his features as he replied, "I'm not allowed to discuss this with you, Emma."

A fear I couldn't place swelled deep inside me, a hazy intuition that maybe the same thing was happening to me, that like Faust, I was just a tool, a chess piece someone much bigger had chosen and was moving around.

You're not wandering around aimlessly . . .

Renewed anger simmered in my stomach. "It's too easy! You just stumble around in the dark, and you got no idea why, where you're going, or how long it's gonna last. That's the name of the game?"

Faust ducked his head with a bitter smile. "Congratulations on figuring out the meaning of life, Emma. Some people live up to be a hundred without realizing this."

I fidgeted, tapping my feet on Termini's gum-studded asphalt. "That's just bullshit . . ." I muttered. "What about Montecito? Say she rang that Perses guy, and he picked up, what do we do?"

He rolled his eyes. "We run and hide—especially me."

I gulped the last of my soda and kicked the can to send it rolling toward a couple of pigeons. "You got bad blood with him?"

Faust blinked in amazement, before a warm laugh burst from him, which infuriated me as much as it eased my tension. "No, don't worry. I'm but a comma in the pages of history; I don't battle titans."

"Okay, if you say so . . ." I eyed him warily. "So why do you need to hide? Why would he go after you? Why . . ." My eyes popped wide open as those damn puzzle pieces finally started to come together. "*Montecito* is after you, and you said no one controls titans—it's pretty much the other way around. You think Perses is holding the remote, right?" I asked, my pulse increasing steadily.

Faust's brow knotted as if something still didn't quite compute for him. "It would explain a few things . . ."

As good as a yes. I gazed down at the coffee cup sitting between us, mentally picturing the silvery threads of a spiderweb made visible by beads of dew. *Perses* was after Chronos's Table—an old titan preying on another old titan's turf, both manipulating their respective goons on a chess board to achieve their goal. That, at least, made some amount of sense. Except I stood in the middle of this shit storm, and if I couldn't get Lily away from Montecito and Lucius . . . "This is not gonna end well," I murmured, the certainty coming from a deeply buried part of me I preferred not to inspect too closely. I clasped my hands together, wrenching my fingers. "Faust, you know what I'm gonna ask next, right?"

He turned his head my way and gave a single nod. His milky pupils stared past me, through me. "And you know what I'm going to answer."

Christ, I wanted to shove that paper cup up his ass so bad. "It's not fair," I ground out. "I'm part of this, somehow. There's something inside me messing with your power—with the table's power. If you don't tell me why Perses wants the table and how you fit into all this . . ." My voice faltered. "I can never know where *I* fit."

He reached for my arm. I tensed, but let him feel his way to my hand, covering it. I shivered from the warmth seeping between us. A tender smile cracked through the blond bristles of his beard. "Are we still discussing titan business, or is this perhaps a broader question?"

"You tell me," I replied, right before he raised the cup just in time to catch another coin—how the hell could he manage that?

"I honestly don't know where you fit into all this, Emma. But I have a friend who might be able to answer that." His Fausty grin returned. "She's an expert in titan matters."

I jumped to my feet. "Titan expert. Is that an actual job?" To be honest, I played it cool, but my head was still reeling—along with the rest of me, in fact.

Faust dropped the contents of the McDonald's cup in his palm, shoved the change in his pocket, and rose to his feet with a wink in my direction. "Everything is a real job if you're brave enough. I used to know a Parmesan whisperer. Now let's . . ." He paused mid-sentence, his eyes turning to slits. His fingers tightened around his cane. "We're being watched."

I crashed down to earth and darted a panicked look around, before my eyes met a pair of big brown ones, staring hard in our direction. A little girl no more than six or seven, whose fuzzy cornrows ended in bright pink beads. My shoulders slumped in relief, and I grinned. "It's okay. I think you got yourself a new admirer, but she looks way too young for a bowl of faxkrispies."

But Faust didn't relax one bit. "No, Emma. There's someone else."

I rolled my eyes. "How do you . . ." The words remained stuck in my throat when I caught the girl's mother's eyes on us too— empty, like those of the old man standing next to them, about to bite into a panini. I scanned the crowd, nostrils flaring. Every single pair of eyes was . . . "Faust, they're all staring at us like they're high or something," I hissed, slowly backing against the wall.

Faust raised his cane and hummed a few words that sounded like a verse. "Oh, beware of the many eyes of the strix . . ."

His cane hit the floor barely a second after I caught a familiar sleek black sedan glide down the street and park in front of the station. Lucius had the time to open the Mercedes's door, but not to step out.

"How did they find us?" I panted behind Faust across the silent hall.

"The owl's eyes," he replied, slaloming near-effortlessly between frozen tourists and their suitcases with the help of his cane. "A nasty little spell. Didn't I say we should have gone back to my place? My fascinus doesn't only protect the laundry, you know."

I stumbled, caught myself. "The winged dick? Is it some kind of magic shield?"

"This old infirm needs his privacy," Faust grunted. "Now I'm taking you back there, and you won't step out of that attic until I'm done with Montecito. Are we clear, Emma?"

Under any other circumstances I would have blistered at his uncharacteristic burst of alpha douchebaggery, but we were being hunted by the goons of an immortal witch. I shut up and walked faster. We were almost out of the station. Beyond the hall's gigantic mouth, a line of cars and colorful Vespas had been stopped in their course in front of a café where patrons held their cup of espresso to their lips without drinking. When a dark shape slithered at the edge of my vision, I thought Faust had released the flow of time already. I broke my stride to glance around.

His sixth sense kicked in instantly. "Emma? Are you coming?"

"Yeah, I thought I saw something . . ." *move.* But everyone stood petrified in the hall, and a couple of pigeons hung still above our heads, their wings stretched to their fullest.

He stopped, his eyes half-closed, listening to the void. His nostrils flared. I couldn't pinpoint the sensation, but I, too, felt the hall stir alive around us. A trail of goose bumps bloomed down my back. The shadows . . . it was the people's shadows. Now I could see it. On the floor, the walls—they were shivering, stretching, crawling toward us with a will of their own. Sudden pressure welled in my chest, exploding in a single scream. "Faust! Run!"

I raced to him, but it was too late already; the shadows whirled around us like tendrils of smoke, trapping us in a column that roared all the way to the station's ceiling. I clung to Faust's arm, dug my fingers into his coat. "Please tell me you can still that shit like you did back in London!"

There was an undercurrent of amazement in his voice as he admitted, "I don't think so. Not without breaking a lot of rules . . ."

"Then break them all!" I screamed.

"Yes, Faustus, why don't you unseal the table for us?" The voice was silk filtering through the chaos, all too familiar.

Crushing fear vised me to the floor as her pale face and golden shawl appeared behind the walls of the vortex imprisoning us. She walked through the spinning shadows as if they were just a cloud of ink. Lady Montecito had found us after all. My eyes flitted between her and Faust. So that was what she wanted from him? What did she mean by unsealing Chronos's Table anyway?

Her pale eyes swept over Faust's ratty clothes. Her dark red lips curved in a parody of a smile. "I've wanted to meet you for a long time, Faustus. Every time I saw a piece of human waste lying around in the street, I wondered if it might be you, hiding under the rags."

He rewarded her greeting with an easy grin of his own. "I, on the other hand, can't say I ever thought about you until recently . . ." His eyes darkened. "Tell me, my lady, who's lending you that kind of power?"

The corners of her lips quivered. "Your worst nightmare."

Faust's expression didn't waver, but knuckles went white around the wood knots of his cane. "Oh, my lady," he murmured darkly. "What have you done?"

Her tongue darted to swipe across her lips, and there was this bone-chilling edge of excitement in her voice as she hissed, "He chose me." Her eyes briefly fluttered closed, like she was high. "He wants to unseal the table, and there is no place in this world where you could *ever* hide from him."

Faust's eyebrows quivered a fraction, so fast it could have been a trick of the light. Every single hair on my body raised on end in response. When Montecito's mouth opened again, I shrank behind him, but it was my name she spoke, dripping from her tongue like honey. "Emma . . . you must be so confused. He knows you're looking for your place in this world. He knows how much you've suffered. Lucius told you the truth last night; there is a place for you among us." Her lips quivered. "At his side."

In a demented cult, basically.

Faust's cane came up to shield me, giving me the strength to lash at her. "Don't get near me; I saw what's in the Libro too! I saw McKeanney's office, and I heard Lily crying! What are you planning to do with her?"

Her features remained a waxen mask, but her mouth curved, and a soft laugh escaped her. "I'm going to help her earn her PhD in reward for finding the table for us. Her grandfather wasn't as indispensable as he liked to think."

"You killed him . . ." I managed out.

She arched a perfectly trimmed eyebrow. "I did not. McKeanney made the conscious decision to end his life because the poor man was so conceited he believed we wouldn't find the table without him." She gave an eye roll. "He dreamed up a mediocre play in which I was a gorgon, and his sacrifice served to thwart my nefarious plans."

"He discovered your true nature and tried to escape Katharos's claws," Faust corrected icily.

"He made us waste two years, and for what?" She shook her head in mock disapproval. "Lily turned out to be much brighter than her grandfather ever was. She decoded all his notes for me, combed through thousands of pages in a matter of weeks." Montecito's gaze fell on me, mocking. "And she loves working for us."

I snarled. "Don't look at me, you fucking waste of oxygen."

She sighed. "You see, Faustus, how it frightens humans, the power our kind wields."

He rewarded her with a feral sneer. "Make no mistake, my lady: you're not immortal, and Perses can't make you. You're a lovely rotting body, nothing more."

The corners of her lips quivered down. "He *will* grant me the gift of eternity, with the power of the table."

My jaw hurt from the effort to stay clenched and not let shock show on my features. There it was, the missing piece. A fraction of the secret Faust wasn't allowed to reveal. He'd hinted at it last night though, perhaps unconsciously. *Time can't be stolen, only given*—by Chronos's Table. Perses wanted the table, and his shadows had promised the impossible to Lady Montecito: more than just a wonky embalming spell, as Faust had called it—true immortality.

I wrestled my fear under control, forcing myself to look past her at the swirling black wall trapping us. What was in it for *him*, though? For that mysterious titan whose power Montecito had borrowed, and whose voice she claimed to hear inside her head?

"Emma," she called softly, locking her gaze with mine.

Faust's free hand grappled for mine, squeezing it tight. "Don't fall for it. She's trying to manipulate you."

"As you are!" she hissed back at him. Her gaze cut back to me. "Emma, he's figured out you can break the table's seal. Eventually, he'll have no choice but to kill you."

Her words cracked in the air between us. In a split second, I was standing again in Katharos's lab. My palm rested on the table, and I knew nothing but the contact between me and the table's granite as I unwittingly broke Faust's time-stopping spell. I let go of him, barely aware of the victorious curl of Montecito's lips. "What does she mean? What is . . . what's *wrong* with me?"

Faust's Adam's apple rolled in his throat. "There's nothing wrong with you, and all you need to know is that I *will* keep you safe."

I shook my head in panic. "Safe from *what?*"

Montecito shot him a disdainful glance. "Himself. He's bound to the table, Emma. He guards it and must destroy any threat to it." Her eyebrows drew together in mock-confusion. "He's just a slave. Have you forgotten that already?"

I hadn't. The tattoo around Faust's wrist served as a constant reminder of his 'contract,' as he called it. But I'd been so desperate to find an ally against Katharos, that I'd chosen to ignore the obvious. I wasn't Faust's sidekick or whatever. I was just another pawn in this game, another threat to the table he guarded. My lungs tightened as if there were a mass growing in my ribcage, a tangible symptom of the nameless disease inside me. I wobbled away from Faust, my lips trembling without a sound. I couldn't find a way out of this nightmare.

Faust's hand reached for mine again, only to claw at thin air.

Anger twisted his features, transformed him. "Emma, stay close!" he shouted.

His bark only served to make me jump back even farther until it was just him facing Montecito. It wasn't until her right arm moved to direct the swirling shadows at him that I realized this had been her goal all along. The shadows gathered and waved to form a hissing spear flying toward him. Faust raised his cane to block the attack just as fast.

My feet remained paralyzed as the dark howling mass ripped through his torso and dissipated in the same instant. The second after, he was still standing, cane in hand. His eyes were wide and unblinking, their pupils paler than ever. My lips worked to croak his name in vain. His body reeled, and the moment he collapsed, the wail trapped behind my lips burst out. "Faust!"

I lunged to kneel by his side and froze as if I'd been struck in my turn. My hands hovered, shaking above the scorched hole in his chest, bigger than a fist. I tried to breathe, to keep myself together, but I could see the floor through Faust's chest, where his heart had been seconds ago. His lips remained parted in surprise, unmoving.

I gasped for air under Montecito's cold gaze. "Oh God . . . *Oh no* . . ." He couldn't be dead; he was immortal! He'd been feeding cats and roaming the streets for twenty centuries! I couldn't bring myself to touch his lifeless body. My hand felt for his cane instead, seeking reassurance in the solid knots of wood. My fingers closed on dust as it disintegrated with a whisper.

"It is arrogance that killed him, Emma," Montecito cooed, creeping closer.

Time was streaming again. Life had resumed around us in the station, but no one noticed us. Faust lay dead at their feet, my jeans and hands stained black from the ashes of his cane, and they just hurried by, dragging their kids, their suitcases—all under Montecito and Perses's spell.

She called my name softly. "Emma?"

My head snapped up, and adrenaline rushed back to my blood, lacing with rage in my veins. Lucius had joined her. He stood behind her with a bunch of his suited gorillas as she spoke. "Let's head back to the villa."

I scrambled away, raising my hands to shield myself. She stiffened, and seeing the way her fingers twitched, it dawned on me that this magical disease of mine was the only weapon I had left. "Y-you know what will happen if you touch me," I warned.

Oh yes, she did. Montecito snorted and clenched her right fist. I rolled terrified eyes at her pale skin as it went taut over her knuckles. No veins underneath, just a lifeless envelope. What would happen if she used the spear on me too? Could I possibly dispel it like Lucius's shadow whip thing, back at the mausoleum?

Tense seconds ticked between us. Her prune lips curved. "I know you only meant to help Lily." She didn't need to add anything else; the threat was crystal clear.

I lowered my arms with a trembling exhale.

Lucius snapped gloved fingers at his bodyguards. "Take care of the trash."

Two men stepped forward to take hold of Faust's prone body. I lunged over to shield him. "Don't touch him—"

"Emma." The kindness dripping from Montecito's had frozen into sharp icicles. She flourished a graceful hand at the oblivious crowd bustling in the hall. "There's no point in making a scene. You don't exist for them."

My hands clung to Faust's coat, my eyes begging the travelers in vain. Two cops were helping a Japanese tourist clad in a colorful kimono, mere feet away from us. They didn't see a fricking thing, wouldn't spare even a glance at Faust's corpse. The rest of Lucius's henchmen shuffled to surround me as I got up on shaky legs. Montecito's favorite goon wasn't stupid; he knew I could do nothing against regular beefy dudes. I watched from the corner of my eyes as their cronies lifted Faust's body. No way out, and even if I tried to run, they had Lily. I squeezed my eyes shut at the memory of her agonizing wails in the Libro, pounding in my skull, crawling under my skin. It had been more than just grief; her voice had been raw with horror and despair. I sensed, bone-deep that the Libro had tried to warn us about something.

Maybe once Montecito's spell wore off I could just spot a cop . . .

My eyes darted left and right as our gloomy bunch made its way out of Roma Termini through an indifferent crowd. Once we were on the street, though, I caught fleeting glances at Faust and the guys carrying him to a black SUV. Kids would look up from their gelato cone to stare; a pack of bums clustered around a shopping cart full of trash bags side-eyed us. My pulse raced with renewed hope. The spell had been lifted, maybe because Montecito was so sure she'd won anyway.

One of Lucius's men went to open the trunk. Within seconds they'd crammed Faust in there, with the ease of true professionals. Barely a few people noticed them, or the way my shoulders jerked in response to the door slamming shut. Done with Faust, they unlocked the rear door, and an unidentified hand gave me a discreet shove. I twisted my neck to catch one last look at Montecito as she folded into the backseat of a black Mercedes.

Silver flashed at the edge of my vision.

There was a sudden cool sensation on my nape, a few drops of liquid hitting my skin as a can whizzed past me to hit one of my captors in the chest. Beer splashed all over his pristine shirt. He drew out his gun before the projectile had even touched the ground. I went rigid. Lucius's eyes scanned the street behind his sunglasses, right before a single scream set the dominos of utter mayhem in motion.

"Ha una pistola! Aiuto!" He has a gun! Help! The voice was unusually shrill—almost childlike—and belonged to that girl in the kimono I'd seen in the station moments ago. She pointed out our group to a pair of policemen running toward the cars. Montecito's Mercedes took off with a roar of its powerful engine while Lucius threw caution to the wind and lunged to push me inside the SUV. I flung awkward arms at him with a war cry and howled for help in my turn. "Don't touch me! Help! Someone, help me!"

His men tried to grab me, but suddenly it wasn't one can being thrown at them; it was a fricking storm of the cheapest, nastiest booze a euro could buy you in Rome hailing from all directions. Bums in their dirt-stiffened rags popped up all around us, yelling insults and hurling cans at Lucius and his men, which clattered against the SUV's sides and showered the windshield with stinky foam.

Another bodyguard tried to pull out his gun, only for the policemen to do the same and yell for Lucius's goons to drop their weapons. And through all this, no one seemed to notice the flash of black and gold making a dash for the driver's door. It was no magic, no mysterious ancient power, just an Uber driver with a sketchy resume doing what he knew best—jacking a car. By the time I realized the surreal chaos unfolding around me had been orchestrated by Silvio and his secret bum network, he was behind the wheel, barking, *"Salta!"* Jump in!

Powered by pure adrenaline, I grabbed the open rear door, but a crushing pain in my shoulder stopped me before I could climb in the backseat. Lucius. Throwing caution to the wind, he'd sunk his claws in me with an inhuman roar. I screeched my lungs out, writhed to free myself while cans still rained on him. I arched until my spine might break, reaching behind me to pry his arm off. My fear was a remote, insignificant particle of myself, washed away by the rage pumping in my veins. I squeezed his forearm as hard as I could and felt the muscular flesh shrink and dry up under the fabric of his suit.

Foam seethed through his clenched teeth as he fought to retain his hold. A ribbon of colors shimmered at the edge of my vision, and for a millisecond, I thought someone had punched me, but instead, a pair of lean and unbelievably strong kimono-clad arms hauled me into the backseat. I registered a loud crack, like a worm-eaten floorboard snapping off before the door slammed shut.

Lucius's enraged howl kept ringing in my ears even as Silvio slammed the gas and we bulleted away from the station. Crushed into the seat by the sudden acceleration, unable to breathe, it took me a good ten seconds to realize that the weird branch I still clung onto was Lucius's dried up arm.

XXIII

I tossed the arm with a shriek of horror. The Japanese girl—when the hell had she climbed in the car? Before or after the beer fight?—caught it and shoved it into her embroidered silk bag. "I keep. I like. For research."

Curled against the door, I gawked at the bony fingers now poking out of her bag while Silvio raced down a busy avenue. "W-who are you?"

She fastened her seatbelt without looking at me, her face and voice void of any emotion beneath the long bangs of her ebony bob. "I am Ryuuko. I am the dragon who guards the Porta Alchemica." Her brow creased a fraction. "I don't like cars. I like animals." Her gaze set on Lucius's hand. "And research."

This particular moment called for a resounding "What the fuck?" but the wheel spun in Silvio's hands before I could speak, and I went flying into Ryuuko as the SUV took a sharp turn right.

I found myself sprawled across her lap, my nose *inches* from the hand. She shoved me away with the strength of a wrestler. "You buckle up."

Oh, I did, with hands that were shaking so badly you'd think I had Parkinson's. And it was a good thing because we were supposed to share the street with a tram car, but Silvio didn't feel like it. He nearly snapped the gear stick in half as he sent the car spinning across the road to cut the tram off. I saw myself die. Twice, when a bus barreled from the right, honking madly. I *swear* I felt it graze us.

We kept speeding along the tram tracks toward a patch of green. Ryuuko told Silvio, "Is the park. You go ahead, I open the Porta for you."

Ahead. Straight into that low wall and the iron fence atop, then. I gripped my seatbelt and yelled, "Silvio, hit the brakes!"

Surely, he must have mistaken one pedal for the other, because we kept gaining speed. I squeezed my eyes shut and prayed, bracing myself for the impact. And he fricking did it; we crashed straight into the wall at full speed with Katharos's evidently armored SUV. Bricks flew all over the place, hitting the windows without managing to shatter them. The fence clanked under our wheels as we bulldozed over it. Through the cracked windshield, I saw that we were tearing across a deserted park, straight to another obstacle—another wall, or rather the ruins of one, *much* thicker, and on which the shape of a single stone gate remained. Except it was just concrete filling it. No way through. That . . . that would definitely smash the car—and us.

"Stop! You'll kill us!" I pleaded as the pair of stone deities guarding the gate grew ominously closer.

"No, you go full throttle," Ryuuko ordered him, clutching her grim treasure tightly.

I heard Silvio slam the gas and I shrank back in the seat, gasping for air. This time the impact never came. The wall ahead seemed to shimmer and ripple as we made contact, letting us through as if it were shiny Jell-O. I think I closed my eyes for a second, maybe even less, and when I reopened them everything around us was white.

My head lolled on my chest, and by then, I was pretty sure my eyes had popped out of my skull; I could feel them dangling out of my eye sockets, hanging by a thread. Okay, maybe it's a metaphor. What I'm trying to say is I brushed death here. Licked it. Tasted it.

Yet after the shadows, Faust's death, the bum commando, the car chase, and our subsequent crashing through a magic Jell-O wall, I was somehow still alive. I blinked my eyeballs back in place and took a dizzy look through the windows. The ground under our wheels had become soft and squishy. The snow was everywhere, coating centenary trees and antique statues. The SUV was driving up a wide alley leading to a villa that reminded me of Katharos's Villa Malespina, only smaller. It was the same nearly flat-tiled roof and rows of ornate windows on all three floors. We drove through an archway, and, at last, he stopped the car in a vast courtyard hemmed by round bushes that looked like ice cream scoops under their cap of snow.

After the engine went quiet, I registered Silvio's ragged sigh, echoing mine. My jaw resting somewhere between my chucks on the floormat, I watched Ryuuko undo her seatbelt. "Is the Villa Palombara," she announced. "I live here. I do research."

Well, all right then.

She stepped out of the car, her tall wooden sandals sinking into the powdery snow when she shuffled around to the trunk. I managed to stop trembling long enough to unbuckle and scramble out of the SUV as well. "Where are we?" I asked, getting up on legs that were dancing the Charleston.

"At the Villa Palombara," Ryuuko repeated tersely.

I ran a hand across my face. "But where is it? Because, I don't know if you noticed, but . . ." I pointed a shaking finger at the white expanse surrounding us. "It's snowing here." Was this some sort of dream thing like the Libro? I glanced down at my feet, buried in snow. This was different. In the Libro, I'd felt nothing, no heat, even as I stood in that burning room. But here, the air was crisp and cold, and melted snow was starting to seep through my Converse, drenching my socks. This place was real . . .

"Here, it's in Rome, but not in Rome," Silvio grunted unhelpfully as he came to stand by me as Ryuuko opened the trunk, revealing Faust's curled form, hastily rolled in black plastic tarp by Montecito's men. My chest grew tight. I gritted my teeth, blinking back the heat in my eyes. Silvio removed his Puma flat cap and pressed it to his heart, his mustache falling over his lower lip in grief.

Unaffected by the solemnity of the moment, Ryuuko single-handedly pulled Faust out of the trunk and hoisted him over her slim shoulders. "I keep him. For research."

Silvio stiffened, his eyes narrowing behind his sunglasses.

"We need to bury him," I said. "You can't . . ." I gave a weak shrug. I couldn't bring myself to say it. I hope she understood—even though that girl or witch or . . . dragon clearly hovered somewhere on the autistic spectrum.

She stared at my chest for endless seconds, before stating, "He's dead. I do research."

When she took a step away from the car, I leaped sideways to bar her path. I balled my fists, wondering what would be left of me if that tiny Japanese hulk decided to take me down. "Ryuuko, you have to put him down and—"

"Yes, Ryuuko, put me down, please."

In the span of a single heartbeat, I went through a roller coaster of emotions at the sound of Faust's muffled voice—horror, relief, and ultimately a sort of panicked joy I could feel throb all over my body and squeeze my lungs. "Oh my God . . . Oh *shit!*"

Ryuuko dropped him in the snow with a fleeting air of disappointment, and the second after, I was on my knees, clawing at the tarp to free him. When his mess of blond curls and a tired smile appeared, I could have slapped him for scaring Silvio and me that badly. I balled my fists not to. My voice cracked before I was done asking him, "You're alive?"

"Emma, I'm immortal."

As he shrugged off the rest of the tarp, his chest appeared. Where the charred wound had been minutes ago was a new patch of skin with a dusting of blond hair, completely healed. I risked trembling fingers to the burned edges of the hole in his T-shirt, grazing the skin beneath. Warm, alive. I snatched my hand back and clasped it over my mouth. It was one thing to accept the notion that Faust had stayed young for two millennia and he couldn't die, but seeing his chest healed like that . . . I thought of Montecito and Lucius and Lucius's waxy, eerie features, preserved by the embalming spell. This was the miracle she had begged Perses for— warm blood and skin, a beating heart, forever.

Faust's face drew close, his forehead almost brushing mine. "See?" he murmured. "It's just like in *Highlander*, when the girl discovers he's immortal."

I swallowed, unable to look away from the disc of skin showcased by the hole in his T-shirt. "What does she do?"

He tilted his head, inching even closer. "She kisses him."

My hands jerked to push him away before he could score. "Um, yeah . . . no." I cleared my throat and got to my feet, dusting snow from my jeans under Silvio's curious gaze and Ryuuko's stony one. "Do you think you can get up?" I asked Faust.

He craned his neck my way, his gaze infinitely tender, as if he could see my cheeks reddening. I bit the inside of my cheek. Maybe if we'd been alone, I'd have let him . . . not because he was growing on me or anything. Just for the sake of kissing an immortal guy once in my life. Bucket list stuff, basically.

"I'm afraid I'm going to need a little help," he said at last, an impish grin piercing through his beard.

His hope was short-lived. Silvio was faster than me. He went to hook his arm under Faust's and hauled him to his feet, before patting his shoulder roughly. *"Nessun diavolo può ucciderti."* No devil can kill you.

Faust's fingers felt at the large hole where the Salvation Army logo used to be on his T-shirt. "Well, they certainly tried."

"It was because I moved," I admitted in a guilty breath, remembering Montecito's victorious smile when I'd let go of Faust. "She wanted me out of the way."

He sobered, but I sensed no reproach in his reply. "I think she's come to understand the nature of your power."

I shivered, suddenly hyperaware of the cold seeping through my hoodie and directly to my bones. "She wouldn't touch me, back at the station. She knows she can't. But she has Lily."

He shook his head. "Lady Montecito won't take the risk to hurt Lily. Not if she's hoping to find us: she knows Lily is her best bargaining chip."

I pondered this, rubbing my arms to fight chills. "Was it true? All that stuff she said about the table, when she said I could . . ." I flicked my wrist. "unseal it, whatever that means."

Faust nodded to himself, his lips working in a visible effort to answer my question without breaking his damn contract. "Not quite. She said she believed you might be able to *break* the seal."

"You see a difference?" I asked bitterly.

"You open your piggybank, or you smash it?" Ryuuko asked, her gaze impassive.

I blinked down at her. "It's empty anyway. So, neither, I guess."

Her eyes became judgmental slits. "You're stupid."

"Hey," I warned her, squaring my shoulders and clenching my fists.

"Ladies, ladies . . ." Faust chided, rubbing his hands together. "Why don't we go inside to discuss matters of the universe?"

I gaped at him, remembered the last thing he'd said before all hell had broken loose in Termini. "The titan expert . . ." I looked between him and Ryuuko. "Come on, don't tell me she's the expert!"

Ryuuko pulled out Lucius's dried up arm out of her silk bag and waved it at me menacingly. "You respect me."

I recoiled in outrage. "Put that shit away!"

Faust ran a hand over his beard and scratched it at length while Silvio stared past us, stoic amidst all the drama. I gave up on my beef with Ryuuko and wobbled around in the snow to follow the direction of his gaze. We weren't alone. I squinted my eyes at the figure standing in the villa's columned doorway, a woman in her late thirties—much younger than her silvery bun hinted—and clad in a long blue petticoat dress. Clutching a lace shawl around her shoulders with one hand, she motioned to us with the other. "Ryuuko dear, bring our guests inside."

The antisocial dragon didn't bother with an explanation or even an introduction; she tucked the arm back in her bag and marched straight to the villa without looking back.

Faust's laid-back smile became a solar grin. "Emma, would you like to meet Lady Palombara?"

Oh.

I gave the woman a perplexed once-over while she kept waving at us excitedly. Open smile, Betty White kind of vibe; Lady Montecito's polar opposite. I knew better than to trust appearances, though. This snowed-in haven was just another door in the house of mirrors that was Faust's reality. The question was: what lay on the other side, this time?

I scratched my hair. "I guess . . . I mean, if she can tell me what's going on in here, yeah, sure."

"Then let's go," he offered.

Lady Palombara called him from across the pristine lawn. "Come, Faust! You'll certainly catch a cold if you stay outside in this weather."

She was right—well, I would catch one, anyway: the sweat cooling on my neck would soon turn into an icy crust, and my fingers were getting numb. Next to me, Silvio had screwed his cap back on his balding skull. He gauged me from behind his sunglasses and said, "Good luck."

I winced. "You're not staying?"

He flicked his wrist at the wrecked SUV, allowing me a glimpse of a tacky red Nike watch. "I'll get rid of the car."

"Thank you, my friend," Faust told him.

Silvio shrugged it off and turned on his heels, his hands shoved deep into the pockets of his tracksuit.

Faust trudged close enough to rest his left hand on my shoulder—so I could guide him, I realized, when I caught the twitch of his empty fingers, seeking his cane out of habit.

"I'm sorry about your cane," I said, while we treaded through the velvety powder across the silent park. "I tried to pick it up after Montecito took you down, but it turned to dust in my hands."

He gave my shoulder a light squeeze. "It's all right, you couldn't know. I wouldn't have wanted my old friend to change hands anyway."

My guilt returned at once, like a dull ache in my belly. "Can you still—"

"Yes, don't worry. I liked to use it to channel my power, but it was never more than a defensive artifact."

Imbued with magic, and which I'd destroyed with a mere touch. "I'm just sorry." I sighed. "I can tell it meant a lot to you, even though you're being cool about it."

"It's all right, Emma. If anyone can help us at this point, it's

Lady Palombara."

"Is she a witch too?" I whispered, eyeing our host's round cheeks and cheerful attitude as she welcomed Ryuuko and bent to marvel at the contents of her bag, clasping her hands in apparent delight.

"Oh no, she's a titan."

Lady Palombara was a titan, and at the moment, she sat on a gilded pink brocade couch among a dozen hat boxes full of multicolored pieces of fabric and just as many different reels of sewing thread. She held up Faust's coat, inspecting the hole in the brown wool against a square of embroidered mauve velvet. "How about this one? Isn't it lovely?"

"I like," Ryuuko noted dryly as she poured a fragrant green tea in four china cups which sat on an antique lacquered coffee table. She took one for herself, supporting the delicate saucer underneath with her palm and went to sit in an armchair whose flowery yellow brocade matched the couch, of course. She raised her head once to acknowledge us, and said, "You drink."

I made no move to touch my cup, staring at the two of them in a state of stupor that was roughly 50% awe, 30% *dude-what?* and 20% . . . okay, let's call it mortal fear in the face of the unknown.

Ryuuko nudged the cup my way. "You drink," she repeated.

My eyeballs slowly rotated south, to the green water sloshing in the cup, before they rolled back up to focus on Ryuuko. "You're a titan too?"

"I'm a dragon."

Sure. I shot her a canted look, scanning her small hands for scales, or the folds of her lavish kimono for a tail. Finding no visual clue, I gave Faust his cup and took mine without daring to drink it. I feared I was reaching my limit and I'd taken all the weird I could.

Lady Palombara set aside Faust's coat to bring her cup to her lips, careful to keep her little finger up and hold the saucer like Ryuuko was. She took a slow sip, then another, before her deep black gaze rose to meet mine. I noticed for the first time that she didn't seem to have pupils; her irises were dark pools that seemed almost navy depending on the angle of the light. I was looking into the eyes of an old goddess, and a tremor in my hand made my cup clatter in its saucer when it dawned on me that no one in this room was entirely human . . . *not even me?*

"Is that something you worry about? Not being human?"

I nearly dropped my cup. Drops of hot tea splashed my wrist, but I barely registered the burn; I was worried about my jaw, which had just unhinged and rolled to the Persian carpet at my feet. She could . . . She could read my fucking mind.

Her head snapped up. "No swearing, Emma dear."

Shhhh—oo . . .

The corners of her eyes crinkled in approval. "Better."

Next to me, Faust suppressed a snicker in the rim of his cup. I kicked him under the coffee table and took a sharp breath before answering Palombara. "Four days ago, I was in New York, serving tuna rolls in a fast-food restaurant. And now," I motioned to the windows, through which I could see snow fall over Lady Palombara's world—which was in Rome, but not in Rome, according to Silvio. "I'm *here*, and you just read my thoughts. So yeah, I got a lot on my mind, and I think this is where I need to start before I can tackle anything else." I massaged the bridge of my nose forcefully to focus, hold on. Just hold on through all this. "I need to understand what's happening to me."

She repeatedly nodded like a doctor. "What are your

symptoms?"

I didn't have time to answer. I just thought about it, the frozen seagulls of my childhood, Lucius's arm, Chronos's Table, the way Faust had grabbed my hand to break the Libro's spell, his cane crumbling to dust . . . It all flashed behind my eyelids at once, a confused mosaic of memories that couldn't have lasted two seconds. Lady Palombara's dark eyes widened slowly. She took a sip of her tea that she seemed to let sit on her tongue as if to better savor it and raised an eyebrow at Ryuuko. "And here you are, pestering me about taking a Netflix subscription because nothing fun ever happens in Rome. There you have it—*fun*."

Ryuuko shrank in her seat, her face bunching in evident displeasure, before dipping her lips in her tea cup as well.

"Look," I told Palombara, "I don't know what you find so funny about all this, but I just need to know what's *wrong* with me, like if I'm cursed, or, I don't know . . ."

Her shoulders hitched. "*Cursed?* That's such a disheartening way to put it. Why not *chosen?*"

I heard Montecito's quivering voice again. *He chose me.* Yeah, no; I didn't want to go there. Besides, no one had ever chosen me for anything in twenty years, except the manager who'd hired me at Tuna Town a year ago. Typing my resume in an internet café and bullshitting my way through the interview afterward—that was more or less when I'd peaked as a human being.

Lady Palombara smiled. "You remind me of Faust when I first met him. Same doubts, same questions." My eyebrows shot up, and I forgot to be pissed that she kept reading my thoughts like that and wouldn't let me say a damn word. I glanced at Faust, whose breathing had slowed down while he listened to our exchange— likely dissecting every subtle nonverbal signal he could pick up. Her expression softened, almost tender as she recounted, "When I met him, he'd just sealed his pact with Chronos, and he wouldn't believe he was immortal.

"I remember that afternoon as if it were yesterday: I sat in the grass by the Tiber, under a bridge we used to call the *Pons Fabricius*, and I watched him jump and jump and jump . . . until he grew tired of it, and when he came out of the water for perhaps the tenth time, I told him, 'Centurion, even if you could die, that bridge wouldn't be high enough to kill you.'"

She covered her hand to stifle a giggle. Faust didn't laugh. He looked fucking sad as the old memory washed over him, and it made my heart ache for him. I set my teacup on the table and brushed his forearm awkwardly. It seemed too intimate to take his hand, and I wasn't sure how to let him know that I got it, that there was nothing funny about hitting rock bottom so hard you jump from a bridge ten times in a row. His muscles twitched when he felt my touch, and he turned his head my way and smiled a little.

I eyed Palombara angrily. Maybe it was funny for a supernatural being like her because human lives made no sense to her anyway . . .

"They do," she replied, once more reading my mind like a prompter. "Much more so than immortal lives; in fact, humans seem to shine brighter in their short time, like shooting stars."

Silence stretched between us as I gave up on speaking and thought my next words. *Very poetic, and also totally useless. If you don't know what's wrong with me, just say it, and we're done.*

Her unfathomable eyes reached deep under my skin. "Such temper . . . but you're right, Emma, enough chitchat."

Ryuuko's cup rattled in her saucer as she placed both on the table. She stared at the window behind me, purposely avoiding my gaze. "You act tough. But are you strong?"

Lady Palombara's lips pinched to stifle a laugh. "Oh, more than you could ever imagine, my love."

The little dragon's almond-shaped eyes became suspicious slits, but she thankfully shut up.

Faust leaned back on the couch, his arms crossed and told Palombara, "So, you believe I'm right?"

Palombara's soft smile grew mischievous. "On occasion."

"Right about what?" I asked, my pulse picking up. We were getting somewhere at last, but I was no longer sure I wanted to take that trip . . .

Lady Palombara set her cup on the coffee table next to Ryuuko's and laced her hands over the blue velvet of her ample dress. "Faust is worried that, at the moment, you might be the Omega. Or rather," she pointed at my chest, "that the Omega might be located inside you."

Faust swallowed, a twitch in his fingers the only cue to his inner tension. I caught Ryuuko's eyes widening a fraction. A cold sweat dampened my T-shirt. It was bad. It *had* to be bad, like . . .

Palombara's features pinched in confusion. "Oh no, it's not Ebola; magic or otherwise."

I gulped slowly. "Please *stop* doing that and tell me what I got. Am I cursed? Is it a curse?" How did you even catch that in the first place? And *why*?

"It's not a curse, and you'll be fine, Emma," Faust reassured me, with a tremor in his voice that pretty much advertised the opposite.

"You're going to live a long and fun life," Lady Palombara confirmed. I didn't miss her fleeting wince, though. "A very fun life."

Okay, now I was panicking. "I don't understand any of this, but I know you're basically implying I'm gonna get in a lot more trouble than I already am."

Her head lolled in hesitation. "Yes. Say, Emma, do you like

theoretical physics?"

"Uh . . . what?"

"Theoretical physics," she insisted.

"I dropped out from high school." I shrugged. "Straight F student here."

Ryuuko pursed her doll lips. "I graduate from Tōdai. Twice."

"Under two different names." Lady Palombara laughed. "But we're not here to brag."

"Good for you," I mouthed at Ryuuko, with an eye roll I hoped spoke volumes—even though I had no fricking idea what or where Tōdai was.

"I never had much patience for studying either," Faust remarked—to rescue me, I gathered, judging by the way he had meticulously annotated his disc covers in braille, it was quite the opposite.

"We'll try to keep it simple for everyone, then." Palombara folded her hands back on her lap and enunciated slowly, "To *almost* everything in this universe and any other, there's a beginning and an end. An Alpha and an Omega."

"Like A to Z," Ryuuko added, with a pointed look my way.

Man, that bitch really thought I was dumber than a rock . . . I shot her a nasty glare but allowed Lady Palombara to go on. "All you've witnessed, Emma, Lady Montecito's abilities, Faust's power, or even mine . . . all this 'magic' as some people may call it, originates from a unique source, a beginning. That place is a forbidden dimension we call Othrys. Othrys is where old titans, like me, took form, a very long time ago."

I listened with a deadpan face, feeling like I'd just popped in a cult meeting. Except no one in this room was crazy, I knew it now. "So, Othrys is where magic basically starts. It's the Alpha," I repeated hesitantly. "And the end is the Omega, and that's . . ."

She smiled, and pointed a finger at my chest, without touching it. "Here. Where all magic ends, and none can exist." She plunged her strange swirling gaze into mine. "Essentially a black hole."

That was not how I expected my day to unfold when I'd shoved Faust's cat off my face this morning. But I took it pretty well—mostly because I barely understood what she was talking about, save for the fact that something inside me sucked magic like a vacuum. I'd have taken Ebola instead, at that point.

Ryuuko's fists clutched tight on her lap as if she were scared, but Faust remained his usual laid-back self, which helped me keep it together. I managed a stiff smile. "I'm a black hole? I mean, I know I'm not exactly a ray of sunshine, but—"

Faust shook his head. "You're not a literal black hole; rather, let's say you contain a tiny one within yourself, capable of absorbing the power emanating from Othrys. That's why my power or Montecito's can't affect you, and it's also why you were able to disintegrate Lucius's external envelope; it was nothing but a spell that could not exist at your direct contact." He took my hand gently. "My body, on the other hand, remains human, even though its healing abilities are not. I probably wouldn't be able to heal while in contact with you." He seemed to realize what he'd just said the moment the words crossed his lips. Shock registered in his eyes.

"I could have killed you," I breathed. "I touched you after Montecito stabbed you with the spear. I'm sorry . . ."

"Don't be. Could explain why it took me so long to heal this time though," he mused. "But I don't know if you could truly kill me."

"She could absorb you, which would amount to the same," Palombara casually warned him, oblivious to the look of horror on

my face. She was talking about me like I was some sort of monster—
Pac-Man, basically.

A million questions whirled in my head, which all boiled down
to two simple words: "But why?"

Palombara caressed her lips with her thumb, gazing at me
fondly. "The greatest of all questions." Her chest heaved in a quasi-
shrug. "To the most powerful gods, the past, present, and future
form a single, simultaneous reality that's clay in their hands. The laws
of Othrys predict that the Omega must exist at any given moment and
that it could be any point of any universe, but if someone chose to
place it inside you, there must be a reason, indeed. There is always one."

My face twisted in dismay. "But that's just a bunch of
philosophical bull . . . *shoo*. You're not actually answering the
question."

"Perhaps you need to seek the answers within yourself."

"Oh, *come on*! You have no idea, right?"

The beat of silence that followed was an answer in itself. I
deflated on the couch and tried to put my thoughts into brittle words
under Faust's sympathetic gaze. "This makes zero f—" I caught
myself when her nostrils flared . . . "fricking sense. This makes no
sense. Why would anyone, a god, a titan or whatever, want to put
that thing inside me?" I motioned to my stomach with trembling
hands. "Why didn't they stick it into someone who actually cares?"

Lady Palombara tilted her head at me. "But you do care. In spite
of all that divides you, you care about Lily."

I went rigid. "How do you know . . ."

Her lips curled. "You hide your memories almost as well as you
do your thoughts."

You're not wandering aimlessly . . . In my mind, the living room and
the tea cups blurred into the sunny streets of Rome. I saw Lily again,

running into me near the coliseum—or had it been the other way around? Lily taking me to visit the site, where I'd met Faust. That cumsock Dante cancelling my booking because he thought my guesthouse wasn't good enough. Lily inviting me to see her lab the day after. The table, Montecito.

Perses.

There's a fate written for you: you're going somewhere, and you'll influence other lives on your way. Things can happen a thousand different ways, you can make a thousand different choices, but eventually, they'll always lead you where your path is taking you.

My hands moved to rest on my stomach as if they might feel the black hole there. A place where Perses's power could no more exist than Montecito's.

A solemn, sorrowful mask fell over Palombara's gentle expression. "You have felt his presence." Not a question, but a statement.

"I'm not sure. I mean, I've seen the Spear of Shadows, and I'm pretty sure Montecito used it, but—"

"You've felt it," Palombara repeated slowly. "And this suffocating power is only a speck of him, dust lingering in his wake. If he ever were to return . . ."

Faust's eyes briefly squeezed in silent horror.

"What would happen?" I asked, a growing pressure squeezing my throat, like an invisible hand strangling me.

Outside, the sun had set. I hadn't noticed. When had Lady Palombara's living room grown so dark? Seconds ago, I'd seen her and the others clear as day, and now the only thing I could make out clearly were her eyes. The shimmering specks in them. As I realized for the first time that her pupils looked in fact like dark galaxies, Lady Palombara murmured, "Let me tell you a story."

Lady Palombara's voice drifted in the darkness, fraught with regret. "In a different world and a different time, we, the old titans, fought a war that shattered the earth and burned the skies."

The air around had grown cold, and that feeling, that shiver up my spine, it was just like . . . I freaked out and jumped from the couch when I realized it was the same as when we'd entered the Libro. I felt Faust's warmth near me, clung to his voice as the roar of an ancient battle threatened to cover it. "There's nothing to fear, Emma."

And yet . . . whereas the Libro's memories had carried fire and death, they couldn't compare to the blaze ravaging Lady Palombara's. Thousands of shadows crashed against each other in a sea of flames, tore each other apart with otherworldly screams.

"Like my brother Chronos had turned against our father Ouranos in another age, our own children turned against us for control of Othrys," Lady Palombara murmured through the chaos ringing in my ears. "Zeus believed our reign had to end, so the age of Olympus could begin."

The howling shadows collapsed one after another, speared and slashed by shimmering figures. Faceless gods wearing blinding golden armors.

"Chronos lost his mind trying to retain control of his realm," she breathed, a cutting edge to her voice. "He sent his armies against Zeus's, and unleashed the worst beast of all, Perses, the God of destruction, son of our foolish brother Crius."

A lone shadow emerged from the hell of the battlefield, dominating the writhing hordes at his feet. He tossed a gigantic spear across the compact mass of tangled bodies that tore a monstrous hole through the chest of one of the golden-armored Gods. I saw Faust again, wounded in the same fashion by Montecito. I needed no confirmation to know I was witnessing the power of the Spear of Shadows, an integral part of Perses. My hand fumbled for his in the flames surrounding us, grazing his palm. He laced his fingers with mine as Palombara went on.

"But we were to lose, and nothing could have changed what had been written. Chronos knew it better than any of us, he who saw all."

Before my eyes, Perses eventually collapsed in his turn, crushed by a shimmering tide as she said, "After our defeat, we were cast away to rot for eternity in Tartarus." Whipped by powerful winds, the scorched battlefield became dust, then a cold, dark desert where ragged ghosts roamed across a rocky immensity. "Those of us who managed to escape found shelter in the worst hell of all . . ." At the edge of the inky night sky, the sun pierced through an incandescent horizon. Dawn's coppery light licked temples and ruins, paved streets, and rickety market stalls, swarmed by a colorful and sweaty crowd. Earth. Rome.

Lady Palombara sighed. "Chronos refused that supreme humiliation. He sealed what was left of his power in the table and vanished, leaving it to immortals such as Faust to guard his legacy. I chose to roam the earth and eventually summoned the remnants of my powers to create this peaceful dimension, a retreat outside of time to spend eternity. As for Perses . . ." Her voice faltered, allowing through a sliver of genuine fear. "Zeus buried his remains in the depths of Tartarus, and for a very long time, I believed him to be trapped there with our brothers and sisters."

"But there's at least a part of him that escaped to Earth, and when someone tries to summon the Spear of Shadows, they're actually channeling that," I completed, remembering Faust's earlier explanation as Palombara's vision dissipated and the living room reappeared around us.

Faust's hand jerked instinctively to brush the hole in his T-shirt. "Montecito is under his control; she made it very clear that she hopes to unseal the table for him."

"I remember that . . ." I frowned. "She kinda sounded like she was hearing voices. Is he calling her long-distance from Tartarus?"

"No," Palombara replied, a twitch of her lips chasing the grief weighing on her features. "A titan's external envelope might seem similar to a human's, but we do not possess a heart or a brain in the same sense human beings do. We *are* in our entirety, at every moment and in every place."

I tried to wrap my head around the concept. "So, he is in Tartarus, but since Montecito summoned a small part of his power, he is also in Rome at the same time, and he's kind of . . . stretching across two dimensions?"

"For the sake of clarity, let's say yes," Palombara acquiesced.

"Okay." My head bobbed slowly as I digested this new barrage of information. "And we know he wants the table. Montecito said he promised her he'd use it to make her truly immortal."

Palombara shook her head with a sigh. "The lure of eternity. Always . . . Since the dawn of mankind."

"It's kind of easy to say that when you're immortal in the first place,"

I shot back. "You'll never know what it's like to want more time."

"We do know, Emma." Palombara's gaze met Faust's, both filled with unfathomable sorrow. "The time of our loved ones is sand in our hands."

He gave a faint nod. I thought of Silvio, who must be over sixty, of the women Faust had maybe loved over the centuries, of the friends he'd watched grow old. Lady Montecito on the other hand probably didn't care for anyone except Lucius—she'd kept him young at her side after all, and he clearly worshipped her in return. "Perses is already immortal, though," I eventually said. "What's in it for him?"

Faust's nostrils flared, but he remained obstinately silent. He wouldn't reply if it meant saying anything about the table . . .

"Power," was Palombara's simple reply. "The power to break his chains, to control the flow of time. See the future and shape it." She gazed through the window, at the now darkened park, asleep under a smooth blanket of snow. "Enough power and enough anger to make many more mistakes . . ."

I crossed my arms, my lips pressed tight. Perses and Montecito were a match made in heaven; two frustrated psychos dreaming big. One of which happened to be the remnants of an old god. What the fuck could go wrong? I eyed Palombara. "Can't you send him back to Tartarus? Or, I mean, cram the part of him that's sticking out back there," I wondered aloud, illustrating my suggestion with a shoving motion in the air. "You're a titan too, and you seem . . . pretty powerful." I flicked my wrist at the living room surrounding us and the park beyond, hoping she'd get my point.

"Only you know how to do that, Emma," she replied softly.

I got to my feet, pacing in front of the coffee table. "More chosen one shit? Is that really what we're going for?"

"Language, young lady," Palombara reminded me, before her

eyes fell to her half-empty cup of tea, the green hue reflected in them. "Even if Ouranos had seen it fit to bestow me with the power to annihilate, there's too little left of me to defeat the Spear of Shadows—and Faust doesn't have that power, either. The Omega, however, could swallow Perses into nothingness."

"And he knows it," Faust said. "Montecito reached out to Emma. She claimed there was a place for her at Perses's side."

A tendril of fear stirred in my chest at the memory of that bitch's victorious smirk as Perses's shadows imprisoned us. I went to plop myself back on the couch at Faust's side. "Montecito said I could break the table's seal. Is it because of the Omega?" A vision of my palm resting flat on Chronos's Table flashed in my mind. "Can I really do that if I touch it for too long?" I asked, a tremor in my voice. I wasn't sure I could process this—accept that there was . . . that thing inside me. It just didn't feel real.

Faust walled himself in silence for the second time, but I noticed the way his Adam's apple rolled in his throat, and I started to wonder if he wouldn't reveal anything about the table because of the contract binding him to Chronos, or if, maybe . . . he physically couldn't.

"It can," Palombara answered for him. "For now, you've witnessed only limited effects of your power. If the Omega were to be unleashed against the table, it would first absorb the defensive power keeping the table sealed, then, likely, keep on absorbing Chronos's power which lies dormant inside."

Unleashed, like it'd . . . burst out of me Alien-style? I gulped softly at the mental image. "What about Perses? Why can't he do that himself?"

Unexpectedly, it was Ryuuko who chimed in while she worked on picking up our teacups and collecting them on a silver tray. She shot an unreadable look at Faust. "Because Chronos bans everyone from using the table. Only the guardian knows the words to unseal it. If Perses wants the power, Faust unseals the table, or you break it. No other option."

I gazed at the tattoo around Faust's wrist. His shackle. "And you can never allow either to happen," I murmured to him.

He mustered a pale copy of his Fausty grin. "I would never stab you."

"Unless you have to," I replied. Yet I couldn't find it in me to be angry over this. It just hurt a little to think that maybe we'd never be able to trust each other completely, because he'd been chosen to guard the table, and I'd been chosen to be the only threat to it. Divine fate sucked giant balls.

Lady Palombara's gaze traveled back and forth between Faust and me. "Perses needs one of you, and he knows it."

I twisted my neck with a grimace, fighting exhaustion. "And we're stuck. They have Lily working on the table at Katharos's HQ. If I try to get near, Montecito will use her against me."

Faust dragged a hand across his face, scratching his beard. "And she'll use *you* against me."

That gave me pause. I turned to him. "You don't have to come with me. Lily is my problem. I chose to stay at the Residenza knowing something was off with Katharos. I chose to get involved. I know I agreed when you offered to help me, but . . ." I glanced at his tattoo. "I understand now . . . that I can't ask you to do anything that would threaten the table."

He leaned forward and rested his elbow his knees, looking drained, just like me. "Emma, if you march to the Villa Malespina with the intent of bargaining with Lady Montecito to save Lily . . . I can't ignore that. There's too much at stake."

"So, you *would* stab me," I joked. My throat was dry though, and it didn't sound that funny.

He didn't reply and instead, clasped his hands and rested his forehead on them. "I'd rather not have to, Emma . . ."

"But we can't just hide here. Faust," I urged. "I'm not immortal, and Lily certainly isn't. There's *no* time. You were in the Libro with me. I didn't dream her voice. Every second she spends around Montecito and Lucius, she's in danger. What if she finds out what they are like her grandpa did?" I stopped there: no need to get graphic.

"You do have time," Lady Palombara countered. "What you sorely lack, Emma, is *patience*."

Maybe. But her lack of fucks to give was starting to piss me off, and I could feel my legendary short fuse start to sizzle. I inhaled through flaring nostrils. "Patience? Are you serious? You're the one who keeps rambling about how dangerous Perses is! Faust and I already escaped Katharos twice, and I can tell you this: those guys are anything but *patient*. We can't stay—"

"Then you go." Ryuuko—who had been observing our exchange in silence until now—leveled her vacant stare at me. "Now we seal the Porta Alchemica, and you do what you want. You fight Perses alone with your black hole if you want." Her eyes narrowing, she thought it useful to add, "Since you're stupid anyway."

I shot up from the couch, every single muscle in my body coiled from the need to fight back, explode. I wouldn't. I could control this, be the bigger person. I mean literally so since she must have weighed ninety pounds. I averted my eyes and said, "I need some air."

Faust rose in his turn to stop me, a wrinkle of concern splitting his brow. "Emma, wait . . ."

Palombara tilted her head, her gaze shining with kindness I suspected was, in fact, condescension. "Suit yourself. I must tell you, however, that your guilt and naïve calculations are clouding your judgment. Saving Lily won't redeem you in your mother's eyes." The galaxies in her eyes bored into me, deepening the wound. "You know nothing can."

Shots fired. I reeled, wobbled a bit on my legs as I tried to process that she'd just casually ripped me open in front of Faust and Ryuuko, and now that aching, gangrened part of my heart I tried my best to protect all the time, was pulsing in the open, defenseless.

Surprise flashed in Faust's eyes; he turned toward Palombara. "Theia, please, don't be so harsh," he told her, his hand fumbling for mine. "I'm sorry, Emma, she can sometimes be—"

"Leave me alone," I snapped. I didn't need his pity. It was worth no more to me than Ryuuko's quiet contempt as she observed our exchange. Faust's fingertips found my knuckles. I pulled my hand away to shove it in my pocket. I glared at Palombara, shivering all over, my stomach lurching like I was seasick. "Open your Jell-O portal. I'm out of here," I barked.

She feigned confusion. "Do you mean the Porta Alchemica? Very well, Ryuuko will open it for you." She chuckled. "What are you planning to do? Hide out on the streets? Or perhaps ask the police to solve titan matters?"

I didn't know. A thousand tons had been dropped on my shoulders over the span of two hours, and I couldn't carry that weight, couldn't take it anymore. My breathing was coming in painful pants. My head hurt, and I needed to kick something or smash it against a wall. The teapot would do. I bent to grab it and hurled it to the floor with all my strength. It shattered at Palombara's feet. Water stained the bottom of her dress. She didn't move an inch from her couch, her patient gaze set on me as I unraveled.

Ryuuko leaped from her armchair to lunge at me, but Faust was in the way. He shielded me with his body. His features were taut with a mixture of surprise and anger I'd seen on a hundred faces before—

he wasn't the first to be disappointed in me. Wouldn't be the last, either. "Emma . . ." My name, nothing more, loaded with reproach. I wasn't sure why it made me feel so shitty to hear it in his mouth.

I couldn't listen; my brain was clouded with too much hate, too much pain. I shoved him aside, challenging Palombara's soft gaze with my blazing one. "Here's what I'm *not* gonna do: stay here and do nothing while you keep reading my thoughts like we're on Dr. Phil! And just for the record, the only reason I want to help Lily is because it's the fucking decent thing to do! I don't give two fucks about her or mom or Richard . . ." My voice broke. I swallowed back the tears I could feel blurring my eyes. "I didn't ask for any of this. I just . . ." *I just came here to see my father.*

But maybe that wasn't in the cards of this life that no longer belonged to me anyway. I'd been designed as a shell for a black hole. How terribly accurate. A tear rolled down my cheek that I wished I could stop.

Faust's eyes were staring through me as if he had no idea who this blistering bitch was, and Lady Palombara apparently had nothing else to say. I barreled out of the living room and across the villa's marble hall without another word, ignoring Faust as he fumbled his way around the furniture and called my name.

Palombara found her voice as I pushed the heavy wooden doors leading out, but it was only to say, "Emma, do you want a cloak to go out in this weather?"

I didn't bother turning around. I just raised my hand and flipped her off.

The funny part is, I really thought Lady Palombara would let me go. I slammed the villa's doors, barreled down a flight of stone steps into the crisp winter air, and took my first steps on the snowy lawn stretching at the building's feet. I covered less than a hundred feet before realizing that my sneakers were no longer cushioned by powdery snow, but rather skidding in sludge, then treading in wet grass.

What the . . . I darted a puzzled look around. The snow was melting, lightning fast. In a matter of seconds, the air had grown warm and the inky night clouds stirred apart to reveal a bright moon above my head. Pure white became a dark green lawn where rose bushes sat, scattered. Freed of their winter coat, naked statues looked down at me, a mocking glint in their empty eyes.

She'd made it a summer night.

I whirled around and yelled at the villa's now-closed doors. "Wow, you're *so* funny! And I'm *so* impressed! Fuck you, by the way! I hope you get mole mounds all over your lawn!"

My curse rose to the sky, echoed by a shrill birdcall somewhere in the trees. The door remained closed. I resumed my walk across the park, searching for the wall we'd crashed through in Katharos's stolen SUV. But it was just darkened woods everywhere I looked, hemming the expanse of fresh grass . . . except where a long archway formed by the canopy met over a trail. There was no end in sight to this creepy bowel though, only a tangle of trunks and shrubs fading into pitch-black.

I buried my face in my hands and massaged my temples slowly, fighting the unpleasant buzz of a headache. I was 100% sure we hadn't come here through the woods, and that trail had "trap" written all over it. Palombara wasn't done playing with me.

I glanced back at the warm light pouring from the windows. The living room remained empty. She, Faust, and Ryuuko had retreated into another room. I sucked in a shuddering breath. I was alone in the dark, trapped somewhere outside reality, at the mercy of an ancient goddess with a shitty sense of humor. I was running on empty, lost in every sense of the term, but my pride and the anger still thrumming in my blood wouldn't let me go back there with my tail between my legs. My molars ground together in aggravation. I would be no one's bitch!

I marched to the trail, inhaling earth and moss. With each cautious step, fear took over the last of my fury as the woods around me came alive. The night breeze whispered in leaves; birdcalls were answered by the lazy croak of a frog somewhere in the thicket. Twigs snapped under my feet, like firecrackers exploding in the silence enveloping me. More than once, I froze and blinked terrified eyes when I thought I saw something stir in the dark, my heart pounding in my throat.

And still, there was no end in sight, only the villa behind me, getting smaller and smaller until its windows were little more than shimmering gems in the distance. There had to be a way out. Palombara couldn't just trap me in here forever. Faust wouldn't let her. I swallowed a painful lump in my throat. I *hoped* he wouldn't, but I'd blown him off when he meant to take my defense; he had every reason to give up on me. Shame tightened my heart for the second time that day, and as usual, after the anger came the regrets. I wasn't sure I truly wanted to push him away, but I knew nothing else: strangers or enemies, nothing in between because I'd never been taught otherwise.

"Then you'll have to learn."

Holy fricking baby Jesus—I jumped out of my skin and whipped around, in the direction of Palombara's voice. My eyes popped so wide my eyeballs damn near rolled out. She was here, standing in the dark in front of a wall that hadn't been there five seconds ago. Light haloed her silhouette, pouring from a sculpted gate encased in ancient mossy stones. On each side, I recognized the statues of two bearded deities I'd glimpsed right before Silvio had sped through the shimmering Jell-O. The Porta Alchemica.

"Is this what you were looking for?" Palombara asked softly, motioning to the open gate. My eyes adjusted to the light splashing from the portal, and moving shapes came into focus. It was the municipal park we'd driven through earlier, bathed in a late afternoon glow. Police uniforms bustled around the gaping hole in the fence, working to close it with yellow tape.

"Go," Palombara offered.

My gaze shuttled back and forth between her and the portal. "It's still day," I chewed out.

"It's been less than twenty minutes out there," she replied, her mouth twisting as if it were totally obvious and, *seriously, Emma, didn't you know that?* "As I tried to tell you, you *do* have time to sit and consider your options before ramming into Perses like Don Quixote. Time flows somewhat more slowly beyond the Porta Alchemica than it does in the outside world."

I gazed at the "crime scene" through the gate, at the lean young policeman scratching his cap and looking around the street.

"So? Are you leaving?" Palombara crossed her arms over the bodice of her blue velvet dress. "Or have you changed your mind?"

"Why did you bother with all the tricks and bullshit instead of just telling me that?" I bristled, all shields up. "What do you *really* want from me?"

"I merely wanted to give you a little time to calm down, and," she looked up at the star-studded veil above us, "you left without a coat."

I didn't reply, just stared at her, my jaw hanging limp.

She chuckled. "Why don't we talk for a moment and try to work out our differences? Sit, Emma."

Hang on, not so fast . . . I glanced around, frowned. Had that stone bench been standing in the middle of the trail a second before? "Uh, did you just . . .?"

She shrugged an eyebrow and went to sit on the long slab of sculpted limestone. "It's my dimension," was the only explanation she offered.

I went to perch on the edge of the bench gingerly, and by the time I looked up again at the Porta Alchemica, sunlight was no longer pouring through from the real world. A slab of plain concrete now walled the gate, just like I'd seen on the other side hours ago. My eyes lingered on the esoteric signs carved in stone all around the door and the Latin inscriptions under the six-pointed star topping the whole thing.

"The dragon of the Hesperides watches over the entrance of the magic garden," Palombara said, smoothing the folds of her ample dress.

"Is that what's written?" I asked, pointing to the Portal with my chin. "Yes."

"And Ryuuko is the dragon," I reasoned.

"She told you so herself," Palombara noted, amusement gleaming in her dark eyes. I'd have wanted to figure out that dragon thing, but she went on to say, "You'll have to excuse me. When I meet someone new, and I smell a fierce temper, I can't help rousing them a little . . . to see who I'm dealing with."

I'd agreed to make peace, but the memory of our conversation in her living room was still fresh in my mind. I muttered, "Like when you laughed at Faust when he was trying to kill himself?"

If she picked up on the jab, she didn't let it show. "No, it was different with him; he was never that volatile." A wistful smile relaxed her features. "He's one of the kindest and most patient souls I've ever met—and truly worthy of guarding Chronos's Table—but he tends to shy from decisions and confrontation."

"I kinda noticed that about him," I admitted with a reluctant smile of my own.

"But you're quite the opposite. Headstrong and bellicose, perhaps too much for your own good."

I shrugged. "You give me shit. I give you shit."

"Spoken like a lady," she noted sourly before her expression sobered. "Emma, I didn't say those things solely to probe old wounds and see what I would find."

No need to answer; I knew she could read on my face what I thought of that claim. She darted a guilty look upward at the moon glimmering through the canopy. "Well, perhaps I *did* try to nudge your demons out. What I'm trying to tell you is that you are wrong . . ." My nostrils flared. ". . . about your path."

You're not wandering aimlessly.

"I know," I murmured, forcing the words past my lips. "I'm not as stupid as Ryuuko thinks. I get it, I think. It was all meant to happen this way. Lily's grandpa killed himself to escape Katharos. Lily took over his work and found the table for them. Montecito wanted to be immortal, so she rung Perses. It was all linked, and meanwhile, I decided to find my father, and I came up with that stupid plan of flying here and showing up at his doorstep, like in a movie or something."

I touched my stomach. "The only reason the black hole is in me is that it needs to be here, right now." My fingers played with one of the holes in my jeans, running along the frayed edge. "It was never about saving Lily. The Omega is only here for Perses because he's trying to snatch the table, right?" Too bad whoever had chosen me over everyone else hadn't bothered checking if I was capable of using that power in the first place . . .

Palombara nodded. "I've considered this possibility. Or perhaps you're meant to accomplish something else entirely. The truth is: you will never know. No one can."

"But you're . . . a goddess. You see things," I countered. "You can't see what's in the cards for me?"

She combed a lock of pale gray hair behind her ear, and her lips pressed into a sorrowful smile. "*No one* can, Emma. I can no more see your future and purpose in this world than I can see mine. There's no point in looking for any signs." She looked at the sky. "Only Chronos and the Parcae are gifted with prescience. The rest of us must walk in the dark."

"The Parcae?"

"Daughters of the all-powerful Nyx. She and Chaos were the first of our kind; all titans descend from them. Perhaps you've heard of them as the fates?"

Actually, I had . . . "Lily was the one who first told me that the fates spin the thread of your life and that you can basically never deviate from that path. Things can happen a thousand different ways, but you'll still go from point A to B."

"Your stepsister is unexpectedly wise," Palombara said, a shadow passing across her features.

"She was always really smart." I shrugged. I stretched with a groan. Man, that bench was hard, and my butt was getting numb. I gazed at the Porta Alchemica absently. "What would you do if you were in my place?"

Palombara's shoulders hitched. "I didn't see that question coming."

I smirked. "Maybe I'm not always that easy to read. Anyway, what would you do? You say if I go pick a fight with Montecito and Perses, I'm screwed. But, of course, Montecito is gonna put Lily's life in the balance, and if I try to break the table's seal to save her, I'm screwed, too, because then Faust has a halberd waiting for me. So, how would you play that hand?"

Her gaze grew unfocused—not the reaction I'd been hoping for. "Faust told you about him?"

"What do you mean?"

"The alchemist he killed," Palombara breathed. Did she sound . . . upset?

"You mean with the halberd? Yeah. He's the one we saw in the Libro, he . . ." I frowned. "He was the last one to try to summon Perses, but Faust killed him before he was done. Faust showed me his embalmment spell too. He thinks Montecito is using the same thing and that she's basically copying that guy's ideas."

"I know," she said. "His was a mind like no other, fascinated by the hidden nature of things, that so few humans understand."

Faust had said the same, and there had been an undercurrent of admiration to his voice, too, as he recounted the story of our mystery dude. They'd both known him, and I had a hunch that to them, he'd been more than just a bad guy to take down like Montecito. "What was his name?" I asked. "Faust never told me."

She wouldn't look at me. A smile returned to her lips. She laced her fingers and nodded once as if she'd come to a decision after some internal debate. "I'll tell you about him someday." She rose from the bench. "For now, you need to apologize to that poor Faust, and I have some crocheting to do."

I tilted my head slowly, my eyes round as an owl's. "I'm sorry, what?"

"Isn't that what you were asking? What I would do in this situation?"

"Um . . . yeah, but—"

"Well, in the face of inevitable confrontation and certain peril, I would choose a kamikaze approach, and that, my dear, requires some preparation."

After the villa's doors creaked shut behind me for the second time that day, Lady Palombara said, "I'll leave you to dine with Faust and Ryuuko. I'll see you at dawn. Good night, Emma."

I stood dumbly in the ornate lobby, the angels painted on the ceiling laughing down at me. "My last meal before I go on your 'kamikaze' mission?"

She brought a finger to her lips. "I certainly hope not. Ryuuko is a terrible cook."

Having stated this, she disappeared up a curved marble staircase I figured must lead to the rooms. It took me a couple seconds to realize she hadn't told me where Ryuuko and Faust were.

I looked around at the painted walls and the columns framing several sets of doors. "Hey? Anyone here?" I called.

Hinges sighed as one of the doors came ajar. Faust appeared in the doorway, a lazy smile peeking through his beard. "Welcome back."

A sense of relief washed over me, loosened my limbs, and I realized I'd kinda missed him, even in such a short lapse of time. I brushed the awkward thought aside and walked to him. "Didn't have much of a choice, I guess." I lowered my voice to a mumble. "I'm sorry. For being . . ." I waved a hand he couldn't see, but I trusted he'd get my meaning. *For being me.*

He ducked his head, his grin widening. "You are forgiven once more. Do you like fox?"

"Like . . . the animal?"

He opened the doors wide to reveal one of those nineteenth-century kitchens you see in period dramas, with a massive chimney stove dominating one side of the room, and a long table in the center. Clad in a blue silk kimono and a long apron, Ryuuko stood near an antiquated cart with large iron wheels atop which sat . . . a microwave. Her gaze was locked on the dish spinning inside. Intense. Unblinking.

Faust entered the kitchen and felt for the back of a chair before sitting in front of one of the two plates set on the table. When the microwave beeped, he rubbed his hands. "We're having fox stew with noodles."

I noticed stacks of plates in the hutch taking most of the wall opposite to the stove. "Can I take one?" I asked Ryuuko.

She opened the microwave and took out a crock dish where a brownish mixture bubbled ominously. She set it on the table in front of Faust, whose ecstatic grin wavered when he got his first whiff of the stew. The feet of her chair scraped the floor as she sat across from him. Through it all, she totally ignored me.

I let my rising aggravation flow out in a deep breath and helped myself to a plate. "I'll eat with my hands, thanks."

"The cutlery is in the drawers," Faust thankfully supplied, while Ryuuko poured a ladle of boiling brown shit in his plate. He grabbed his spoon and cringed.

I padded to the table and sat at his side. Ryuuko wouldn't serve me, but I didn't mind. I actually preferred Faust taste it first, just in case. He did, and his nose wrinkled the moment the piece of fox touched his tongue. He swallowed it with difficulty before a coughing fit shook his frame. "There's . . . a lot of vinegar," he rasped.

"It's because the fox is tough. I boil in vinegar." Her gaze met mine, a challenge burning in their depth. She served me a ladle of stew.

"I'm sorry," I said, looking her in the eye. "I'm allergic to fox."

Her eyes narrowed. The corner of my mouth tugged victoriously.

"Nothing else left," she said icily.

Meanwhile, Faust soldiered through his plate of fox stew with a grimace. He cleared his throat. "Didn't you say you brought back *melon pans* from your last trip to Kyoto?"

Shock and betrayal flashed across Ryuuko's features before her emotionless mask slammed back in place. "I brought for *you*," she replied.

"But I want to share one with Emma," he pleaded. He topped it with his secret cute hobo grin, the one I'd seen him use to extort cash from those two girls yesterday.

Ryuuko averted her eyes. I couldn't be sure since her skin was so pale, but I detected the faintest blush. Interesting. She got up and went to search the pantry, returning to the table with three round cakes wrapped in plastic. She gave us one each. I tore the plastic eagerly and bit into mine with a moan of delight. It was sweet, spongey, and mostly it was food. Faust pushed his plate aside to feast on his melon pan, and told Ryuuko, *"Melon pan o taberu no ga hisashiburidatta."* It's been ages since I had *melon pan*.

I gawked at him. Sure . . . whatever that meant. "How many languages did you learn in your life?"

He shrugged. "I'm not sure. A few, I suppose."

And among those, Japanese, obviously.

"How many languages you speak?" Ryuuko asked me in between two bites of her own cake.

"I know a little Italian from my dad, and I took Spanish in high school, but I can basically say *¿cómo está?* and *soy un burrito,* and that's about it."

She sized me up with absolute contempt. "You're stupid."

Faust frowned in disapproval, but this time the jab glided on me. Because I'd found her weakness. "Are you always that mean to Faust's friends?" I asked slyly.

"He only brings Silvio," was her terse reply.

I flashed her a compassionate smile and patted Faust's shoulder as he finished his cake. "But now I'm here too."

She stared at my hand like she'd have wanted to cut it off. I snatched it back out of caution. The moment she was done eating, she shot up from her chair and cleared the table with fast and efficient moves. She placed the plates in an antique stone sink, rinsed them, and without turning around, said, "Dinner is over. I take you to your rooms."

"Thank you, Ryuuko," Faust replied. "The fox was excellent."

"You lie," she muttered, wiping her hands with a cloth.

He gave her a contrite smile. "Maybe a little less vinegar next time, and it'll be perfect."

After she had removed and folded her apron without a word, she exited the kitchen in a rustle of silk and said, "Follow me."

We crossed the lobby, and she led the way up the marble stairs leading to a long-paneled hallway whose walls were painted with cherry tree branches and birds flying everywhere. My gaze lingered on the details of their delicate feathers. So lifelike, almost as if . . . my heart nearly stopped when a tiny green sparrow stretched its wings to fly from one branch to another.

"Faust," I whispered. "The birds . . . I think they're flying inside the painting."

His lips curved. "I know. A simple, but lovely spell."

"I find in a book I buy from Louison. I like," Ryuuko explained.

I pursed my lips in genuine admiration. "Really cool."

My attempt at breaking the ice was met with arctic silence. She stopped in front of a set of dark wooden doors and opened them, revealing a lavish room whose curtains, armchairs, and bed were all fitted with the same delicate blue brocade. Her hand darted to brush Faust's forearm in a fleeting, awkward touch. "You sleep here," she said, almost—*almost*—gently.

He smiled at her, but it was to me that he asked, "Emma, will you stay a moment? I'd like to talk to you."

Abort! Abort! I had to clench my fist to stop it from performing a facepalm. You'd think a two-thousand-year-old dude had picked up a few things about the mystery of women somewhere along the way. Except not. Ryuuko remained her usual stony self, but I didn't miss the way her lips tightened, just long enough for me to know that my life was on the line here.

"Um . . . maybe later, once I've gotten some sleep." I turned to Ryuuko and forced a friendly smile on my face. "Do I get a room too?"

She gave a sharp nod.

"Good night, Faust," I said, while she was already on her way to open another door, farther down the hallway.

"Good night, Emma . . ." There was no mistaking the undercurrent of confusion and disappointment in his voice, but there wasn't much I could do about it for now. I wasn't above playing with Ryuuko a little—especially given how she'd treated me so far—but full-blown drama was where I drew the line. I just hoped that bitch at least appreciated my modest offering of peace.

I entered the room she'd shown me to, a cozy nest similar to Faust's, save for the soft yellow and cream palette of the walls and furniture. A pleasant smell of beeswax and soap laced the air as if the place had been cleaned recently. Pretty nice. "Thanks," I mumbled.

But Ryuuko wouldn't go. She stood still in the doorway, her dark gaze stabbing mine. Uncomfortable seconds ticked by, until I eventually motioned to the bed. "I'll try to get some sleep now . . . I guess."

She took a single step past the threshold and lowered her voice to a whisper. "I don't like you."

I let out a weary sigh. What else was new?

Pointing to her eyes with two fingers, she added, "I watch you when you sleep."

Oh wow, wow, wow . . . Hang on. Had we just reached a new and unexpected level of creepy here? "Hey—" The door slammed in my face before I could finish—or even begin—my sentence.

XXVIII

I figured Ryuuko would be waiting for me in the hallway wearing a leatherface mask patched together with the skin of a former rival, so I made a beeline for the window. I was no architecture expert, but I remembered that each floor of the villa had a single balcony spanning several windows on the front. I parted the curtains' heavy yellow brocade and turned the knob with excruciating care.

A gentle summer breeze caressed my face as I stepped onto the balcony. If my calculations were correct, the window next to mine should be Faust's. There was no light, but it didn't necessarily mean he was asleep. I crept across a smooth tiling in the dark, covering the few feet separating me from his window. Once I felt cool glass under my fingertips, I rapped. Blood rushed to my head and pounded in my ears as I waited for him to answer. What if Ryuuko had eyes on the balcony too?

Faust's window opened without warning, and I tumbled inside. A silk rug on the floor cushioned my entrance somewhat, and when I tried to scramble up, my hand met a familiar steel toe peeking from a busted leather boot.

"Emma? I take it you changed your mind?"

"She's onto me," I hissed.

"Ryuuko?"

I got to my feet. "You realize she has a crush on you, right?"

"Really?" He felt his way to his nightstand and turned on the lamp there.

I let myself fall on the embroidered covers of his bed with a groan of exhaustion. "Yeah, and guess what? She's watching competition *very* closely."

The mattress sank as he sat next to me, a Fausty grin lighting up his face. "You consider yourself competition?"

I flipped him off tiredly. "That's my middle finger, raised at you, right now."

That earned me a chuckle as he bent to undo the laces on his boots. "Whatcha doin'?"

"Making myself comfortable."

A slight funk tickling my nostrils informed me he'd taken his socks off too. "Man . . . do you ever wash your boots?"

"There's rain for that," Faust said before he laid on the bed and wiggled his toes with evident satisfaction.

"I mean the *inside*," I groaned, kicking off my sneakers to properly stretch alongside him on a sagging mattress that threatened to swallow us whole. So be it. I was too tired to fight it. "Just so you know, you can put baking soda inside your boots to kill the smell."

"Is it that bad?"

"Let's just say it's a great spell to protect yourself against sex," I said, hoping he'd get the underlying message: *just because we're in the same bed doesn't mean you're getting any.*

He sighed, folding his arms behind his head on a frilly lace pillow. "And here I'd been hoping you were here to share one final night of passion before we battle eternal and all-powerful forces."

My eyes snapped open at his reminder of Palombara's ominous promise that confrontation was inevitable and she'd "crochet" a plan to face Perses. "She told you that too? That she had some sort of plan? What is it?"

"She wouldn't share the details with me, but I think I know, and . . ." His lips pursed. "I'm not sure about this."

"About what?"

He remained quiet.

"Jesus . . ." I rubbed my eyes, digging the heels of my palms into them. "It's about the table. You won't talk about the table."

More silence, but a sad twitch of his lips. Yep.

"I've been wondering about that. Is it just you being super committed to a job you're not even getting paid for, or is it, I don't know, physical? Like you couldn't talk about the table even if you wanted to?"

Again, he didn't reply but instead held up his right hand, whose wrist was bound by his tattoo. "We call it an *eterathis*. It means a contract weaved in one's flesh. My *eterathis* compels me to protect the table's secrets. I must not reveal its nature, nor its content." My intuition had been correct, then. The tattoo wasn't just the actual source of his power, it was also the chain that kept him tied to the table.

"But Palombara spilled the beans, so it makes no difference," I remarked.

Faust's chest heaved. Not quite a sigh. "She's not bound by any contract. She's free to reveal what she knows."

"But she doesn't know everything, like how to unseal the table," I completed.

His shoulders shifted in a lazy shrug. "My turn to ask the questions," he announced.

"You can always try," I replied.

The mattress bounced under us as he rolled to his side, resting his weight on one elbow. "You said your father was Italian at dinner."

"Yeah."

"And you told me earlier that you came to visit him, but you haven't seen him yet."

I frowned. "Is there an actual question coming?"

"Yes. Why haven't you seen him yet?" Faust asked, his voice softening.

A shiver spread in my chest, an ache that never really went away. Sometimes the pain would dull, and I'd even forget about it altogether because life was too loud, too fast for me to stop and think about it. But now I was safe, alone in that quiet room with Faust, and he wanted to pick at the scab, see what it concealed. I sat up, gathering my knees to my chest. "I don't know if you've noticed, but I've been pretty busy since I arrived in Rome. I'll see him later—if I live long enough for that."

Faust shifted to prop himself on both elbows, his head raised as if he could see me. "You told me it was complicated. How so?"

Just my luck: the one guy on earth who actually filed every single word you told him. I gritted my teeth and curled tighter as if turning into a compact ball might shield me from his gentle probing. "Why do you care?"

"Because I'm curious about the woman hiding under that coarse shell."

I inched farther toward the edge of the bed, unsettled by his statement. I wasn't sure anyone had ever called me a woman before or suggested that there could be more to me than meets the eye—I always thought I was pretty straightforward about who I was. I caught my reflection in the gilded mirror of a dressing table across the room. A pale girl with messy hair and bitten nails glowered back at me. Not a woman, not frail, nice, or that kind of stuff. More like a sturdy gutter cat, the kind you'd expect to get up and scramble away with a limp after it's been hit by a car. "It's just more shell under the shell," I replied. "And that stuff with my dad, it's not really interesting. There's no huge drama or anything like that. I barely know him, to be honest."

He sat up like I had with his legs crossed. "Shell all the way through, huh? I like a good challenge. So, absent father, correct?"

I could have lied, or even lashed out at him, but oddly I didn't feel like it. I was tired of tasting that sweet release of adrenaline every time I got mad, only to crash down minutes after. I gave a trembling sigh, and said, "He'd visit on weekends once in a while, but he never filed for paternity, and he returned to Italy when I was seven. I haven't seen him since. No calls, nothing. He basically ghosted us."

"I'm sorry to hear that, Emma," Faust murmured.

I shrugged. "That's just life. I did just fine without him, but a few months ago, I started to think maybe I needed closure, to know if he was even still alive. I found him on Facebook, and the rest is just . . ." I flicked my wrist. "A series of bad decisions."

"Did he refuse to see you?" Faust asked, shifting closer on the bed until his arm brushed my shoulder.

I snorted. "Not even that. I landed in Rome, but I didn't have the balls to call him or stalk him, and then I ran into Lily, and I met *you*, and things just went downhill from there, in case you didn't notice."

He ducked his head with a sheepish smile. "I'm sorry for getting in the way."

"Don't be." I gazed at Faust's reflection next to mine in the mirror. He'd always been here. Even when I didn't know he existed, Faust had been part of my life. The mistakes may have been all mine, but he'd set the beat. He'd stilled some of the best and worst moments of my life. My throat went tight. I didn't want to tell him, but the words spilled out. "You stopped time, the last time I saw him."

His eyes widened, but he remained silent.

"It's not really a bad memory," I added quickly. "We ate a hot dog and looked at dumb seagulls on the beach. It was okay. And after that, you got me in and out of trouble a few times when I was older."

His smile returned, mixed with an emotion I couldn't decipher—that was at once pain and happiness. "I didn't want to ask, but I did wonder what it was like . . . for you."

My heart tightened. "I thought I was crazy. So crazy I didn't even dare telling it to the shrinks my mom sent me to. I thought they'd lock me up if I told them I could feel time stop. I'm just glad you didn't do it often. I think it helped me stay sane. I remember that nothing happened for almost a year when I was fourteen, and I thought, 'It's over; I'm cured.'"

He gave a nod of understanding. "I am not allowed to use Chronos's power in vain. What qualifies as vain, however, is left to my appreciation."

I smiled. "No stopping time to catch the bus?"

"Sadly, no."

I ran a hand over my mouth. "You know, I was so fucking angry when it started happening again . . . Good thing we didn't meet when I was fifteen. I'd have kicked your balls real deep up your ass."

Faust winced. "They'd have healed anyway, but I'd rather not think about it."

"Anyway, most of the time I'd just freak out and wait until it was over." I spared him the darkest details. I didn't want to look back on those times of utter distress. "I think it helped me distance myself, being so sure I wasn't sure it wasn't real. But there's been moments . . . moments when I used it to my advantage, and afterwards I'd convince myself things happened differently—that it was just luck with a side of hallucinations." I chewed the inside of my cheek, seeing myself stagger out of a Walgreens with free makeup, or running away from a run-down squat in Hunt Points before a 'friend' could introduce me to her pimp. "Nevermind. Let's just say not everything I ever fucked up was because of you or my mom."

"Your mother?" In the mirror, Faust's double cocked his head, intrigued. I retreated to the head of the bed and huddled against the fluffy lace pillows, mentally smacking myself for the slip. It was too late though. The mattress moaned, and sank as Faust moved to lie closer to me. "Emma?" His voice was infinitely cautious as if he feared I might detonate any second. "What Lady Palombara said this afternoon . . . I think she was only trying to—"

"She was right," I rasped, studying the floral pattern on the blue brocade bedspread to avoid his silvery gaze. "I know she wanted to mess with me, but it worked because she was right . . . about everything."

"You two don't get along?"

At once a simple question and an impossible equation chalked on a blackboard. I'd heard those words so many times from well-meaning counselors and shrinks when they leaned back in their chair and tried to look me in the eye. My best defense had always been stubborn silence; at first to protect myself, then because it was the only way for me to win, to feel powerful. I could never make my mom love me, could never be Lily's equal in her eyes. What I had were two perfectly working middle fingers to flip off the rest of the world.

Faust waited, his head turned toward me on his pillow. Lady Palombara had said that too, that he was one of the most patient persons she knew . . . Words welled in my chest and died just as fast; bubbles of pain and anger that wouldn't come out. I reached to the nightstand and tugged at the chain hanging from a Chinese vase lamp there. I preferred darkness.

I rolled to my side, looking away from him. "We were never close, even when I was a kid. I think she had me too young, and it didn't help that she hated my dad. She thought he was a huge loser. She took care of me, but I noticed we didn't really talk or hug like the other kids did with their parents. We were roommates," I murmured.

"Never more?" Faust asked.

"No," I rasped, a shameful prickling in my eyes. "Not long after my dad disappeared for good, she got a fresh start with Lily's dad. Lily had lost her mom very young, and there was this insta-love between her and my mom, and you know, the great grades, being a cute little girl with a big heart and shit . . . I just couldn't compete with that."

"You were jealous." That wasn't a question, but his tone held no reproach, not even pity; it was almost tender.

I sighed and tossed on the mattress, staring up at the swirls of blue brocade on the canopy bed's ceiling. I couldn't find the courage to look at Faust while I bared myself like that, but it was still better than just having my back to him like he wasn't here. "You bet. I turned into a little turd over the next few years because I was just so pissed there was no room for me in the picture. The three of them were a family, and I was like, 'hold on—what do you mean, 'club's full?'"

Faust gave me a knowing smile, the sort I'd seen all my life, and for a second, I hated him almost as much as I hated myself. "This is very common among children whose parents enter a new relationship. Perhaps your mother—"

"Plot twist. When I turned twelve, she dumped me in a

boarding school upstate, and she kept Lily."

There was a beat of stunned silence before his eyebrows jerked. "Was that . . . a permanent relocation?"

"Sort of. In the first few months, I'd go home every two weeks, but we stopped doing that because I'd just fight with my mom, steal some cash, and spend the rest of the day out. So, she came up with strategies to keep me away: camps, summer schools . . . I think she tried everything except kennels. They had to take me home every year for Christmas though, and it drove her totally insane." I snorted. "I went to three different schools because I kept stirring shit and getting expelled, and when I hit eighteen, I just grabbed my backpack and took off."

Faust shifted closer. Ever closer, in every way. His hand found mine in the dark, grazing it as if to read the lines of my palm.

I swallowed. "And now I'm a waitress at Tuna Town, and most people think I'm joking when I tell them about it. And . . . I guess that's it." I gave an awkward chuckle in a desperate effort to cut through the tension.

He squeezed my hand a little. Heat seeped where our skin touched. I shivered from the foreign, oddly intimate sensation. "I see," he said at last.

I figured we were done. I'd given him a bone to chew, a nice, abridged summary of my life. Twenty years of going nowhere until a capricious god, hiding somewhere in another dimension had decided to place a black hole where all magic ended inside me. I sighed, tried to close my eyes. Maybe I could doze a little, forget until the sun rose over Lady Palombara's secret world.

But then, Faust let go of my hand. His fingers traveled upwards, to brush a stray lock of hair away from my cheek, and he asked, "Emma, how long did you stay on the street?"

I went rigid, my neurons suddenly fast-forwarding through a thousand shitty memories. I rolled to my side to present him with my back—my shell—but I could still feel the warmth of his body, lying inches from mine. He waited, always so fucking patient. A silent pressure built between us, pulsing with the blood under my temples.

My chest hurt, and my eyes were hot with tears that wouldn't come out. A brittle murmur escaped my lips, and I heard myself reply, "I always think it's written all over my face and it's, like, the first thing people see. But you're actually blind . . . so I guess it's kind of a whole new low."

I felt his hand brush down my back, petting me like his cats, I thought. "Few of my dates ever sat down with me for a nice bout of panhandling . . . You seemed in your element."

Did I? Maybe he was right, and I belonged outside no matter what. How long until I unraveled again, and my ass landed back on Madison? My nose prickled, and I wanted to sniff so bad, but I didn't want him to know he'd made me cry over that shit. "I didn't stay that long," I eventually mumbled. "Less than a year and a half, after I dropped out. My school was upstate in Uthica. I took the bus back to New York, and after that, I just . . . hung around, I guess. Got small jobs I didn't keep—probably smoked too much too. I went to a couple shelters, but I figured I was better off on my own. I knew a few squats, so I didn't sleep out on the street that often."

"You didn't ask for your family's help?" Faust probed softly.

"Not a chance," I snapped. I welcomed that zing of anger in my veins; it reminded me that I was strong in spite of it all. "Lily said my mom called the cops after I went AWOL, but they dropped the ball because it wasn't a kidnapping or anything." I shrugged. "Took me a while to get back on my feet, but in the end, I went to see a social worker in a shelter, and I just said, 'look, I'm broke, I'm on the street, I want out, and I'm ready to be serious about it'."

The smile returned in his voice as he noted, "I recognize your tenacity."

I rolled to my side to face him in the dark. "This has to be the longest I've ever discussed my life with anyone, you know . . ."

Faust's head dipped closer to mine. "I've been told I'm a good listener."

"And it's a great way for you to avoid talking about yourself," I sighed, turning my head to avoid his lips. His beard grazed my cheek, soft and rough curls tangled together; goose bumps peppered my nape in response. I bit my lower lip, increasingly aware of the quiet tension lacing the air between us, the way he breathed my hair deeply—we were in a bed, and we'd taken off our socks, after all. "I'm not sleeping with you," I reminded him, allowing my head to drop on a fluffy pillow that smelled faintly of lavender. Man, that was nice, and I was fast losing the struggle to keep my eyes open.

At my side, Faust settled in his half of the bed with a low purr. "I can wait. I have all the time in the world."

XXIX

Tap, tap.

A familiar sound woke me up, the echo of a dream still clinging to me. I couldn't remember what it was I had dreamed of, except Faust had been in it . . . I blinked puffy eyes at the blue brocade tapestry on the walls, the stripe of blinding white peeking between navy curtains. Lady Palombara had changed her mind: it was snowing again in the park. Flakes swirled behind the window, adding to the smooth coat covering the balcony and the park beyond.

My gaze drifted to the golden bowed legs of the dressing table, the mirror atop. I wasn't alone in bed. Faust snored softly at my side. In dawn's bleak light I saw the hole in his T-shirt. I smiled to myself; he really needed a fresh one.

I didn't mean to wake him, but the mattress bounced when I sat up, shaking him slightly. His snoring hitched and ended with a grunt, then a yawn. He propped himself on his elbows with a lazy grin. His voice still husky with sleep, he said, "I dreamed that I woke up in bed with a beautiful woman, after a night of—"

"Nothing. It was a night of nothing, and . . ." I wrinkled my nose. "You need to wash your feet and everything else too."

His eyebrows wiggled under the mess of blond curls. "As you do. I can think of a solution that would solve both our problems."

I let myself fall back and sink into the feather duvet with a groan.

"You never give up, do you?"

"Et res non semper spes mihi semper adest," he declaimed in his singing Latin accent, with a dramatic flourish of his hand.

"Sure . . ." I agreed, then rubbed my eyes.

"My hopes are not always realized, but I always hope—from the great Ovid."

I chuckled. "I'll stick to Aerosmith's version if that's okay with you."

His brow creased but then he got it, and there it was, his Faustiest smile. "Dream until your dreams come true? Oh Emma, Emma . . ." he purred. "How can I ever give up when you wile me so?"

"That's me, wiling all the time." I sighed, dragging myself out of bed to inspect a delicately painted door near the dressing table. Naked girls around a fountain—I turned the porcelain knob and peeked inside—Yup, that was the bathroom. I raised an eyebrow at the massive clawfoot tub peeking from behind an ancient Chinese screen where colorful fish swam against a golden background; that looked like the most expensive bath I'd ever take in my life . . . "Calling dibs on the bathroom," I announced.

Faust fell back on the bed, silver peeking between his half-closed lids. "This old infirm will wait for his turn, and dream of the silk of your skin."

I leaned against the door, a lopsided grin dancing on my lips. "You know that's basically harassment, right?"

He winked. "Only if you ask me to stop."

My mouth opened, only to close without a sound. There was a foreign flutter in my chest, and maybe he had a point.

I was tying my hair in a high ponytail when Faust came out of the bathroom, smelling of the same flowery soap I'd used not long ago. I glanced over my shoulder. My eyes went wide, and laughter erupted from my throat before I could stop it. "Please don't bite me," I managed in between chuckles.

He felt for the balloon sleeves and neck ruffles of his clean white shirt—kindly provided by either Palombara or Ryuuko to replace his holed-out tee. "These used to be all the rage you know."

I crossed the room to inspect his new look. "In the Middle Ages?"

"How provincial of you." He rolled amused eyes and sobered. "Do you feel better?"

"You mean ready?"

"Yes," he admitted.

"I don't even know what I need to be ready for, so ignorance is bliss, I guess."

He went to sit on the bed to slip on his boots, which lay near the bed. I winced when he pulled yesterday's dirty socks from his pants pocket and slipped them back on. "Theia won't leave us in the dark much longer."

"Theia, that's how you called her yesterday. It's her first name?" I nudged one of the boots closer, so he could grab it.

He took it with a grateful smile. "Theia the Bright, yes."

I sat by his side on the fluffy duvet, watching him fasten his laces. "And Palombara, it's just a pseudo?"

His fingers paused in their work, and I realized that a solemn expression had chased his usual smile. "It was her husband's name. Massimiliano Palombara, Marquis of Pietraforte. All you see here was built by him."

I went through several stages of shock and disbelief before I managed to reply. "Like, he built the dimension?"

"No," Faust corrected. "He was human. He had the villa and the park built in 1650, as a green retreat on the Esquiline for Theia and himself." He let out an unsteady breath. "After his death, Theia used most of the power she had left to create this place, a dimension where the villa would forever remain preserved from the ravages of time."

My brow lifted in amazement. "So, it's a copy?"

"The original building fell to ruins and was destroyed by the city at the end of the nineteenth century to rebuild the Esquiline district."

I pondered Faust's revelation and the sorrow creasing lines around his mouth in stunned silence. "She must have loved him a lot, to marry him even though she knew he'd grow old . . ."

"He did not," Faust said. His hand searched mine. "He was the man you saw in the Libro."

I gripped his fingers tight, holding onto him as the room seemed to tilt around. *His was a mind like no other, fascinated by the hidden nature of things, that so few humans understand. I'll tell you about him someday.* The mystery sorcerer. The man who had defied death with an embalming spell and tried to summon Perses in his fight against Faust . . . was Lady Palombara's late husband? Maybe that was her other, hidden reason for helping us. Montecito was barreling down the same slope which had killed the man she loved. Palombara knew better than any of us what kind of pull Perses exerted over those he chose. But . . . "You're the one who killed him," I murmured, struggling aloud to make sense of all this. "And she's still your friend?"

Faust brought our joined hands to his heart, almost unconsciously, it seemed. His skin was warm against my palm through the fine linen; the feeling sent my pulse racing. "She couldn't, so I did it for her. He wanted things Theia could never give him, and that desperate need destroyed him." His jaw clenched. "It had to end, and he left me no choice when he tried to summon Perses."

"He wanted true immortality?"

"More than this." Faust shook his head. "He wanted a child."

The oldest human instinct. I studied Faust's hand, still holding mine on his lap. My heart broke a little for Palombara, even though we barely knew each other. I wasn't exactly great at the whole feelings and empathy game, but this, I could understand: the unbearable grief of loving someone and knowing you can never be enough for them. "She lives in her memories," I said, my voice brittle. And that was the real reason Palombara was unable to fight Perses: because she had wasted all she had—all of herself—to preserve a memory of the villa and her husband.

"I envy her," Faust admitted.

I looked up at him, my brow furrowed in mild shock.

"Only a great love can hurt so much."

"There's nothing to envy," I replied, snatching my hand back from his grasp. "Anyone is better off alone than going through that kind of emotional meatgrinder." It scared me just thinking about it. I never wanted to experience the kind of love that had wrecked Palombara—or turned Lily's brain into oatmeal whenever that bag of dicks Dante was around.

Not that I even understood it in the first place; I didn't have that kind of love in me. Mine was a tiny rotten fruit my parents had spit out long ago. It was full of jealousy and disappointment, of spite and heartache. As a result, the longest I'd ever stayed with a guy was a couple of months back in high school—serious relationship and all—and my definition of romance was to flirt with a lone customer at closing time, follow him home and nail him savagely on his couch before grabbing the last beer in his fridge and going home to sleep in my own bed.

And it was just fine like that. It was . . .

I jolted when Faust's fingers reached to thread in a strand of my hair. He thumbed it with a sense of wonder on his features. "What is she thinking about, this fearsome blue-haired princess I can't still?"

This, right here, was the kind of trouble I needed to stay clear from. The rational part of me recognized his silky murmur and cheesy lines for what they were: a not-so-elaborate tactic to bang me, but, if I was being honest with myself, I liked the way his voice caressed my skin. I liked that he was always so calm, that he could peel my layers off so easily and soothe me in the same breath, without even trying.

"Nothing . . ." I mumbled.

He smiled, as if he didn't really need to ask because he could read my thoughts like Palombara. I chewed the inside of my lip. Maybe I was overthinking this; Faust didn't exactly have Prince Charming written all over him, and he wasn't trying to sell me forever after. He just wanted a little bit of now. I risked a hand to his cheek, grazing his beard. It was rough in places but overall softer than I expected, and so many shades of golden, sandy here, a few near-silvery hairs there. He purred and turned to mouth my fingertips, sending a warm shiver sizzling all the way to my toes.

Normally, this was the part where I rolled atop him and took things in hand—all of them. But I wanted to stay like this a little longer, sitting on a big bed somewhere inside a snow globe as his face inched closer, and pretend it was romantic. Faust cupped my face, his fingertips tracing my jaw, the bridge of my nose. My lips. I let him. My eyes half-closed in a daze. I basked in the unexpected tenderness of the moment, listened to the rhythm of our quiet breathing.

It's complicated, but basically, we didn't make it to first base because of a badly taxidermized fox.

The fox was in Ryuuko's hand when the bedroom door slammed open. Faust and I jerked apart awkwardly. She saw us. Froze. It was beyond awkward, fricking embarrassing really, and I felt even shittier because I knew it must have hurt her, walking onto us . . . well, technically we hadn't kissed.

She took a sharp breath and marched to the bed. My cheeks were blazing while Faust scratched his hair in mild confusion. She tossed the fox onto the bedspread, her brown gaze burning with repressed rage. "I made as a gift."

Wow. What a coincidence, since she'd served us *fox* for dinner. Of course, Ryuuko was an adult—possibly an immortal one, at that—surely, she wouldn't taxidermize dinner's fox to gift it to me and make things even weirder between us. I squirmed away from the mangled mess of orange fur covering stiff limbs that stuck out at odd angles. Faust grappled for it and ran his fingers over the fox's grimacing maw, tracing bulging glass eyes and the long pink tongue dangling from its wide-open mouth. "It's a masterpiece. Another raccoon?"

Ryuuko's bob rippled like black silk as she shook her head. "*Fox.*"

His fingers skittered down the creature's back to meet a fluffy tail. "Obviously. My bad."

She took the fox from his hands abruptly and shoved it in mine.

"For you. Now we're friends."

Yeah, right . . . My gaze traveled between her and the monstrosity sitting on my lap. "Thanks, I guess. It'll look great," *In the garbage.* "atop my fridge."

She gave a sharp nod. "You do that. You put it on your fridge."

"Ryuuko has a passion for taxidermy," Faust thought it useful to explain. "And the skill to go with it."

Another brutal nod. "I like research."

The stiff smile I'd been trying to keep on my lips unhooked with a sinister creaking sound only I could hear. Research. The kind of research she'd been planning to do with Faust's body. I peeked down at the fox's canted snarl, a sinking feeling in my stomach. I wasn't staying alone in a room with her. Ever.

She narrowed her eyes at me—gauging what I'd look like once taxidermized?—and said, "Now she wants to see you. You leave your gift here."

No need to ask twice. I dropped Ryuuko's masterpiece on the bed, and Faust and I got up to follow her. She pivoted on her heels without another look, leading us down the hallway where birds still shivered and flew from one branch to another. I hadn't dared last night, but this time I ventured trembling fingers toward the living painting.

Ryuuko's voice cracked like a whip. "You don't touch."

She glared at me over her shoulder. I pursed my lips and mumbled, "Sorry."

We went down a flight of stairs, crossed the salon, and a deserted two-level library, crammed with ancient books all the way to the ceiling. Ryuuko eventually stopped in front of a set of massive, red-lacquer doors. She pressed her palm to a golden disc-shaped lock with one of those complicated Asian symmetrical patterns. The lock gave a faint click, and she pushed the doors open, revealing a laboratory from another time.

My gaze was immediately drawn upward, to the vast canopy dome looming over our heads, some twenty feet high. A coat of snow had gathered all around it like a milky crown, but in its center was a splash of pearly sky. Once I'd managed to tear my eyes away from the sight, I took in the hundreds of shelves and drawers lining the walls all around me from floor to ceiling: more boxes, jars, books, and . . . more taxidermized shit than I had ever seen in my entire life.

Standing in the middle of this madness was Lady Palombara, her hands demurely folded over a salmon silk dress and the long white apron covering it. I couldn't help it, the moment our eyes met, everything Faust had said came back to me. Was she thinking about her husband right now? How did it feel for her to help us face Perses and Montecito? Was it a form of revenge, or maybe after so long, the pain had turned into something else, the lingering ache of dull grief? The corner of her mouth twitched, and I remembered too late that it was a bad idea to think around her.

"I would do it all over again," she said, answering the question simmering at the back of my mind, "and if it had been possible, I would have turned my Ichor into blood for him, not the other way around."

"Ichor?" I asked.

"It is the name we give to our essence. Long ago, humans pictured Ichor flowing in the veins of titans, instead of all too mortal blood." She smiled. "Poetic, but quite incorrect: we would need veins for that to be possible."

My eyes fell to her pale hands and widened a fraction. Smooth, save for the delicate outline of her knuckles. Like Montecito's, Palombara's body was an envelope, nothing more. I looked down at the back of Faust's hands in contrast, and the lines snaking under his skin, chaotic paths that reassured me there was still a part of humanity in him—as he'd claimed earlier.

"Faust's nature is different than mine," Palombara confirmed softly.

Whereas she merely possessed a human appearance, Faust remained flesh and blood. Did that mean he could . . .

"No," Palombara answered before the question could truly take shape in my mind. "Chronos spared him the torment of having to bury his children."

I registered the shadow passing in Faust's gaze when she said that, thought of his unknown child killed so long ago, and it was all it took for anger to flare in my veins. "Like he spared him the torment of seeing again?"

"Emma," he sighed. "There's no point . . ."

"No point in ever asking why?" I replied, fighting the frustration mounting inside me, that made my head feel too hot and my skin too tight.

He gave a nod.

I swallowed the lump in my throat. "It's not fair! It's worse than just living your life thinking your luck is shit. It's someone . . . something out there, who decided for you that you'd be bumping into furniture for the next two-thousand years, and you're not allowed to question that, only bear with it?"

"Fate works like that." His voice sounded weary, defeated, but then his smile returned, chasing the clouds in his eyes. He winked. "Not all of it is bad."

I wanted to stay pissed, but I feared his brand of lazy optimism was getting to me; I could see he had a point. No matter how rough, our roads were peppered with tiny blessings: great weed, cheap beer . . . new friends. "If you say so," I muttered.

Palombara's hands clapping put an end to our debate. She

tucked a pearly gray curl behind her ear. "As humans like to say, idle hands are the devil's workshop. Let's get to work."

I took another look around at the bizarre junk and thousands of jars crammed on the shelves. "This is your magic lab?"

"We do *research*," Ryuuko corrected, her back to a lone table where stood an unfinished . . . okay, I had no idea what that was. A platypus maybe? With teeth?

"But that's not why I brought you here," Lady Palombara chided her. She glided to Faust, her face glowing with a sort of motherly love that made me uncomfortable because I didn't fully understand it. He had killed her husband when she didn't have the strength to, and somehow, it only deepened their bond instead of shattering it. She told him, "I wanted to give you something I thought you might need soon enough."

He cocked a curious eyebrow as she went to open a long drawer labeled with Greek signs and retrieved a shiny golden crochet vest. "We wouldn't want you to catch a cold." She placed the garment in his hands. "Put it on; I'm sure it'll fit you like a glove."

Faust couldn't see how tacky his new vest was, but he seemed troubled nonetheless as his fingers felt for the soft material. "May I ask where the wool came from?" he asked, buttoning the front over the ruffles of his shirt. Man, he looked like a lighthouse.

"With this, he doesn't make a hole in your chest again," Ryuuko stated icily.

He—as in *Perses*? I stiffened, my gaze fleeting between the two women. Lady Palombara gave a soft chuckle. "He's decided to become a hero; let him fight his war wearing the golden fleece."

My jaw fell all the way down to my chest. She'd given him . . . a divine Kevlar.

Faust patted the vest with hesitant hands. "Theia, it's very precious. Are you sure?"

She feigned a pout. "Don't you like it? I found the pattern on the Internet."

Since his mouth appeared unable to form words at the moment, I stepped in to express the proper level of shock. "Hang on; rewind. What do you mean Faust decided to become a hero?"

"He disagreed with me at first, but he's been thinking about it since last night." She grazed his forearm tenderly. "You don't guard the table; you guard Chronos's power. Wherever it lives."

His left hand rose to thumb the tattoo circling his right one, almost like an unconscious gesture. "I hope you're right."

She reached to tap said tattoo with her forefinger. "Your *eterathis* would stop you if it wasn't the right thing to do," she countered.

So, it *was* physical. That tattoo could control him if he strayed from his contract . . . I looked back and forth between them. "What do you want him to do? Is it about your kamikaze plan, like you said last night?"

Palombara laid kind eyes on me. "Yes. If neither hiding nor leaving the table at Lady Montecito and Perses's mercy is an option, then perhaps the time has come to unseal it once and for all."

My brow shot up to meet my hairline. "Isn't that exactly what we're trying to avoid?"

"We unseal the table and put all the power in the testicle. We give Faust a new baetylus. A better one," Ryuuko explained.

My arms dangling at my sides, I could almost hear the cogs whirring in my brain in a desperate bid to process both halves of her sentence. "Should I ask what's a baetylus first, or are we going to unpack that testicle comment?"

"Both excellent questions," Palombara agreed. "But first,

Ryuuko dear, bring us the cane."

I swear I caught a disdainful sneer on Ryuuko's lips, but it happened so fast, and a millisecond after she had already reverted to her default deadpan self. She went to fetch a wooden cane I hadn't noticed lying behind her mangled platypus. She took Faust's right hand gently and placed the cane in it. "To replace." The corners of her lips lifted a fraction. "Now you have a vine staff again, centurion."

I wasn't sure why a centurion would specifically need a vine staff, but . . . Ryuuko could smile, which was the biggest news here. I pursed my lips tightly, so they wouldn't part in amazement.

"Thank you, Ryuuko," Faust said. He seemed just as troubled by this new gift. His fingers trailed up and down the tormented curves of the long cane.

"It looks exactly the same," I noted.

Faust shook his head. "Not quite."

He turned the staff in his hands, revealing a rough purple gem encased in the hilt, buried in a wood knot as if the vine had grown around it. Judging by the shape, the whole thing must be the size of an egg. Despite its grainy surface, it caught the light in places, casting odd lavender flares on his hand.

I nearly raised a hand to touch it, but I remembered what had happened to Faust's previous cane and shoved guilty fingers back in my hoodie pocket. "What kind of stone is it?" I asked, studying the careful movement of Faust's thumb as it brushed the gem over and over.

"It's for our plan," Ryuuko informed me.

Lady Palombara rested her pale fingers over Faust's rugged and tanned ones. "I have no idea what became of its twin, but I managed to hold on to this one for all those years. Perhaps my greatest treasure, and yet I never imagined it would be of any use. But now

I see there will never be a better purpose for it."

I eyed the purple gem doubtfully. "It's not really a testicle, right?"

Lady Palombara's mouth pursed to stifle a guilty chortle. "Oh, it is. It was once one of our father Ouranos's . . . attributes. But it's long been petrified," she quickly added, as if that made it okay.

I shot her a look of silent outrage. She had given him her dad's ball. Like, literally.

Faust winced. "It's somewhat metaphorical, Emma. Ouranos was an entity so vast and so complex you can't really describe him in human terms. What you see is a fragment of a primordial deity, a stone imbued with an infinitesimal fraction of its power—in short, a baetylus."

Exactly like the table, I realized—except this one appeared to be portable.

In Lady Palombara's eyes, the galaxies darkened, swirling menacingly. "Chronos cut them off; it's a fitting fate that his power should be sealed in them." When she noticed the consternation on my face, she plastered her sweet mask back on and waved my unspoken concern off. "We titans were a rowdy bunch in our youth."

Faust cleared his throat. "Chronos overthrew his father, and well . . . he wanted to make a clear point."

"That he'd nut whoever tried to resist him?"

He grimaced. "Sort of, but in truth, there wasn't much left of Ouranos when Chronos took his remains apart. It was more a symbol, to take away that which made him his father in the first place."

I shook my head slowly. "I don't understand any of this. *What's the plan?*"

"Oh, you two are going to surrender to Lady Montecito," Palombara replied, like an afterthought. "And once you have and she takes you to the table, Faust will unseal it."

I eyed the purple nut. "And you think that thing could suck in the table's power before Montecito or Perses does?" Her lips stirred—as good as a yes. I went on, "But what happens once it's done? Can Faust kill Perses with his new cane?"

"Of course not." She plunged her gaze into mine but didn't bother completing her explanation.

"So, I need to cover for the two of us," I ventured. "If he tries to get Faust, I step in, and I buy us time to escape."

"You're stupid." Ryuuko's voice knifed me.

"Hey, I thought we were over that shit—"

Faust thankfully spoke before I could yell, 'You wanna go at me?' and subsequently bludgeon her with her half-assed platypus. "Emma doesn't need to come. If I manage to channel the table's power into the baetylus, I may not be able to kill Perses, but . . ." His eyes narrowed in a determined glare, but his throat worked in vain. God, I wished I could have ripped that fucking contract off his wrist. "I can do this," he said at last. "No one wins against time."

I studied him, intrigued by the implications. What were the table's true powers, once unleashed? Could he control time entirely? Kick Perses's ass all the way back to Jurassic Park or that kind of thing?

"Are you sure you can beat him?" I darted a guilty glance at Palombara, before adding, "You were able to stop Massimiliano because he never managed to summon the Spear; he tried, but you got him before it appeared completely. It's different for Montecito; obviously, she went all the way, and back at the station, you couldn't freeze her or Perses's shadows," I recounted, trying—and likely failing—to filter the worry out of my voice.

Ryuuko's lips quivered with barely repressed anger, but she didn't speak to me. She turned to Lady Palombara instead. "She doesn't see; she's too stupid."

Okay, the truce was over for good. She could shove her fox up her ass. "Hey," I snarled. "How about we sort this shit out with a good old arm wrestling match?"

She balled her small fists. Lady Palombara took a step aside to shield her. "Emma, dear, *language*." Her posture relaxed, her hands folding back over her apron. "And to answer your question: no, Faust can't hope to succeed alone. He'll need you."

Our quiet exchange in front of the Porta Alchemica came back to me. *The only reason the black hole is in me is because it needs to be here, right now.* A shudder cascaded from the top of my scalp to the small of my back. Far as I knew, the Omega would only suck in power upon direct contact: Faust could still heal or stop time as long as he didn't touch me or I didn't touch the table—So, if Palombara was so sure Faust would need me, it meant she believed I would have to . . . to—

"Are you afraid?" Palombara asked.

There was no point in lying to her. "I don't want to touch him," I said, my skin crawling at the idea of coming in contact with the dark mass I'd seen swarming around Montecito.

Faust shifted closer to me, his arm brushing mine in silent reassurance. "You won't, Emma."

"I will," I murmured, hating the certainty coiling in my belly. "The only way he can be stopped is if he butts against the Omega. The black hole just wouldn't be in me, right now, if it weren't meant to stop Perses." I shook my head as I tried to work out my thoughts coherently and clutched my middle. "Otherwise, it'd make no sense that it's in me."

Faust's hand skimmed up my arm to rest on my shoulder. "Then it means everything will be all right." He smiled at me then, that soft, radiant smile that melted the heart of gullible Chinese tourists and thawed mine just a little. "I've always been very lucky."

Except there was no luck—only that mysterious path we

followed blindly without knowing where it led—or even why we were walking in the first place. A future was written already, by someone who had decided my purpose for me, and I had never felt so powerless.

"It's quite the opposite, really," Lady Palombara remarked. It took me a second of puzzlement to figure out that she had fricking done it again and read my thoughts. My lips parted to plead her for the umpteenth time *not* to do that, but she swiveled around to go search her shelves before I could start my sentence.

Her fingers fluttered up and down a series of identical wooden drawers, pausing on each painted label before stopping to open a specific one. "I have a magical artifact for you, too, Emma. Something very powerful."

Holy shit—magic that would work even in *my* hands? My shoulders hitched in anticipation, and I had to clasp my hands to prevent their fidgeting as she returned with a black object. A cap. She handed it to me with an infinitely benevolent smile. Faust's curiosity prickled my nape as he bent to me, obviously expecting me to describe the precious gift to him.

I sucked in a sharp breath, my fingers playing on the black visor. The sinister masked figure embroidered on the front of the cap was sadly familiar. *Ha ha ha . . . Fucking hilarious. No, really.*

"It's not magic," I stated, each word wound with offense. "It's Kylo Ren. You gave me a Kylo Ren cap."

Her hand flew to her mouth to suppress a giggle. Ryuuko grinned. *Grinned.*

Faust had the good grace to say, "I liked him in the movies. He's a very interesting character." *And a high-maintenance emo literally no one likes*, I thought.

My gaze snapped up to Lady Palombara, loaded with reproach.

"Thank you. I'm sure it's gonna help. Like, if it rains."

"It may," was her reply.

I considered the cap, my nostrils flaring. When Ryuuko's mocking gaze met mine, I shoved the cap on my head defiantly. "If you say so."

Palombara sighed, one of her hands reaching out. Without touching me. "Emma, the truth is, I have nothing else to give you, no help, no advice. Never in my existence have I stood so close to the Omega; I never even considered the possibility that it might exist inside a human being. I don't understand your power, and to tell it all, it frightens me. The only certainty I have"—she looked at Faust fondly—"is that there is a path."

A path to Faust, a path back to Lily after all those years spent resenting her . . . I looked deep into the stars swirling in Palombara's strange eyes. "But you have no idea what it really is."

Her lips twitched. "Do you want to know what I see?"

"Well, yeah!"

"An Uber."

XXXI

Lady Palombara was an okay psychic. When Ryuuko walked us back to the wall and the Porta Alchemica turned to glittery Jell-O to let us through for the second time, the first thing I noticed was that night had fallen over Rome, and the second was a red Honda minivan conspicuously parked in the street. Silvio stepped out of the van, wearing a camo tracksuit and coordinated Air Max. Yup, we were going to war, indeed.

Once Ryuuko had disappeared behind the walled gate, I darted an anxious look around the deserted street. "Can they find us now that we're outside Lady Palombara's dimension?" I asked Faust.

His lips curled. "I don't think so."

As he said this, Silvio unzipped his jacket, revealing a most unusual piece of bling hanging from a golden chain around his neck. The winged dick guarding Faust's bathroom door—and a crucifix too, just to cover all bases, I figured. "I'm the sacred ground, now," he announced.

Faust raised his palm for Silvio to high-five. A complicated routine ensued during which their fingers twirled, hooked and unhooked several times before Silvio concluded the ritual with a bro punch to Faust's shoulder. "Nice vest," he noted soberly, lowering his sunglasses to check the crocheted golden fleece.

"Have you been able to locate Lily?" Faust inquired.

Silvio pulled out his phone and checked a GPS map. "She's back at the Malespina, working late."

Shit. I'd hoped she'd stay at the Residenza—out of the way. I glanced at the screen. Past midnight; working unusually late, indeed. "The lab is underground," I explained. "If we can get inside the villa, I know the way. But it's probably heavily guarded, and Dante is basically glued to Lily . . ." And I couldn't call her to try and get her away from him because I no longer had her number. I kinda wished Faust hadn't smashed my phone two days ago—admittedly to make it impossible for Katharos to track me. I asked Silvio, "Do you think you could find the lab's extension? Katharos probably listens to the calls, but I just need to bullshit her to get her away from the lab."

He nodded, and his thumbs rapped on the screen, texting someone, I gathered. "Can try to find that."

"Once Lily is out of the way, Dante and the guards won't be a problem either," Faust replied, patting the hilt of his new cane.

"The shadows will be another matter," I reminded him. "You can't still them."

He thumped his chest with a wink. "But this will stop them."

Silvio's mustache twitched in appreciation—he definitely liked Faust's disco vest. "Then jump in. Once you get the girl out of there, I'll take her to safety." He adjusted his glasses as he climbed into the driver seat. "Fast."

I settled next to Faust in the backseat, gripping my door handle to brace myself. Silvio's right hand slammed on the gear stick, and the minivan took off. We bulleted through empty streets and squares, ripped along the ribbon of centenary trees and elegant buildings lining the Tiber. We crossed a bridge, drifted right so hard the tires screeched, and within minutes I recognized the dark pines canopy overlooking the brick wall, the cameras sitting atop and watching everything . . .

Silvio pulled the brakes and pulled out his smartphone. His thumb repeatedly flicked to type in a phone number, and he handed me the phone. "Lab extension. See if you can get her out."

I waited as it rang. Over and over, until a voice in Italian greeted me. My lips parted, but before I could speak, I realized I was listening to a voicemail asking me to leave a message. *Shit.* "Voicemail," I said, giving the phone back to Silvio.

Faust turned to me. "Then we'll have to improvise that part."

Silvio glanced at Faust in the mirror, expecting what came next. Faust nodded back as the rear doors slid open. He unbuckled and raised his cane. When it hit the floor mat, I wondered how it felt for Silvio to know what Faust could do without ever being able to experience it himself. When time restarted, he'd have a split second to come to terms with a whole new reality and act on it.

The shockwave washed over me. Silvio went still. I swallowed the lump in my throat and stepped out of the minivan, into the eerie silence.

"Follow me." I guided Faust down the street, to the iron gates. In the security booth, a pair of guards I didn't recognize sat frozen as we walked past them. Night team, probably. I tried to describe our environment to Faust in tight whispers as we entered the park, should he need to find his way out . . . alone. He picked up on the tremors in my voice, my unsteady breathing. His hand squeezed mine. "We can do this, Emma."

"There's a path," I murmured back, sweat beading under my Kylo cap.

"There is," Faust reassured me.

There was. I mean, literally. Once we'd climbed the stairs leading to the terrace, I saw that the glass doors of the palazzo's first floor were open. The lights were on, bathing the courtyard in a soft golden hue. The Villa Malespina awaited us.

"Everything is open," I told Faust. "I-I think they know we're here."

"Lady Montecito never disappoints . . ."

"Please tell me again Ouranos's magic nut will work," I hissed, setting a trembling foot on the lobby's multicolored marble pattern.

"It will."

Yeah, it better, because already shadows glided across the walls, detaching themselves from frescoes and columns. "There's a welcome committee," I gasped.

"I feel them," Faust replied, his eyes closed. "We must follow them."

I gripped his hand tighter and let him take the lead. His stride was steady, strangely attuned to the ghosts slithering and whispering all around us, shrouding statues like smoke veils, snaking through rooms where Katharos employees' glass desks stood empty.

I recognized the dramatic flight of stairs, the elevator tucked away in a corner. The shadows crawled down the steps, inviting us to the underground level. The lobby's bright spotlight became a dim glow sculpting familiar stone walls. Faust's cane clattered against a final marble step before meeting soft gray carpet. Like the rest of Katharos's building, the floor was empty, its glass and steel curtains wide open.

I drew a shaky breath, watching the shadows glide along crowded bookshelves to disappear down the hallway leading to the lab. "They're taking us to the table," I told Faust.

His mouth curved into a wry smile. "Of course they are . . ."

I readjusted my cap with trembling fingers. "Okay, let's do this."

We stepped into the dark through a gaping steel doorway and took a few steps along the windows encircling the lab. I saw the table first, resting a few feet above the ground on its giant platform, a sleek black curve painted by the glare of the surgical lamps above.

Then I saw her.

Paler than ever, Montecito stood near the table, one hand casually resting on its menacing granite edge. Behind her, Lucius loomed in the shadows, frozen, as were Lily and Dante, caught by Faust's spell while they'd been gazing at the table. Like the lights reflected on the table's surface, the white of their lab coats was almost blinding.

As I feared, Montecito moved, her soft smile freezing the blood in my veins. She gave us a scornful glance over. "By every titan in Othrys, you two look more and more *pathetic* every time I see you . . ."

Faust waved at her, an easy grin cracking through his beard. "Are you surprised to see me, my lady?"

The corner of her mouth quivered into a sneer. "No. He whispered to me you still lived."

I contracted the muscles in my legs to stop my knees from buckling. "Perses?"

She shrugged an eyebrow, the movement creasing not a single wrinkle in the pearly skin of her forehead. "He knows what you know too," she breathed, like a secret.

Each word crawled under my skin, and I couldn't help but dart a look around the room, wondering if unseen eyes were watching me right now. "He speaks to you in your head, right?"

"We're bound," was her reply. But she wasn't looking at me; she was looking at Faust.

He gave a slow nod. "So I see."

She took a single step forward. "You've come to unseal the table. He *knows*."

My heart stopped and became a rock that plopped down directly to the pit of my stomach. No plan, no path—just a fucking trap. I shot a desperate look at Faust, who clung to his enigmatic smile like a shield. "And he's so smart. But then, he also knows we're here to trade our services in exchange for Lily's freedom."

Montecito damn near rolled her eyes, which looked supremely weird on her waxy features. "Must we absolutely drag human concerns in matters of immortals and titans?" she huffed, flicking an imaginary speck of dust from her skintight black turtleneck.

"Then let her go," I managed. "We have a car waiting outside. I'm sure *he* knows that too."

Faust confirmed. "Emma will take Lily with her. Once they're in the car, I'll unseal the table for you."

I looked up at him, renewed fear roaring in my skull. That wasn't the plan. If Montecito was fighting with Perses's power, I *needed* to stay here. Leaving Faust to face her alone sure wasn't the fricking path.

The bitch crossed her arms, allowing a beat of unbearable silence to drift our way. She shook her head. "Emma stays with us. He knows exactly what you have in mind . . ."

"Does he?" Faust asked. "Then how about we throw a little chaos in our plan?"

She understood before I did, and the quiver of her eyebrows was my only warning. Faust's fist curled tight around the gem encrusted in the hilt, and he hit the floor once. The second after was a bang as time roared back to life. Lucius, Dante, and Lily came alive in the same instant. Anger flashed in Lucius's eyes, while in Lily's I read shock and, almost immediately, fear. Dante's eyebrows, on the other hand . . . they barely twitched. He took in Faust's and my sudden presence with supreme self-control, resting a proprietary hand on Lily's shoulder—out of habit, maybe. My calves tensed from the urge to leap at her and shove him away.

Montecito switched to damage-control mode faster than me,

shifting closer to Lily with a compassionate smile. "Allow me to explain. You must be so scared . . ."

But Lily said, "No." Her entire body shook like a leaf, and she wouldn't stop blinking in obvious panic, but she found her voice and gritted out that same word a second time. "No. I am . . . not scared."

Renewed tension whipped across the room, painted on Montecito's smooth features, thrumming through Faust's rigid posture. I saw the shadows swirl and gather around them . . . flying to Lily's tightly curled fist. I'm not sure if it happened incredibly fast, or if time stretched and thickened as Lily's hand moved. I recognized the terrifying edge of Perses's hissing spear, but I couldn't process that it was now *Lily* wielding it.

Montecito's eyes went wide. Her lips parted in a silent gasp. A tremor zinged up my legs in response, but I couldn't move. I couldn't lift a finger as Lily stabbed her straight through the heart.

For the first time, I saw wrinkles appear on Leonora Montecito's skin, spreading fast like a disease around her eyes and mouth, painting a mask of agony.

Montecito reeled as the spear plunged deeper and eventually dissipated in Lily's hands. The moment it was gone, Lily staggered back into Dante's arms. They closed around her, as tender as his eyes were cold.

Faust seemed just as shocked and lost as I was—likely even more so since he couldn't see them. When his cane rose to shield me from whatever was happening, I managed to croak out. "Lily . . . what the fuck?"

A grimace of pain clawed at her features. Tears came, rolled down her cheeks, pooled at the corners of her lips as she struggled for air, but she wouldn't answer. She watched Montecito collapse near the table and clutch at the gaping hole in her chest. In the second that followed, Lucius snapped out of his own shock and lunged to his knees to catch her. I noticed for the first time that the arm I'd torn off in the morning was still missing, replaced by a dark prosthetic.

The shadows reappeared, slithered out of the darkness, and hissed toward Lucius like snakes, ripping through him from all directions like arrows. He didn't scream, only coughed a surprised groan, before his skin, too, started to lose its smooth texture. Inexorably, deep wrinkles ravaged their faces, and their hair became sparse silvery strands.

"Lily!" I screamed, this time. "What's going on?"

Her head lolled against Dante's shoulder. He pressed a kiss to her temple and left her side to move closer to Montecito and Lucius's rotting embrace. His lips stirred. Not quite a smile, the expression of an icy kindness. And his eyes . . . I thought they were brown, but now all I saw were dark pools where stars shimmered faintly. Two galaxies swirled in his pupils, same as in Lady Palombara's, and I was afraid to understand what it meant. His voice turned my spine to brittle ice as he told Montecito. "You've served your purpose, but now you must pay for what you did to Lily's grandfather, Leonora. Go now. I set you free." He gave the slightest flick of his forefinger, a twitch really. It was all it took for Montecito and Lucius to sizzle to pitch-black dust that scattered across the lab's floor. Returned to *nothing*.

I tried to ball my fists, but I was so fucking petrified, my fingers wouldn't even curl. *Oh God. Oh . . . shit.* It wasn't just a severe case of douche boyfriend. He was . . . he was seriously . . .

"Perses," Faust stated, a tremor belying his cordial tone.

I sent Lily a pleading look. "Did you know? *Lily,* did you know from the start?"

She managed to sniff her tears back long enough to gasp out a brittle answer. "I found a letter in his book. He knew . . . and she left him no choice but to kill himself. It was her fault!" Her face twisted in rage and I no longer recognized her. "Em, she was a monster!"

She'd known. From the moment she'd introduced him to me, every time he'd nuzzle her neck when we had talked in her bedroom, when they'd whisper to each other and speak with their eyes. She knew, and I saw now, as blinding evidence, that none of this had ever been about Montecito.

Dante—no, Perses—drew her back to him, combing damp bangs away from her eyes. "You were stronger in the face of evil than I ever imagined you could be." His features softened as he hypnotized me with his inhuman eyes. "Your gifts have no equal."

Lily's . . . gifts? I mentally pictured her, standing among her grandpa's notes and books. The table, the ancient spells she wanted to understand so much. I heard her desperate wails in the Libro again. Not fear, not horror. A plea. *You beg, lay all you have, all you are at their feet in exchange for the fulfillment of a meaningless human wish.*

It was Faust who said it. I could never have; I could barely breathe as it was. "Lily," he asked, his voice pure velvet. "Was it Lady Montecito who called him?"

Her lips trembled. Perses chuckled, keeping her close to his body. "Leonora begged like a child for someone to give her more than bandages to wrap her decaying body into. But she could barely read our words, and much less understand them."

His laughter stopped as his gaze locked on Lily. "Lily, on the other hand, had nothing but her grandfather's notes: old, incomplete spells carved in stones by the many worms who'd called my name over the centuries, but I heard her voice, begging me to avenge her grandfather." He closed his eyes briefly as if heavenly music were playing in his head. "And I saw a path. She had something the others didn't. She understood . . ."

The hidden nature of things that so few humans understand, I mentally completed. Like Massimiliano, straight-A Lily had a mind made to learn, brilliant enough to pierce secrets none of us were supposed to.

Faust snorted, his nostrils flaring in disdain. "Or rather, you saw that she had located the table. You saw that you could use her and Katharos, to seize what you were forbidden to."

"No!" Lily's angry scream sliced the air. "You don't understand him! No one does!"

"One learns a few things about human and divine nature in two millennia, Lily," Faust reminded her softly.

She bared her teeth—Lily McKeanney roared at another human being. "You roam *alone*! Forsaken by all! How can you—" Her breath faltered as she forced her rage out. Tears welled in her eyes, rolled down her cheeks. "How can you ever understand what it is to love someone and be loved, so completely?"

She was making my own eyes burn, and at that moment, I hated her so fucking much for reminding me that *she* was loved—had always been—and even that couldn't stop her from blowing it all. "What about me? All that shit about a second chance?" I glared at Dante, Perses, or whatever that cancerous assbag wanted to be called.

Her lips mouthed, "I'm sorry" but I barely heard the words.

Of course she was sorry. Everyone was always sorry; billions of people who were sorry but didn't give a shit who they had to step on to get what they wanted.

"You know what happened to me? You know what I fucking *am*?" I yelled, clasping a trembling hand over my stomach. "Did he tell you about the black hole inside me?" I shouted. "Do you understand what *your* path did to me?" I wasn't sure this was about eternal gods anymore; maybe it all boiled down to that old wound between us now, and as usual, only one of us could win. This time, though, the stakes were a notch higher. I wouldn't just end up sleeping on a bench if I lost.

"Em, we don't have to fight," she whimpered, huddling in the safety of Perses's arms. "He doesn't mean to hurt you. You don't understand what he wants—"

"Emma understands perfectly, as I do," Faust retorted coolly. "She came here to save you." His eyes narrowed. "But you don't need any saving. Do you, Lily?"

"She does," Perses replied. "From humans' greatest enemy." His gaze swallowed mine, soft and infinitely cold. "Emma, all I want is for Lily to live a long life."

An immortal life. The words rang loud in my head. I thought of Lady Palombara who'd lost Massimiliano because he was mortal, and he was willing to destroy himself to live just a little longer until he could figure out how to give her a child. I wanted to believe Perses was just an eternal turd, but . . . it was possible for ancient gods who were but shells of their former selves to love too. Lily was the one he wanted to use the table for, to give her the most precious gift of all: true immortality.

Faust's jaw tightened. "So she can spend eternity in Tartarus with you? How long can you remain incarnated on Earth when the rest of you is chained there?"

Perses's dark irises expanded like wells of pure fury. Faust had hit a sore spot, and the answer was probably: not long.

He squeezed Lily's shoulder. "I need her at my side. Faustus, you of all people should understand the meaning of eternal loneliness." His expression warmed a fraction, as if a sliver of humanity existed deep inside him. "What I want to give Lily . . . I could offer to Emma as well, as a reward for your obedience. Think about it," he crooned. "I don't need anything else. Help me with this, and you'll never hear about me again."

I glared at him. "What about Lily? Will she vanish too?"

She gripped Perses's arm a little tighter like he was her raft. "Em, even that tiny drop of Chronos's power inside the table would be enough to break his chains." Her eyes begged me. "He could live *free*, after being trapped in hell for so long."

There it was, the detail in Perses's happily ever after. The table's power wouldn't just serve to make Lily his bitch for eternity, it would release a monstrous god-killer, a titan nasty enough that no one wanted him out—and for a good reason. I already knew what Faust had to answer to that.

A sorrowful smile ghosted across his lips. "I'm sorry, Lily. You don't measure the significance of what he's asking. Chronos's power can't be unleashed." He seemed to hesitate before he told her, "There can be no exception, no deal."

There went our plan to unseal the table and transfer its power to the nut; with Perses standing ten feet away, it would pretty much be suicide. I glanced at the pile of blackened ashes on the ground, fighting a shudder. If we couldn't unseal the table for Lily's psycho-god-boyfriend, and there was no hope to beat him either . . . This was probably our last stand. Like, really the last, and I didn't want to die here, at barely twenty. I searched Faust's taut features for any sign that he had some sort of backup plan.

"Emma." My gaze snapped to the gentle asshole I'd known as Dante less than an hour ago. He held out a hand to me. "You have nothing to fear, Emma. I know yours is a heavy burden, but there's no need for us to be enemies. I don't know what Theia told you, but"—he shook his head with a boyish smile—"I'm not as terrible as some would like you to believe."

I inched back, closer to Faust. "Oh yeah, you are."

That didn't deter him. "I knew you'd lead Faust to me, just as I know he came here thinking he would defeat me with that ridiculous armor and an empty, powerless baetylus." Perses didn't give me the time to panic over this revelation. His arm shot out to call the shadows.

"Faust!" I shouted to warn him.

He raised his cane, as he had against Montecito. This time the spear couldn't make it through, crashing against Lady Palombara's indestructible crochet work instead. But the impact itself was powerful enough to send Faust flying backward and slamming into the lab's windows. A star-shaped crack bloomed where he'd hit the shatterproof glass, and he slid to the floor, coughing blood all over the golden vest.

I ran to his side, falling to my knees to check on him. Obviously, that wouldn't kill him, but air wheezed from his throat like he could barely breathe from the strength of Perses's blow. Meanwhile, the shadows drew back to coil around their master. He was through negotiating. There wasn't an ounce of mercy left in his eyes. "If he won't do it, you're going to unseal the table for me, Emma. Because if you don't . . ." the shadows slithered back toward us with a vengeance, circling Faust like vultures. "I will flay him. And when he heals, I'll do it again and again, until you can't stand his screams anymore."

"Please . . ." Lily's whimper broke through the emotionless hum of his voice, and the maddening whisper of the shadows. "I'll follow you there," she sobbed. "I don't care about being truly immortal if I can stay with you."

He mellowed, bent to brush his mouth to hers feverishly. "No. I *want* this for us." His voice grew husky, desperate. "There's a path. I see it."

There's a path. I clutched Faust's crimson-stained coat, feeling sticky blood transfer to my fingers. Lady Palombara had said no one could ever see the truth of their own path. Maybe Perses was the one who had it all wrong. Faust's cane still rested in his right hand, his fingers clutching it tightly. He would be okay; he could do this.

"I'm doing this," I murmured, for him only to hear.

Whether Faust had heard me or not, whether he was ready or not, it was too late to back out. With one last stroke to the golden fleece for good luck, I got to my feet and told Perses, "Okay. If all you need from me is to touch the table long enough to break the seal . . . I think I can do that."

He flourished a hand to the massive slab of granite. "I would be eternally grateful."

I took hesitant steps toward the table. Beyond the flare of the surgical light, Lily's silhouette shook in Perses's arms as she watched me lower my palms to the table. I flinched under the flare of the surgical light kissing the concentric circles of ancient characters. Through it all, Perses's eyes were on me, in me, searing me.

I registered the cool contact of granite under my fingertips, and the tide of time rose and pulsed inside me. At first, I thought I saw the signs swirl before my eyes again, like the first time I'd touched the table. But I had it wrong: there was nothing random about the movement. The circles were spinning fast in opposite directions, aligning the characters to form words and speak long-forgotten secrets, that only Faust was allowed to know. I didn't understand the whispers echoing in my skull, but I knew, in my bones, that I'd broken the seal, and the power flowing through my blood was forbidden.

The table, the Alpha, the source, all spiraling toward a single point, the Omega. Me. Inside me. I tumbled into blessed darkness and soothing silence, the room blurring fast around me as I started to absorb Chronos's power. I couldn't move my hands, couldn't even feel them anymore.

My senses returned with a flash of pain as I flew away from the table and crashed to the ground, rammed by Perses. I blinked up at the glittering sequins above me. The surgical lights. He'd shoved me across the room before I could suck in the precious power he wanted so bad. I had this weird thought that I'd just been roughed up by an actual titan and I was probably gonna die—if it wasn't done already. But then, I realized the light wasn't just coming from the ceiling, it was a blinding blue flow pouring all around me from the table. Perses's dark silhouette stood against the glow. His hands were on the table, touching the forbidden power, and somewhere in my head, Lily wouldn't stop crying.

I managed to roll to my stomach and saw Faust lying in the corner of the room, moving as if we were on a boat, sailing on the roaring sea of Chronos's power. He raised his cane. A purple flash tore through all the blue, that swelled into a sizzling ball of . . . pure energy, something abstract I could feel zinging all over my body, in my teeth, my heart. I had no strength to smile, but a little part of me wanted to. Faust had done it: no more blue light, only the purple glow of his brand new baetylus, sealing Chronos's power.

Perses probably understood too late he had underestimated Ouranos's nut. He whirled around to face Faust, his eyes blazing. Literally. That's when Lily should have taken the hint—when the stars in her boyfriend's eyes caught fire, when his skin started to crack in places from the ancient power it tried to contain in vain and he lit up like a fucking Christmas tree. Or maybe the true deal-breaker should have been when his voice grew unnaturally deep and boomed ominously in the cavernous vault of the lab, and he roared at Faust, "Know your place, slave!"

I struggled to get to my knees. I tried, *tried* with everything I had, but I couldn't find in me the secret strength Lady Palombara thought I possessed. I wasn't even worthy of that shitty Kylo Ren cap, incapable of stopping Perses's spear of shadows as he hurled it at Faust.

This time the Golden Fleece wasn't enough. Faust's scream of agony tore through me at the same time that I saw the cane spinning away from him. The hellish flow of power had stopped. The table was silent again, just a dead disc of stone. Similarly dead, the nut had stopped glowing, and only a few bolts of electricity still arced here and there in the lab. I scanned my surroundings, my heart pounding like a marching band in my ears. Lily lay curled into a tight ball near the table, unmoving, and Perses . . . Perses stood a few feet away from Faust, the shadows coiled around his hand like a gauntlet.

My gaze traveled from the cane resting on the ground, to the trail of blood connecting it to . . . "Faust!" I let out a broken scream, crawling toward Faust's severed right arm, and his prone form lying next to it.

Perses extended his arm toward the cane. When I saw it slide across the blood-soaked floor of its own volition, called by the shadows, I found the strength I needed at last, felt it thunder in my legs. I leaped forward and managed to kick the cane all the way across the room.

Crap idea. Perses turned his flaming irises to me instead. In his fist, the spear of shadows stretched again, ready. "I'll take care of him later," he growled, his eyes darting to Faust's maimed body. "For now . . ."

Yeah. For now, it was my turn. I scrambled back, my hands and feet slipping in a sickening mixture of Faust's blood and Montecito's ashes. Dark red coated my fingers, my sneakers as my back hit a wall. Panic crushed my lungs as Perses closed in on me, the shadows howling in his hand. A snarl bared a row of sharp white teeth. "I wanted you to come back. I wanted this moment . . . to measure my strength against absolute darkness. Can you give me that, Emma?"

I raised my arms to shield myself from Perses's spear hissing toward me. I had a vision of one of the shimmering gods he'd killed in the past, saw myself torn apart in the same way. But this was different. When it started, I almost wished he'd pierced me and ended it instead. Just like when I had touched the table, I felt the shadows being drawn to me, inside me, and I couldn't stop this unbearable flow ripping my body apart.

My fingers clawed at the air in vain to stop the agony in my chest, tearing through nothing but smoke. I sensed him, one with the shadows, ever closer, until his forehead was pressed to mine. All I could see was the fire in his irises, burning deep within, and the spear in his hand, incapable of transpiercing me, endlessly sucked into my heart instead.

"How much . . . can you take?" he ground out.

I didn't know. I could feel myself go, the pain too great, throbbing in every part of my body at once. Black crept at the edge of my vision. I thought of the table, of the darkness and the silence inside me. Like a pitch-black pearl nested in my heart, a secret place I might collapse into. A black hole.

I didn't consciously feel the pearl grow; I just had a glimpse of that infinitely dark bubble right before it engulfed us. The pain inside me stopped. I was . . . I *no longer* was. Everything and everywhere, pure silence and pure darkness. In the absence of light, I had lost myself and dragged Perses down the hole with me. I could still feel him, struggling in my depths, drowning. He was in me. He was me, an integral part of me.

Hey . . .

Hey, Em . . . Wake up.

Wasn't I already awake? The Ikea couch I sat in was familiar, fitted with stained red velvet. My pink duvet and pillow lay in a heap at my side. I slept here because, man, we didn't have three grand to shell out on a two bedroom in New York. The box of my *Cinderella 3: A Twist in Time* DVD sat on the coffee table. The clock on the wall above our TV wasn't ticking, and onscreen, Cinderella's evil stepmom appeared frozen, holding the magic wand she'd stolen from the fairy godmother to go back in time.

"Do you like it here? I thought you'd like it."

My gaze drifted to the little girl who lay sprawled across two red cushions on the floor, watching the movie. I knew her messy blonde hair and denim bib overalls, the gray sweater underneath. It was the only piece of clothing her dad had ever bought her. There was a drawing of Minnie Mouse on the front, and we never called him Dad at home, just Gabriele. The little girl rolled to her side and sat up to face me across the coffee table. Her big blue eyes studied me coldly. She couldn't be more than seven . . . I looked down at my hands—adult ones, with a few scratches and bitten nails. I combed a turquoise strand away from my eyes. She was me, and I was her, in my mom's living room in Brooklyn.

She glanced at the still frame on the screen over her shoulder. "Bippity boppity boo. Bullshit. No one can turn back time." She focused her cruel cornflower gaze back to me. "Except me."

I stared in incomprehension, struggling to tear through the

white noise in my brain. "You . . ."

She rolled her eyes and grinned, baring randomly placed milk teeth. "*Me.* I thought you wanted to meet me." She quivered, balling her small fists. "Aren't you excited? Don't you have a million questions?"

Slowly, my mind emerged. She wasn't Em, wasn't me. She was . . . *Chronos?*

"Well, yeah!" She squeaked. "Obviously it's not gonna be that poor Perses, 'cause," her voice dwindled to a secretive whisper, "you fucked him up."

Had I? Was she reading my thoughts too?

She shook her head. "He never understood the nature of the Omega—now I think he does."

At last, thoughts clanked in place in my head. I stirred awake. "You did this to me . . . You put it in me!" I gasped.

She gave an exaggerated wince. "Not exactly. But I knew it would be in you before time began, and I knew it'd be fun. I told Faust, you know. Ask him about that someday. Ask him what I told him."

"You told him . . . about me?"

"Sort of. I thought it'd give him some sort of goal in life, waiting for you. But he didn't really believe me." She grimaced. "He freaked out when you showed up, huh?"

He had. I remembered the way he'd nodded to himself and kept repeating my presence with him outside time was "new." But he'd said he had no idea why it was happening. He'd said he had no idea it was even possible . . .

Chronos considered the Chip & Dale stickers stuck to my mom's coffee table. "He's a man; he lies. Get over it."

My mouth worked in silence until I managed to ask, "Why?"

"Now we're talking! Why? The great question! Why me? You?

The universe—"

"Why the fuck are you playing with me?" I spat, cutting her off.

She smirked. "Not afraid to challenge the gods, I see. I like that." She shoved a finger up her nose, picking it thoroughly. "I'm just here to say hi, you know, chat a bit before you disappear."

Panic exploded in my chest, but I remained stuck to that couch like I was paralyzed. "What do you mean?"

"You've fulfilled your purpose. You won! Yay, you!"

I blinked over and over as if it might help me see the line between dream and reality. I was in my own head after all, right? "You mean . . . I killed Perses?"

She sighed. "Think so. He bites the dust, in about a jiffy from now."

"A . . . jiffy?"

She pinched her thumb and forefinger together and held them up for me to see. "It's a very small and very long amount of time."

Perses was going to die—soon, apparently—and I would . . . disappear?

"Like I said, you won, you big winner. And now, since you're expanding pretty fast, I'd say you're about to absorb yourself along with everything else around. It's gonna get nasty."

I just shook my head dumbly, incapable of processing any of this. I was coming apart like a dandelion.

Chronos sighed, cringed. "I made him immortal, but trust me, Faust won't survive that one. Lily won't make it either, by the way. You're about to suck them into a needle eye of infinite gravity and spit them out in another universe, in confetti." She stuck out her tongue as she mimicked something being crushed in her hands. "You're losing control, girl, I'm telling ya."

The meaning of her words didn't fully register: I was stuck behind in our conversation, at the moment when she'd said . . .

"Faust was waiting for me?"

She looked up from the sticker she'd been busy peeling off from the coffee table's glass top. Her head bobbed up and down. "Yeah."

I gazed down at my reflection in the dark glass. A girl who looked completely out of it. "So . . . I was waiting for him too?"

Chronos shrugged. "Dunno. Maybe. It's not like I was in your head."

I didn't know either, and I never would if he . . . died. Her words registered, at last, whipped me hard. Blood resumed flowing to my brain, pounding hard in my temples, and my legs obeyed me when I decided to shoot up from the couch. "No. *No!* I want out!"

I staggered around the frozen living room of my childhood. "Take me *out!*" I shouted.

Chronos tilted her head at me, a puzzled look on her round face. "Girl, whatcha freaking about?" She raised her small palms, to which a Dale sticker still clung. "Do I look like I'm holding the wheel here? I'm six, for fuck's sake, and *you're* the Omega. You don't want to absorb Faust and Lily, cool; do something about it."

"Do what?" I roared. "How do I control this?"

She pressed her lips together in a cunning grin. "That's what I've been telling you for like, ten eons: *wake up, Em.*"

I did.

Or rather, a part of my conscience returned. It's not like I had eyes anymore to open, but there was this tiny fiber of me that still thought like a human being, who still tried to be aware of her body, her own existence. Somewhere in this absolute peace, I remembered fear, and with it came the awareness of my body and Perses's, merging with me. Absorbed. I felt his howl of agony as his limbs disintegrated to become part of my void, and I thought, "he's *inside* me." It was the ultimate horror, the boost I needed to fight back.

I thrashed in the dark, reached for the edge of me, the safe limits of my physical envelope, somewhere to swim back to. Pain and light returned to me, and I'd never been so relieved that every breath hurt.

My knees were the first thing I saw clearly—my torn jeans, bloodstained. I was still curled against the wall in the corner of the lab. Lily spotted Perses before I did. Her wail achieved to clear the fog in my mind. I blinked at the shape . . . the *thing* lying a few feet away from me. A head, half a torso with an arm still attached. Shreds of his lab coat and shirt clinging to blackened skin. *Shit* . . . My hands jerked to feel frantically at my chest and belly, terrified at the idea that maybe I'd feel him crawl under my skin. *Inside me.* Oh my God, I had absorbed him, for real. That was just sick.

Lily scrambled to her feet and ran to him. She fell to her knees, a hand clasped over her mouth in horror. She didn't dare touch him. Her trembling fingers hovered, powerless, over what was left of the mighty Perses. "Oh no, no, no . . . please, *no* . . ." Her voice cracked into a sob so earnest, so desperate, it reached straight to my heart and clawed at it.

My head lolled as I tried to remember why my own chest hurt like that, and I saw Faust. I could no longer get to my feet, just crawl. I dragged my body across the bloodstained floor, my legs a deadweight. The fingers of his left hand twitched. I reached to touch them, feel him. His eyelids fluttered open.

"It's me," I croaked. "I'm here. I think . . . I think I killed him. With the black hole." I crept closer and, with a grunt of effort, managed to get to my knees.

His lips quivered and curved upward. "I told you we'd be lucky," he said weakly. Renewed panic flared in my blood when his smile wavered. "Emma, he's . . ."

My head flipped back to Perses's charred body and Lily cradling his face in her hands, stroking it. The arm he had left moved. *Shit.* I stood up on shaky legs, while behind me Faust attempted to get to a sitting position with a groan of agony. A ring of flaming signs sizzled across the floor around Perses and Lily, trapping them. She took a single look at them and collapsed over him, pressing her cheek to his. "I love you," she murmured. "Take me there with you . . . Please."

Faust grappled blindly for his cane with his remaining arm. "Lily, no! Don't!"

His hoarse shout whipped me into action: I ran back to them and plunged to the ground, my hand straining for her even as a column of swirling shadows engulfed them. I felt her arm, grazed it. I could have grabbed her if I'd been just a little faster, a little stronger, but my fingers closed over thin air as the shadows vanished with a final howl.

I sat in a state of shock, shaking all over, staring at the charred outline of a few characters lingering on the floor. Once I was able to breathe, I screamed, "Where did he take her? Where is she?"

Faust let himself fall back to the ground with a gasp of agony. "In the only place he can heal safely away from you . . . In Tartarus."

Lily's pleas rang back in my ears as I returned to Faust's side. "She asked him. She kept saying she didn't mind if he took her there."

His head turned my way, looking for me. I scooted closer, allowing him to rest his cheek on my knees. He sighed. "I'm sorry, Emma. Tartarus is a death sentence for humans. Her physical body can't survive there."

Pain exploded in my chest, tears building fast in its wake. "Oh God . . . she can't be dead."

"I'm so sorry," he repeated softly.

I wiped my eyes with the back of my hand. "We'll come up with something. Lady Palombara will know what to do."

"Emma—"

The ear-splitting screech of a security alarm cut him off. I looked up to see an orange strobe blinking fast on the ceiling. Faust raised his head at me. "Would you mind helping me up? I think we need to leave. Fast."

My stomach heaved. "Your arm . . ."

"That's definitely a problem," he rasped. "But my cane is a more urgent one."

"Okay." I leaped to my feet and ran around the table to where I'd sent it flying earlier. It still lay in the exact same place, looking every bit like an ordinary vine staff with a purple egg encased in the hilt. Yet Chronos's legendary table belonged in the past: all that remained was a dead slab of granite, a pretty archeological piece for a museum, and a fun enigma for the many scientists who'd try to figure out the meaning of its inscriptions. The power and the whispered secrets all rested in Ouranos's nut now, for Faust to guard more closely than ever . . .

"I can't touch your cane," I reminded him. "I'll kick it your way." I wasn't sure how much contact might trigger its disintegration, so I kinda toed it awkwardly a couple times, nudging it toward Faust until he was able to grab it.

The strobe above our heads stopped flashing almost instantly.

"That should make our life a little easier." He let out a pained grunt. "I'm afraid I'm going to need more help, Emma."

I closed my eyes briefly. *Please don't ask me to pick up your arm . . . Please—*

"My arm . . ."

Oh God.

I would have done pretty much anything for him at that point of our non-relationship, but picking up his severed arm was still the second-grossest thing I'd ever accomplished in my life—that crazy shit with *Lucius's* arm being the first.

"Just bring it close and try not to touch me while it heals," he instructed. "It should do the trick."

I did as he asked, fighting a wave of nausea as I nudged the arm closer to his body with the very tip of my fingers, until it was more or less back in place. "Now what?" I asked, a tremor in my voice.

He let go of his cane to hold the arm in place with his left hand. "We wait."

"How long?"

Amazingly, much faster than I imagined. But then again, time had stopped, so I'm not sure how long I stared at Faust, biting my nails while his flesh kind of . . . grew back together in bloody tendrils straining for each other. Bon appetit. After a while, he declared that it was good enough for now. I didn't dare help him up—terrified that the arm might come off again if we touched—and watched him struggle with the help of his cane. Once Faust stood on his legs, we limped our way out of Katharos's headquarters, past frozen security guards. Gives a whole new meaning to the expression "a close brush with the law."

Once on the street, I spotted Silvio's red minivan and guided Faust to it. We crashed in the backseat barely five seconds after he'd released time. Silvio glanced at our blood-soaked clothes in the mirror. Nodded. And crushed the gas.

It was only when he parked in a tiny paved street near the Trevi Fountain that he asked, "Your sister?"

I shook my head, unable to form words as my eyes grew hot again.

His gaze unreadable behind his glasses, he ducked his head to remove the fascinus around his neck. He turned in his seat to drop it in Faust's trembling left hand, and looked at me. "Be strong and get some sleep."

Faust flashed him a weary smile. "Five stars."

XXXIV

"Are you sure you don't want to come to bed with me?"

Faust's tired voice came muffled from the general direction of his canopy bed, where he lay buried under his Spiderman duvet and approximately a hundred cats. I'm not sure how they could possibly know something had happened to him—or if cats routinely communicated about that kind of stuff for that matter—but somehow, nearly every feline from the neighborhood had gathered on his balcony as I helped him up the ladder leading to his attic, and they'd soon piled up atop of him in the bed.

"I'm good," I mumbled from the couch, tossing under a scratchy blanket, in my underwear and Faust's weird bible T-shirt.

It was still dark, but outside the sky was turning a deep shade of indigo, and stripes of pink peeked between the roofs. Faust and I had crashed up here and gone to sleep almost immediately because, at this point, it was the only thing to do. With dawn would come more problems than I wanted to think of anyway . . .

"Dante" and Lily's disappearance had probably been discovered by now, along with a pile of ashes in the ruins of the lab. For Lily, the cops would call Richard and my mother—if it wasn't done already. It wouldn't take long before all authorities involved learned that I was in Rome and that I'd seen her. They were going to want to question me—to suspect me, even? The prospect only scared me half as much as a potential confrontation with my mom and stepfather. It was easy to imagine how things would look to them: Lily getting in trouble and vanishing right after I showed up in Rome and stuck my nose in her business . . .

Every time I tried to close my eyes, I saw her tear-streaked face, heard her screams. She'd lied to me, and she'd have let Perses use me to obtain Chronos's power, but now that my anger was turning into grief, I could see that she'd done it all out of love for him, and maybe he had loved her a little too, in his inhumane way. I couldn't find it in me to truly hate Lily for what she'd done. I just wanted to undo it all, see her back and safe—so I could tell her to fuck off and never call me again.

In the bed, Faust's good arm moved to scratch one of his cats. He wouldn't go back to sleep yet. "How's your arm?" I asked.

"Connected to my torso," he replied with a yawn.

"Does it still hurt?"

"It's not that bad," he mused, as Arrancino—or was this one Confucius?—moved to sit on his pillow and kneaded his hair with an exaggerated yawn. "I lost my head once, during the Hundred Years' War."

I stretched on the couch's busted leather cushions. "Holy shit!"

"I know, right? Let me tell you, the recovery was something else."

"Emma?" he called softly.

"Yeah?"

"I think it'd heal faster if you joined me under the covers."

I rubbed my eyes, torn between laughter and aggravation. "Are you seriously still trying to bang me? Right now?"

"Yes," he admitted in a small, guilty voice. "But I'm more than willing to settle for a little platonic intimacy."

"No," I said with a chuckle, even as my heart tightened.

Definitively no, considering what had happened tonight. I rested a hand on my stomach under the blanket, swallowing back a wave of nausea at the memory of Perses disintegrating inside me. I felt monstrous, violated. I was no longer a human being, but a walking black hole, a danger to everyone who tried to get too close—starting with Faust.

"Emma," he called again from under his duvet. "Why won't you talk to me?"

I huffed. "Because you need to sleep."

"Are you scared because of what happened in the lab?" he probed gently.

He must have eyes on his dick; that had to be his secret. "I'm not . . . look, I don't want to talk about it. I'm freaked out."

"But you're safe, and you defeated him," he replied, admiration tinging his voice. "I'm almost scared of you now," he joked.

Except it wasn't funny at all. I jackknifed up. "Faust, I nearly killed you!"

His tone grew wistful. "I know. But you didn't."

"And I have no idea why, how, or what actually happened. I basically felt myself drowning . . . inside myself with Perses, which is the worst mindfuck I ever experienced in my life."

He rolled to his side, stirring the living, furry mass blanketing him. "You don't remember anything?"

I squeezed my eyes shut. "No. I know I went somewhere . . . inside my head, but it's like I'm hungover. My head hurts, I feel like shit, and I know I'm gonna regret everything I did last night." A thought arced through my skull, out of the blue. The rattle of the cane and the seagulls. "Faust?"

"Yes?"

"Have you ever been to New York?"

"I have, a few times actually." My pulse picked up. I squinted at his shape in the bed. "Last time was in 1978 when Queen played in Madison Square Garden. Believe me, you wish you had been born to witness that."

I drew the scratchy blanket over my thighs, contemplating his answer with a pang of disappointment. "Okay, I just wondered." I wasn't about to tell him I'd dreamt of him before knowing he was the one responsible for stilling time. He'd be quick to conclude that we were fated to bang with his cats watching and Umberto Tozzi wailing *ti amo* in the background.

"Emma?"

"Yeah?"

"Is it still no?" he pleaded.

I lay back on the couch with a chuckle. "No."

A heavy sigh. Some tossing around. Cats meowing weakly, until one of them jumped from the bed to go perch on a chair. "Emma?"

"What?" I tried hard to be pissed, but my lips were curving already in dawn's blueish light. He was relentless, impossible.

"I'm hungry."

A box of Cocoa Krispies in hand, I studied Faust's newly reattached right arm while the pile of cats curled on his lap watched me fix our unsung hero a well-deserved bowl of faxkrispies.

He laid his tablet aside, which had been reading him an email from Silvio moments ago. "I usually have a good nose, but I just didn't see it coming. All it'd have taken was a call to Sapienza."

"The university where he was supposed to have gotten his PhD? It was fake after all?" I padded to the bed to give him the bowl.

Faust sat up, disrupting the cats piled up on his lap and chest. They rolled and crawled out of the way, only to resettle on his legs and coil around his waist. I stole a guilty glance at the lean muscles of his bare chest while he smelled his breakfast with a blissful smile. Nothing wrong with a little eye candy, as long as I didn't eat the whole bag, I reassured myself.

"No, and that's the amazing part: Dante Alessandri appears in their records, but his doctoral advisor can't remember his face, his name, or even the subject of his thesis—a copy of which can be found in the university's archive."

"Do you think it's because Perses is gone and can no longer control the guy?"

He nodded and held out the bowl. "Likely. Do you want to try it?"

I considered the spoon, last night's nightmare still fresh in my mind. Yeah, this was a beer for breakfast kind of morning. "Thanks," I said, bringing the faxkrispies to my mouth. I chewed on the crunchy mixture with a grimace. "Next time, *I* pick the booze."

"So, there will be a next time?" he teased in between mouthfuls. "I knew you wouldn't resist me for long. Very well, I'll make room for your clothes in the wardrobe, and we'll put your fox next to my raccoon."

I closed my eyes with a tired sigh, ignoring the fleeting jolt of my heart at the idea of us living together. Being together. A memory of Perses and me dissolving in absolute darkness flashed behind my eyelids. I couldn't control it, this terrifying void inside me. Maybe it would happen again, and it'd be worse, and I wouldn't find my way out of the dark. I could never take the risk of the same happening to Faust . . .

"Cool your jets," I chided. "*If* I stay in Rome a *little* longer, I'll find myself a place. I saw crazy cheap dormitories on Airbnb." Which would solve at least one of my ninety-nine problems—the rest of them including the fact that my passport was probably still at the Residenza, or that I could kiss Tuna Town goodbye if I wasn't back at work in three days for my Monday shift, and that meant losing my apartment too, as soon as my meager savings ran out. Just thinking about it made my head hurt, but I didn't want to get there with Faust; I knew the solutions he'd offer were far too tempting . . .

His eyes narrowed over his bowl of cereal as an awkward silence set between us. "Trying to friendzone me, I see."

I huffed loudly, signaling the fun was over. "Faust, I'm serious. There's something I need to ask you."

He gulped down the rest of the beer and placed the empty bowl on his nightstand, an easy smile lingering in his beard as he wiped it with the back of his hand. "Anything you want."

"Say I buy, like, really cool playmobils, do you think Louison would ever consider letting me back into his shop?"

His brow creased a fraction. "I can certainly help you find him a fix, but why do you want to return there?"

My fingers threaded in the thick fur of a white and black gutter boy I'd first seen lounging with Faust on the street near the Residenza. "To check his books . . . I mean, if I can understand them."

His chest heaved. "Emma, there's no way into Tartarus."

And yet I'd have to find one, because I wasn't sure I wanted to see Lily's crying face at night until the day I died . . . The worst part was the guilt, branded into my skin despite what she'd done. I had failed to catch her hand in that final moment, and no matter how much I turned this around in my head, I couldn't process that she was gone for good—couldn't shake the irrational gut feeling that she was still there, somewhere, right under the surface of my reality. "At least part of Perses found a way out, and Lady Palombara escaped too. I could ask her—"

"Even if it was possible, Lily was human; her physical body can't survive in that dimension. All Perses took with him is a soul that's now trapped there." The muscles in his neck tightened. "And I think he knew it. He knowingly killed her rather than giving her up."

"Maybe you're right, but there's no harm in doing a little research. I think it'll help me get some closure if I know I really did all I could."

He rubbed a hand over his chin, blinking his exhaustion away. "All right. I suppose a couple of playmobils won't bring about the end of times. We better find good ones, though; you threw up all over the place."

"I know . . ." I groaned at the memory, and got up from the bed, followed by half a dozen cats who officially believed I was now in charge of feeding everyone in this attic. "There's something else I need to do first."

"What is it?"

"Do you have a supermarket where I can buy a box of chocolate?"

I tucked a stray lock of turquoise hair back under my Kylo Ren cap. "Okay, how do I look?"

Faust winced.

"I was asking the cats," I said in the guise of an apology, glancing down at the pair of tabbies wrapped around his legs. They had no comment to offer as I sniffed my hoodie to check whether that ten-minute wash in Faust's bathroom sink had done the job. Yeah, good enough. I smoothed the cheap golden plastic ribbon decorating a box of Ferrero Rochers, eyeing the gates of a nondescript sixties residence across the street.

Faust grinned. "We'll be waiting here. Do you want my phone to film one of those reunion videos?"

"I think I'll be good," I said, giggling my stress away.

He patted my shoulder awkwardly. "Well, there you go, champ."

I bit my lower lip not to burst out laughing again—he actually sounded more nervous than I was. Okay, no . . . my hands wouldn't stop shaking, and I was a thousand times edgier than he or anyone could ever be as I crossed the street and searched for my father's name on the intercom. Gabriele Lombardi. *Emma Lombardi*, I thought with a secret smile, before inwardly slapping myself for being so damn cheesy. I pressed once and waited, fidgeting on the sidewalk.

"*Pronto.*" A female voice.

I steadied my voice to reply, "*Sono qui per vedere Gabriele Lombardi.*" I'm here to see Gabriele Lombardi.

"*Chi è?*" Who are you?

I froze, aware of the blood drumming in my temples, of Faust, still standing across the street. "*Sono . . .*" My mouth worked in silence. His daughter? A friend? An acquaintance? How did you say that in Italian?

In the intercom, the voice grew impatient. "*Non riesco a sentirti . . .*" I can't hear you. Then she whispered, maybe to someone else. "*Si è rotto di nuovo!*" It's broken again!

I jerked in surprise when the door clicked open with a bipping sound, and the woman said, "*Secondo piano.*" Second floor.

No going back now. I entered the building and took cautious steps across the lobby's checkered tiling. Once I'd called the elevator, I bounce-stepped to calm down as the steel door slid open. I closed my eyes during the short ride. They re-opened in sync with the elevator's door, and I saw him.

He had come to answer the door. He looked older than on Facebook. The lines around his mouth gave him a stern air when he wasn't smiling. But his kind blue eyes were the same as in my childhood memories; the same as mine. His brow furrowed, and I read the confusion on his face. I glimpsed a long hallway behind him. A dark-haired woman shuttled from one door to another, followed by a teenage boy. Blond like my dad and me. I drew in a shaky breath as their voices echoed in that foreign apartment.

Awkward seconds stretched, and my dad still wasn't saying anything. I swallowed hard and murmured, "It's me . . . Emma."

His eyes went wide; he stepped out into the hallway, and nearly slammed the door behind him. His lips moved, and for the first time in thirteen years I heard my father's voice, a soft gravel coated with his singing Italian accent. "Your mother didn't tell me you were coming."

He didn't look happy—terrified, actually—and the growing anguish in his eyes reached deep inside me, squeezing my heart. "I'm sorry . . . It was kind of a spur of the moment thing, and I"—I shoved the box of Ferrero in his hands— "I brought you this."

He looked down at the golden bow, his own reflection in the transparent plastic. His cheeks grew pale, his lips quivered. His gaze wouldn't meet mine as he said, "You should have contacted me first. Emma . . ." His eyes darted at the door behind him. "This is a very difficult situation for me."

You'd think even a moron like me would have figured it out instantly, but it did take me a few seconds of staring blankly at the door to understand what he meant. They didn't know. The dark-haired woman and the blond-haired boy, he had never told them, and in this life, this apartment, this family . . . I didn't exist.

The pain was sudden, sharper than I'd expected. It was a wave surging from deep within, tearing everything as it roared under my ribs. Even more bruising was the realization that I'd never seriously considered it'd end like this. Even in my hours of deepest loneliness, when I would replay our last walk along the beach over and over in my head and tell myself he didn't give a shit about me, there was still a part of me who'd kept hoping. After all, there could have been a thousand reasons why he'd ghosted us. Maybe he was scarred from years of fighting with my mom; maybe he was in trouble, ill or wounded at the other end of the world—dead even.

But the simple truth was that he'd erased me and moved on.

Sweat beaded on his brow as he braced himself for my reaction. He must be terrified I'd yell, that the dark-haired woman would hear us, and his secret would ooze out, stain everything in his new life.

I nodded to myself, once, twice. It was fine. Just a little awkward, maybe. I was cool . . . mostly. Sometimes emotions can be so huge, so devastating that you need to contain them in small words, so they won't overflow and spill all over the place. I was an expert; I could do this. I had tiny, empty words for every heartbreak, every earthquake. I gulped down a lump of pure agony, blinked up to dry the dampness burning my eyes. I hoped he wouldn't notice; he'd probably think it was emotional blackmail or something shitty like that.

Of all the shrugs I ever gave, this one cost me the most. "I get it," I said at last. "I won't come back again. We're cool."

"Emma." The plea in his voice made my heart rev—he still cared. "If you need money, we can talk. Just not here, please."

Oh. He wanted to pay me to leave him alone. My chest grew unbearably tight, and I got scared I wouldn't be strong enough to weather the storm inside me. I was a balloon stretched to the limit, and I had no idea what would happen when I burst, what big, irreversible words might geyser out. I shook my head, trying to avert my eyes so he wouldn't see I was coming apart fast. "No . . . It's fine. I don't need your money."

The door came ajar, and the pretty woman with the jet curls appeared behind him. *"Cosa sta succedendo?"* What's going on?

He gave a tight chuckle and shoved the Ferrero box back in my hands. *"Niente. Soltanto un errore di consegna."* Nothing, it's a delivery error.

She scanned me, a tinge of suspicion in her eyes as he retreated inside the apartment. He mumbled a vague apology and slammed the door just in time. I wouldn't have been able to take another second of this nightmare. I took the stairs to leave the building faster, breathing fast and hard through my nose. When I barreled through the door, Faust was still there, sitting cross-legged on the sidewalk with his cats while above us, lead-colored clouds swelled with the promise of rain.

His head snapped up the moment I stepped out. The hole in my heart hurt too much, and I had no strength left to face him, to lie that my father wasn't home or whatever. I hurried down the deserted street, praying he wouldn't guess it was me.

"Emma?"

I walked faster, my shoulders hunched in shame as tears streamed down my cheeks. The fucking cats betrayed me. One of them left the comfort of Faust's lap to trot after me. I should have never fed them this morning . . .

Faust got up and closed the distance between us in a few quick strides, rhythmed by the familiar clatter of his cane against the pavement. "Emma, wait! What's going on?"

"Leave me alone," I hissed.

He caught up with me instead, worry written all over his features. "Emma, *stop*. What happened?"

"Nothing. I'm . . . fine." Except it came out as a sob, my pain bare for Faust to hear.

I thought he'd insist—secretly hoped he would, to be honest—but he gave up like everyone else. The clatter of Faust's cane stopped as he let me walk away alone, just as I'd asked. I'm not gonna lie; it made me cry even harder, that after all we'd been through, I'd driven him away too. I couldn't blame him. No point in fighting to get close to a human porcupine.

The first raindrops hit my cap, spotted my shoulders. I still held on to my box of chocolate as it progressively got drenched, and the realization came with a wave of nausea. I stopped and hurled it in the air, bracing myself for the satisfying sound of plastic crashing on the asphalt.

Nothing came. The rain had stopped, and a million diamonds hung still in the air that would no more hit the ground than my box would. I looked over my shoulder. His hands resting on his new cane, Faust was waiting. He knew you didn't run after a stray cat; you held out a hand and let it come to you once it trusted you. Once it knew you were home.

I stopped thinking. I walked, then ran back toward him through the frozen raindrops I couldn't feel.

How long had it been since I'd hugged anyone? I couldn't fucking remember. I could only recall a thousand snarky comebacks and just as many shrugs, lashing out at people and shoving them away before they could reject me first. But Faust was here. He opened his arms and pulled me to him when no one else would, and I let him. I hugged him back, squeezed his torso and buried my tears in his T-shirt as he closed his big coat over me like a safe cocoon.

His chin came to rest atop my head as a final sob raked through my chest. He rubbed my back in slow, soothing circles. "Let's go home."

And I said, "Okay."

WHO THE FUCK IS SILVIO? ARE WE GONNA LEARN MORE ABOUT LADY PALOMBARA'S HUSBAND? IS RYUUKO AN ACTUAL DRAGON? CAN YOU BUY ECONOMY TICKETS TO TARTARUS? IS IT HOT THERE? CAN FAUST MAKE IT OUT OF THE FRIENDZONE?

STAY TUNED TO FIND OUT!

STUFF YOU CAN GOOGLE

Constantine the Great (27 February c. 272 AD – 22 May 337 AD)

Not my favorite Roman emperor, but his arch can be still admired in Rome near the Colosseum. Constantine was the last "great" Roman emperor to rule over a reunited empire comprising both eastern and western halves. He was also the first Roman emperor to convert to Christianity—on his deathbed, and after a life spent actively promoting the development of the religion in the empire.

Proto-Canaanite gibberish

In *Still,* the mysterious language of the text written on Chronos's table is presumably the Titans' original language, which was later transcribed using an enriched proto-Canaanite script. While the table and Titans belong to the realm of awkward fiction by yours truly, Proto-Canaanite script does exist and is an ancestor of Greek and Latin. Proto-Canaanite was first derived from hieroglyphs as a simplified alphabet meant to translate Semitic languages. Its descendant, the Phoenician alphabet, would later become the founding base of the Greek, old Italic—used by the Etruscans—and Latin alphabets.

Your friends are weird: Faust and Vespasian

According to historian Tacitus, Emperor Vespasian (17 November AD 9 – 23 June AD 79) can be credited for not one but two dubious miracles. He reportedly healed a man's lame leg with his touch and cured another's blindness by rubbing his spit over his eyes. Icky.

Was that man Faust? Was he joking? One thing is certain: Vespasian got his medical license from a diploma mill.

Faust...us

Believe itus or notus, I didn't just add the suffix 'us' to the name of the infamous Faust to make it sound Roman. Nopus. Faustus was, in fact, a relatively common Latin name, used both a praenomen and cognomen—meaning it was used either as a first name or a surname. You can check Wikipedia for a list of Fausti who left their name in the pages of History.

Malespina or Farnesina?

Still's Villa Malespina is heavily inspired by the Villa Farnesina in Rome, a famous Renaissance villa in the district of Trastevere. I chose to keep it in the same location; the only thing I made up is the lab. :)

Faust's Batavian roots

According to Lady Montecito, Faust used to be a Praetorian, and specifically, an imperial bodyguard, hailing from a Batavi tribe—which explains his somewhat Nordic looks. But why would such a bodyguard hail from what is now known as the Netherlands? Because many, in fact, did. Germania and Batavia's renowned horsemen provided a contingent of Germanic bodyguards to the emperors of the Julio-Claudian dynasty for several decades. They were considered exceptional horsemen, reportedly capable of crossing a river in full battle gear without dismounting. Hardcore.

Another perhaps crucial quality of these Nordic bruisers was that they came with little political connections in Rome, which made them safer than Roman soldiers who may or may not be indebted to ill-meaning politicians.

Faust however, was born in Rome and served as a Praetorian rather than a Germanic bodyguard, leading us to assume that his father was one such Batavian horsemen whose family later settled in Rome toward the end of the first century BC.

Winged dicks to protect your laundry

Ancient Romans relied on amulets and effigies of the divine phallus—Yes, that's a thing—to invoke the deity's protection. The term *Fascinus* can refer either to the talisman itself—often a tiny winged dick pendant you could wear around your neck—or the deity himself—basically a sentient wiener. Phallic images were also carried during religious processions and celebrations, and, ironically, the vestals themselves were in charge of the cult of Fascinus, who incarnated a virile power protecting the state and its citizens.

The villa Palombara, home of the Porta Alchemica

It's—almost—real! Erected on the Esquiline in the 1600's by Marquis Massimiliano Palombara di Pietraforte, the villa was his summer retreat, and mostly, a haven for the marquis to indulge in his passion for Alchemy. He invited famous alchemists there, among them Giuseppe Francesco Borri, Athanasius Kircher and Gian Lorenzo Bernini, who supposedly designed the Porta Alchemica and came up with the arcane symbols and secret verses engraved around the gate. The villa did get destroyed sometime after 1883 when the city of Rome created the modern district of the Esquiline, but to this day, the mysterious Porta Alchemica still stands on Piazza Vittorio Emanuele, and can be admired from behind closed gates, sadly.

Ryuuko in Tōdai

Ryuuko's English may leave something to be desired—although it does efficiently convey her intent and meaning under all circumstances—but she's actually a brain: Tōdai, short for Tōkyō Daigaku—University of Tokyo—is the most prestigious university in Japan. The entrance exams are legendarily selective, so it's no small feat that she made it through this rigorous selection process twice under two different names.

Ouranos's nuts

Again, I'm not making any of this up. According to Greek poet Hesiod's *Theogony*, Ouranos was the incarnation of the sky, and a complete douchewaffle, who gave twelve children—the titans—to his consort, earth goddess Gaia. Ouranos, however, disliked his children and feared that they'd try to overthrow him. When Ouranos imprisoned his youngest children in Tartarus, Gaia asked her sons to take action, and Chronos was the only one brave enough to turn against his father: he castrated him with a sickle. Nice.

Chronos subsequently deposed his father and threw his testicles into the sea, and from them came Aphrodite—don't wanna know how. The blood Chronos spilled on the earth when cutting the nuts gave birth to the Giants, the Erinyes—the avenging Furies—the Meliae—the ash-tree nymphs—and, in some versions of the story to the Telchines—the original inhabitants of the island of Rhodes.

OTHER BOOKS BY CAMILLA MONK

Island Chaptal—nerdy IT engineer by day, romance novel junkie by night—just walked into her messy New York apartment to find Mr. Right waiting for her. No, wait…Mr. Clean.

In a fresh, witty series that blends fast-moving action with romantic suspense, a romance book–addicted computer engineer and a charming, cleaning-obsessed professional killer team up to take on the bad guys…and forge a highly unconventional working relationship. With a splash of James Bond's sophistication and a heaping helping of Stephanie Plum's spunkiness, Camilla Monk's *Spotless* series combines high stakes and plenty of humor with lushly exotic settings and a funny, relatable heroine readers can't help but cheer for.

ACKNOWLEDGMENTS

This book wouldn't have happened without Tiffany Yates Martin—who more or less made me rewrite it, and she was right about that—Mitzi Carroll and Risa Nichols—who did a fantastic job editing *Still* despite an incredibly tight deadline—and Orsola Gelpi, who kindly reviewed my Italian dialogues: guys, I don't deserve you.

I'd also like to thank the many bums in Paris, New York and Tokyo who inspired me to write this book: I owe them some of the funniest and most humbling moments of my life.

Lastly, special thanks are owed to B. who puts up with me and my crazy deadlines.

Addendum: Jesus, Regina, you end up in the acknowledgments again, you big winner!

About the Author

Camilla Monk is a French native who grew up in a Franco-American family. After studying business and advertising in Paris, she taught English and French in Tokyo before returning to France, where she spent eight years building rickety websites for financial companies.

Today, she lives in Montreal, where she keeps a close watch on the squirrels and complains on a daily basis about the egregious number of Tim Hortons.

Visit camillamonk.com for more information on new releases!